I0700980

ADVICE FROM A JILTED BRIDE

PIPER RAYNE

This book is a work of fiction. Names, characters, places and incidents either are products of the author's imagination or are used fictitiously. Any resemblance to actual events or locales or persons, living or dead, is entirely coincidental.

© 2019 by Piper Rayne

All rights reserved, including the right to reproduce this book or portions thereof in any form whatsoever.

Cover Design: By Hang Le

Line Editor: Gray Ink Editing

Proofreader: Shawna Gavas, Behind The Writer

What's a girl to do after being ditched at the altar by text message? That's right. Text. Message.

How does she pick up the pieces and move on? I'm no Dear Abby but here's a little free advice...

Advice #1 – First, purge your apartment of all things him —by tossing his belongings off the balcony.

Advice #2 – Do not, I repeat do not, throw anything out into the hallway because you'll injure your hot new neighbor.

Advice #3 – When said neighbor brings over Chinese Food do not let him stay and keep you company. It's awkward when you realize he's your boss.

Advice #4 – Accept his offer to help you with your side business but think twice before using a date to his sister's wedding as collateral.

Advice #5 – Investigate who your mystery neighbor *really* is. Don't trust his word even if he's the world's best kisser.

If you listen to nothing else, pay attention to that last one. It's the most important and will save you a lot of heartache.

Xo,
LOVESICK IN LAKE STARLIGHT

Advice from a *Jilted Bride*

The Baileys

Austin Bailey - 31 years old
(*Biology Teacher/Baseball Coach*)
Savannah Bailey - 29 years old
(*Runs Bailey Timber Corp*)
Brooklyn Bailey - 26 years old
(*Hotel Maid*)
Rome Bailey - 24 years old
(*Chef*)
Denver Bailey - 24 years old
(*Bush Pilot*)
Juno Bailey - 23 years old
(*Matchmaker*)
Kingston Bailey - 20 years old
(*Smokejumper*)
Phoenix Bailey - 18 years old
(*Student*)
Sedona Bailey - 18 years old
(*Student*)

ONE

Brooklyn

Abandoned.
Deserted.
Unwanted.

All those words run through my head as my younger sister Juno shoves my puffy white dress and me into the back seat of my older sister, Savannah's, SUV.

There had to have been signs that my fiancé, Jeff, wasn't happy, but all I recall are the smiles and the kisses and the hugs and the laughs. Well, there weren't a ton of laughs, but Jeff isn't a lighthearted or laughing kind of guy—the complete opposite of my brothers. Though they aren't laughing or cracking jokes right this minute.

"Don't do anything stupid!" Juno screams over the hood at the boys and climbs into the passenger seat next to Savannah.

"He obviously has a death wish," Austin says, climbing into his Jeep with my three other brothers, their suit jackets stripped off, ties hanging around their necks. His Jeep peels out of the small church parking lot, fishtailing before it rounds the corner, almost on two wheels, and disappears down Main Street.

They're kind of protective, and my oldest brother, Austin, never liked Jeff.

"It's going to be okay." Juno extends her hand into the back seat, rubbing my knee through the million layers of tulle.

Savannah looks at me through the rearview mirror, a reassuring smile perma-plastered on her face. She wanted to stay and inform our friends and family, but I think Juno was scared to handle me by herself, so we left the job of telling all the guests there'd be no wedding in the hands of our uncle, Brian. My grandma Dori, my twin sisters Phoenix and Sedona, and Austin's girlfriend, Holly, stayed behind to help remove the flowers from inside the church.

"I'm fine. I'm good." It's a lie. I know that. They know that. But I'm fighting to keep it together. Falling apart and having a mental breakdown will only add to the level of humiliation I already feel.

I look out the back window of the SUV and watch as the church doors open. Guests walk down the concrete stairs, confusion and surprise laced in their expressions.

Thanks, Uncle Brian.

Juno straightens in the passenger seat and looks at Savannah. They've been doing their whole non-verbal talking thing since Jeff's text came through. That's right— the asshole ditched me on our wedding day via text.

My eerie calmness must set off alarm bells for my

sisters. Don't mistake my composure as a good sign. I want to scream and rant, and if Jeff was in front of me, I might actually beat him with my bouquet like Carrie did to Big when he left her looking like the fool on their wedding day in the *Sex and the City* movie.

Jeff's not here though, because he's a coward.

All I have is the text message he sent me five minutes before I was supposed to walk down the aisle. After my family spent a shit-ton of money on a huge-ass wedding I didn't even want. I would've been happy with a small affair, but nooo, Jeff wanted practically the entire town to bear witness to our nuptials, and now my humiliation.

A text... after I got up at the butt-crack of dawn to get my hair done. After I slipped into a pair of white silk panties, imagining him sliding them down my legs tonight. After a nice Belgium lady ripped all the hair out from between my legs to give me a smooth Brazilian wax.

What a fucker! The fact I did that for him stokes the rage inside me.

"We'll go back to the house." Savannah flips the turn signal to head to the house I grew up in.

Yeah, I'm not going there. "No, go to the apartment."

Juno glances at me, her eyes expressing her uncertainty. "I don't think that's a good idea. We'll go to the house, wait for the guys."

"Hopefully none of them get arrested," Savannah mumbles. "The last thing Bailey Timber needs right now is one of us getting arrested... again."

"Well, now that you've switched to those disposable coffee cups, we should be good." Juno laughs, nailing Savannah with a dig about the time she threw a coffee mug at her enemy's face and spent a few hours in jail.

Savannah flips her off.

Leave it to my family to bring up another sore subject right after my life has fallen apart. Maybe it's because we've dealt with so much tragedy that we search for anything to make a serious situation feel less severe.

Savannah turns toward the house, ignoring my instructions.

"Sav, the apartment."

"I don't thin—"

"*Now!*"

Her gaze shoots to mine through the rearview mirror. She's never been afraid of me, and it's hard to tell if she is now. She's had to play mama bear a lot over the years since my parents died a decade ago.

I soften my voice. "I need to see if he's there. I want answers."

I look at my phone still clasped in my hands. A damn text message. I'm not surprised he didn't have the balls to tell me face to face. Jeff's not a confrontational type of guy. Still, I thought he loved me. That's what hurts the most—I obviously had it all wrong.

"Screw the bastard," Savannah says.

Juno's kind eyes look back over the side of the headrest once more. "If closure is what you need, then let's go." She squeezes my hand and flips back around, shooting a look to Savannah to say *listen to the girl*.

Savannah huffs, forever the control freak, but she does a U-turn and heads toward the apartment I signed a lease for with Jeff only last week.

Why didn't he say something then? Like, "Hey, this whole wedding thing? I'm not so sure I want to be a husband."

We drive for ten minutes and pull up to the cluster of white buildings, each one bearing a small balcony, some overlooking Lake Starlight. We paid a little more money in rent for the view. Jeff said he thought the app he's been developing for the past year was about to sell and we'd be able to afford it.

"I'm going on record that this is not a good idea." Savannah pulls the keys from the ignition.

The three of us sit looking up at where my future was supposed to start. When we signed the lease, I'd thought of the apartment as our starter place. I pictured Jeff and me driving by years from now, after we could afford to move, our kids in the back seat while we pointed out where it all began. They'd roll their eyes as though they couldn't care less, then we'd make our way back to a single-family home with a large yard and a cute sign on the front door that said "The Brickles."

What a crock of shit.

I open the vehicle door. I really should have thought about the size of my dress when I was trying them on, but then again, I wasn't thinking I'd be making a walk of shame in it.

My eyes are set on that small balcony on the side of the building. The one where Jeff said he'd put a grill and a chair for me to keep him company as he cooked his famous burgers.

My sisters exit the SUV and murmur behind me. Savannah's still going on about how this is the wrong call and Juno's arguing that I have to do this sometime.

Digging into my purse, I find the keys. Two keys on a heart keyring. How naïve was I? I roll my eyes, inserting my key into the main door of the building and turning the knob. The foyer smelled of flowers and a future when we moved our stuff in last week. Now it smells of loneliness and despair as I walk up the first flight of stairs.

"Watch your dress," Juno says.

"Why? We'll be burning it tonight," Savannah says.

I pick up the front of the big skirt. Why did I decide on the Cinderella princess style again? What a waste of money.

When we reach the top floor, I look at the numbers on the outside of my apartment door. Three twenty-two. I thought it was a sign—my parents' anniversary date. They married on March twenty-second and that number was magic for them. I had hoped it'd be the same for me. Shaking my head, I insert my key.

Juno's hand covers mine. "Are you sure you're ready?"

I look at her. No one would imagine we're sisters. Her auburn hair is contrary to my blond, her green eyes to my blue. But if you look closely, our noses slope the same way and our lips hold the same smile. But that's where our similarities end.

I nod. "I told you. I'm good."

Juno steps back, and I open the door to what was supposed to be my future home. We all walk into the apartment, and the door shuts behind us.

The light in here isn't nearly as bright as I remember. The space looks smaller and older.

"I'm going down to talk to the landlord. I'm getting you out of this lease," Savannah says, and the door opens and closes with her departure.

"She's in fix-it mode." Juno's hand lands on my shoulder, and I ignore the tingling in my nose. "Want me to go down to Liquory Split and get us something to take the edge off?"

My gaze veers to the couch we bought one another as a

wedding gift before I smile at her. "That'd be great. Thanks."

"Consider it done." Her heels click on the hardwood while she makes her way to the door. Another selling point for the apartment. "Are you sure? I mean, you'll be okay?"

I circle back around, keeping the smile on my face. "Yeah. I'm sure Savannah will be back soon."

Appeased by my answer and my smile, she opens the door and leaves the apartment.

The silence that cloaks the room feels like nails on a chalkboard. I scour the small apartment. Jeff's suit jacket from yesterday still hangs off the chair. The coffee cup he drank out of this morning sits in the sink. Did he sip that while typing that text? I look at my phone again.

"Coward," I say, my voice echoing through the half-empty apartment.

I pick up the coffee mug, inspecting it for lipstick. What other reason could there be for him to break every promise he ever made to me? There has to be someone else. It'd be easier for me to handle this if someone convinced him to leave me, rather than thinking he came to some realization himself between the time he kissed me goodbye on my family's porch last night and texting me this morning to tell me I'm just not what he wants. But I don't find the evidence I'm seeking.

I toss my phone on the table and blindly throw the coffee mug with no thought of direction. The smashing sound lifts my mood slightly. A piece of him. A piece of our promised future gone. God, it feels so good.

I grab his jacket, pulling hard on one sleeve. It rips, and I throw the scrap of fabric to the floor. I search his pockets for any evidence of a cocktail napkin with a woman's name and phone number scrawled on it. Nothing.

After stepping out of my heels, I run down the short hallway into our master bedroom. I pounce on the disheveled bed like a puma, burying my nose in the pillow, wanting to smell the perfume of a woman. I toss it, smell the other one, and toss that one to the floor as well. I open every drawer, only finding the box of condoms we bought the night we moved our stuff in.

In the bathroom, I open the medicine cabinet; cologne and aspirin bottles crash to the bathroom floor. I dig madly through the trash, finding nothing except a small piece of bloody toilet paper he must have used when he cut himself shaving. Is that when he decided I wasn't who he wanted?

Coming up empty of any evidence that there's another woman, I head into our closet, the main reason I decided to sign a lease on this apartment. His clothes are on one side, mine on the other. I smiled like a fairy princess after we hung up our clothes. I'd dreamed of the whole his-and-hers closet since I was sixteen.

I yank his V-neck sweaters and his horrendous collection of *Star Wars* T-shirts from the shelf. Opening the built-in drawers, I pull out socks, underwear, and every other stitch of his clothing and throw them onto the floor. "Screw you, Jeff Brickle!"

Still without a sign of any other woman, I sit in the middle of our closet, looking at my neat and orderly side and the pile of his belongings on the floor in front of me. My throat locks up, and I struggle to breathe as my chest constricts.

I pick up an armful of his clothes and stomp out of the closet and into the living room. I open the patio door to our small balcony, throw the clothes over the banister, and head back inside for another load.

"I'm throwing *you* out of *my* life!" I toss another pile of his shitty wardrobe.

"Brook!" Savannah screams from below.

I ignore her and snatch up every other belonging of Jeff's. His precious collection of *Star Wars* movies. His stupid alarm clock that blares his shitty music.

I'm heading back to the balcony when Savannah rushes in through the apartment door. Her hair has fallen out of her perfectly styled updo. "Brooklyn. Stop."

The man to her right is the guy we signed the lease with.

I toss everything in my hands over the balcony.

"Please, Miss Bailey, you need to stop. You could injure another resident."

I inhale a deep breath. "How could you let me sign this lease? Surely you have some sense of these things? I mean, he called off our wedding! You had no inkling of that happening when you pointed at that dotted line?"

"Sorry," Savannah says to the man.

"I'm not sorry." I point at the building manager. "You should let me out of this lease. It's the least you can do!"

I pick up the sci-fi novel Jeff claimed was better than any of my romance books. Should have figured out then that we weren't compatible.

The manager runs over and locks the screen door. "Please."

He blocks it, but there's fear in his eyes. If I step closer, he'll move. Somewhere in my sensible brain, I know I need to calm down, but it feels impossible at the moment.

"What the hell?" Juno rushes in, a brown paper bag in each hand. Her hair has also fallen out of the pretty bobby pins with little flowers I glued to the ends. What a waste of fucking time!

I chuck the book at the open apartment door. Juno dodges it, thank God. Her reflexes always were stellar in our adolescent fights.

"*Fuck!*" a man yells from the hallway.

Savannah's eyes widen, and she turns toward the sound.

I nibble on my lip, praying that was one of my brothers.

Juno places the two bags on the table and follows Savannah.

The manager slides along the wall so he doesn't have to come close to the possessed bride as he heads toward the door.

"What the hell?" the same deep voice says.

Nobody has to leave the apartment though, because the person I hit walks in, holding Jeff's book in one hand while rubbing his head with his other. A small trickle of blood runs through the crease of his fingers.

Savannah takes the reins because she's the one who handles any crisis in the Bailey family. "Oh, we're so sorry!"

"Are you really?" His tall figure eats up the entire doorway. He's in a pair of slacks and an untucked button-down shirt. You'd think he was a guest invited to my wedding. His dark beard is scruffy, his hair neatly gelled—except one chunk that's fallen loose, probably from the book hitting him.

"I'm sorry, really," I say and step forward.

His gaze moves from Savannah to me. He blinks three times as though he can't believe what he's seeing. After a few seconds, he looks down at himself and chuckles. "Nope. I'm not naked or in a tux... thank fuck. For a second, I thought my worst nightmare had come true."

I raise my arms. "Great, just what I need. Another man afraid of commitment!"

"Let me grab you some ice." Juno breezes into the

kitchen. "Oh, a broken coffee mug." She picks up a piece and holds the evidence up to Savannah. "What does our family have against coffee mugs?"

The laughter Juno's going for never arrives.

I disappear down the hall and slam my bedroom door. I know this is only the second worst day of my life. The first was the day I lost my parents, but at the moment, it sure feels a hell of a lot like things couldn't be worse.

TWO

Wyatt

I crack my neck, passing the sign on the side of the road that welcomes me to Lake Starlight. According to it, it's "My new home and I just don't know it yet."

Whatever.

Small-town life isn't meant for me. The only exciting thing to happen since I rented my car at the airport and drove an hour west were the goats walking up a cliff on the side of a mountain. I took the bait and parked my car next to the scattered line of vehicles alongside the highway, joining the rest of the people watching a baby mountain goat try to follow its mama or daddy. I'm not sure which. Does one sex have horns and the other doesn't?

See, I'm not meant for this life. I'll admit it was interesting though. Not a moose, but it beats the ass cracks I see from the street vendors in New York on a daily basis.

My phone rings through the Bluetooth speaker.

"Hey, Mom," I answer.

"Wyatt. You landed safely, I presume?"

"Yeah, sorry. Everything here is like extracting a tooth with a pair of pliers and no drugs."

She giggles. "Enjoy it. Maybe you'll like a slower-paced life."

"Doubtful." I'm no sooner in Lake Starlight than I'm in their "downtown," which I think might have been inspired by Stars Hollow.

Yes, I know Stars Hollow from *Gilmore Girls*. I have a sister who used to spy on me then blackmail me in order to force me to cede control of the television to her. Mom had this ridiculous rule about having only one television in a ten-bedroom brownstone. Mom was a reader, so now that I'm an adult, I can understand her reasoning a little more. Luckily, Haylee is her fiancé, Bradley's, problem now.

"You'll be back for the wedding?" my mom asks.

Right now, only two things matter in my mom's life: my sister's nuptials and who'll be my date for the big event.

"Yes. We've been over this." I bring the car to a stop at the stoplight.

"And?"

"And I'm probably coming stag."

"Unless you find someone in that cute town." Eagerness fills her voice.

"Doubtful."

A long, exasperated breath flows through the receiver. "I don't know why you insist on this bachelor life. Weren't your father and I a good example of how much a committed relationship can bring to your life? I know we've had our fights, but we love one another. Your sister is doing great."

I roll my eyes and press the gas when the light turns

green. "It's not off the table, but I have a lot more I want to do before I'm stuck in Connecticut, playing house."

"Most people don't feel like marriage is being stuck."

"See, I'm not like most people. I'm the exception. Remember?"

She giggles again. One thing I'm great at is making my mother laugh. "You've always been the exception to every rule. I think I've convinced your dad to come out there after the wedding. I'm eager to see the new place."

I roll my eyes, turning right to head toward the latest hotel my dad has added to his empire. "It's a podunk hotel. Probably a three-star."

"I've spoiled you. When I was younger—"

"Yeah, you were a poor peasant girl begging for a crumb of bread on a corner."

"Wyatt Whitmore, you better take back that tone. I'm serious. You need to find a wife. Fall in love. Live for someone else besides yourself. You do what you want, when you want without any regard for anyone else."

"That's the whole point of being single."

I blow out a breath. Man, she must be stressed to ping between moods so fast. I'm not sure why my mom is so obsessed with the idea that I get married. If I did, I'd be divorced after the lust phase ended a month later.

I pull up in front of Glacier Point Resort. *Resort* is being used loosely here. It could probably be torn down and rebuilt, but my dad bought it to have a presence in Alaska before anyone else. He wants to buy up these small, independent hotels before his competition does. Thinks Alaska is the next great escape everyone will be flocking to. This isn't a year or two operation though—his clear instructions were to get my assessment done in six months. Before ski season starts.

"You make me feel like I'm a bad mom."

I swear, menopause is no fun for either my mother or myself. "You're not. I'm not even thirty."

"A couple months shy," she mumbles, but I hear the thickness in her voice from crying.

"A couple months? Mom, don't buy me a walker yet. I have ten months before I'm thirty."

She giggles.

Thank fuck she's back to happy. For a second, I was going to tell her I'd marry the first girl I saw here. That thought moves my thinking from the resort to who I'll spend my nights with here. Six months in Alaska and only one weekend with an excuse to head back to New York. Maybe I should take a vow of celibacy while I'm here and see if it helps me concentrate more. I could get out of here in four months.

"Where is your dad having you start?" Mom asks.

"Bellhop. For a man who doesn't watch television, it's odd that I'm doing something that feels like a reality show."

"He just wants you to appreciate what you have. He didn't have an easy road, you know? When he bought his first place, he had five investors—"

"I know, Mom. You and Dad had a horrible upbringing. I gotcha."

Look at the line of pick-up trucks. My rental might be the only sedan in the parking lot.

"I just want you to be happy."

"Which I am. Well, I will be once I finish here and Dad finally hands over what he promised."

She's quiet. We both know there's a chance my dad could change his mind. He swore to me that if I proved myself, he'd finally release the reins and let me own one of his many hotel chains. Not that I want whatever this chain in Alaska will be. I'd settle for our high-priced skyscraper hotels in the theatre district though.

"I know. But after this, maybe you'll think about finding someone."

I chuckle. "Isn't love supposed to plow you over, take you by surprise? I don't think I'm supposed to pencil in time to meet the love of my life."

She laughs again. When I was younger, I'd always try to make her laugh with silly magic tricks or goofy faces. Same goal these days, just different tactic.

"I suppose not, but things nowadays have changed."

I drive out of the parking lot of the resort, even if I'm anxious to get started on getting it back in the black. According to everyone in that building, come Monday morning, I'm the new manager/bellhop. Do they even have a bellhop? Probably not. My dad's ludicrous idea is for me to work in every department while relaying to him what needs to be done and who should stay and who should go. I'm basically doing an untelevised version of *Undercover Boss*.

"Okay, Mom, I promise to put a little more effort into finding 'the one' after Dad signs some properties over to me." I fail to mention that means I'll need to interview a lot of women, and when I say interview, I mean in my bed.

"There's the boy I love so much. You have way too big of a heart. You need to find someone who appreciates it."

"All right, I'm going to go and get settled. I have to find this landlord guy at the new place. I pray he got it furnished like he promised."

"Okay, remember to keep your eye out. Your bride could pop up at any time."

"Bye, Mom, love you."

"Love you."

I click off the Bluetooth as I pull into the parking lot of the apartment building I'm renting a unit in for a year, even though I'll be here for six months. The landlord was a stickler on the length of the lease. Then he huffed and puffed when I asked about a furnished place, so I threw a few more thousand his way.

I hit the key fob to lock the doors of my rental sedan. No bells or whistles this far north. I haven't sat in cloth seats in... well, maybe ever.

As I'm walking to the apartment number the landlord told me to go to, I dig in my pocket for the keys he sent me. At least he was nice enough to overnight them to me. I guess they haven't progressed to key code entries up in this mountain town.

A piece of clothing falls on my head. I pluck it off, finding some guy's boxer shorts.

"What the—what the fuck kind of place is this?" I glare at the pile of men's clothes on the ground in front of me.

"Brooklyn," a girl pleads right before a door above me shuts.

Great. I look up to see a man splayed along the glass door on the third floor. I glance at the keys in my hand. Three twenty-three, which means I'm on the same floor as whatever's going on up there. I sure hope there's more than one cop in this town.

I open the front door of the building and walk up the stairs. The carpet is slightly stained, but I can't imagine it gets much reprieve with the shit weather in this part of the country.

I'm halfway up the second stairway and I really wish I would've brought my suitcase with me. Where's the elevator in this place?

The screaming grows louder the higher I get, which isn't really a surprise.

I catch my breath when I reach the third floor and spot the door to another apartment open, a short redhead standing in the doorway. No one pays me any attention as I insert the key into my apartment's door.

Thank fuck. I don't want to be a witness to something and spend the rest of the day telling the police what I witnessed. I'm incognito in this town from this point forward.

"*Ugh!*" I hear a woman scream.

I can't help but turn toward the sound. It's like a reflex, even though I should mind my own business.

Something hits my head with a huge thud.

"*Fuck!*" I yell.

What have I gotten myself into by living here?

I bend down, retrieving my keys and the weapon of choice. A book depicting an alien invasion on the cover.

I stomp across the hall. "What the hell?"

Three women and a man are inside the apartment. The man looks scared shitless, sliding along the wall, his eyes frantic.

A tall blonde meets me before I can fully step into the apartment. The redhead's eyes flick to mine then concentrate on her shoes.

"We're so sorry," the blonde says.

I blink a few times to clear my vision, probably looking as if I have a twitch in my eyes. "Are you really?"

I stare between the blonde and the redhead, wondering which of them should be pitching in major league baseball.

"I am." A soft voice reminds me someone else is here.

I look away from the two women trying to give me some

type of nonverbal communication with their eyes, and I blink.

I blink again.

I blink one more time because my mom's words from ten minutes ago haunt me like the ghost from Christmas past.

"Your bride could pop up at any time."

The blond bride is cute as hell, and if it wasn't for the flushed, angry look on her face and loose strands of hair going in every direction, she'd probably be the most beautiful bride I've ever seen. Forget that. I kind of like the runaway bride look.

I look down at myself, wondering if I was knocked out and am now dreaming, then I release a long breath.

"Nope. I'm not naked or in a tux. Thank fuck. For a second I thought my worst nightmare had come true." I speak the truth, though I probably should've kept that thought to myself.

"Great, just what I need. Another man afraid of commitment." The bride raises her arms then disappears down the hall, slamming a door in the process.

"Let me get you some ice." The redhead breezes past me to the kitchen.

"Have a seat." The blonde pulls out a chair.

I step over a ripped sports coat and sit down. "Should I watch for flying books every time I leave my apartment?"

The redhead puts a bag of ice on the table. "I'm Juno Bailey, and this is my sister, Savannah." She points down the hall. "That's Brooklyn, and um... it's just not a good day for her today." She folds her small frame into the chair next to me, patting my wound with a wet paper towel. "It's just a surface cut. I think you'll be fine."

"Are you the town doctor?" I deadpan.

She laughs and gives her sister a look. "Town matchmaker."

"What?" Obviously the hit to my head has affected my hearing.

"Is this the groom?" The guy, who now has color back in his face, walks over.

"I'm definitely no groom."

He laughs. "Just messing with you."

Juno rolls her eyes, and a sound comes from Savannah's throat. One that means she agrees with her sister. If I stick around long enough, maybe I'll figure out their native tongue.

"Who are you?" Savannah asks.

"I'm Wyatt W—Moore. Someone here's neighbor for the next year."

Again, Juno looks at Savannah, but this time she smiles. Wide and welcoming. Another grunt comes from Savannah. They're disagreeing now.

Look at me, I'm understanding how the natives communicate.

"So who's my neighbor?" I ask.

The guy thumbs toward the hallway. "The jilted bride in there."

"We still need to negotiate," Savannah interrupts.

"I told you, she's not getting out of the lease." He puts his hand in front of me. "I'm Joel, your landlord. Nice to finally meet you."

I hold out my free hand while holding the bag of ice to my forehead with the other.

"You good to walk? I can show you the apartment and go through everything with you now."

Joel is eager to leave and I'm his excuse. Not that I want to stick around with three chicks who are probably moments away from raising pitchforks toward anyone with a member between their legs.

"Thanks for the head wound and the ice." I nod, stepping toward the door.

"Any time. And we do apologize. Just a bad day," Juno says.

Savannah doesn't say anything.

"We're going to have pizza later tonight if you'd like to join us." Juno follows us to the door.

"Juno, stop," Savannah says.

Juno glances over her shoulder, and her sister rolls her eyes. "Brooklyn really is a sweet girl. You'll see, she'll be a great neighbor."

Juno's smile is so bright, I feel as though I'm in a remake of *The Stepford Wives* movie.

"Sure. Whatever you say."

"Yeah, bye, girls." Joel shuts their door. "Can you believe it? Left at the altar. And a Bailey at that. What a moron," he says, as though I understand any of it other than her being left at the altar.

What the hell does her being a Bailey have to do with it?

He inserts a key into my door and opens the apartment for me. "The Baileys own the big lumber company in town." He thumbs toward the other apartment. "That's three of them. There are six more."

I nod, inspecting the furniture. Not the best, but not the worst either. I do a quick sweep of the apartment and see that he's left the mail key on the kitchen counter, along with a sheet giving instructions for garbage, etc. "Thanks a lot, Joel. I'll let you know if I need anything."

"Sure thing. I'm glad this worked out. Normally this is a

quiet apartment building. I don't know what kind of idiot stands up Brooklyn Bailey."

I huff. Joel obviously thinks I care about whatever happened to the bride. I have no interest in involving myself in any small-town gossip. I'm here to do a job. Get in. Get out.

Not that I disagree with him. Brooklyn's gorgeous, but you have to watch out for a girl with an arm like that. I'm not sure how things are here, but in New York, nothing is ever as good as it seems. Maybe that's the case with my new neighbor too.

THREE

Brooklyn

"What do you mean he's not letting me out of the lease?" I direct my question to Savannah. No isn't a word in her vocabulary, but she accepted his denial?

I line the scissors up on the next seam of my dress, clipping away thread by thread while I sit on the floor in front of the coffee table.

"Can we please just rip it?" Savannah asks, her hands inching toward the dress.

I scowl, and she rolls her eyes.

"I think we should talk about the hottie with the head wound. I got this incredible energy when he walked in." Juno props her feet up on the coffee table Holly restored for Jeff and me as a wedding gift. Poor Holly, putting all that work into something for nothing.

Savannah shoots her a death glare. "Juno. Focus."

"If I wasn't a scorned bride and hell-bent on making the

entire male population pay, I'd be all over that." I can't deny the guy is heart-pounding, belly-flipping goodness. I might not want to head to bed with the man, but he has that air about him. You know what I mean. He walks, talks, and looks like he'd make you come three times in one night.

"What?" Savannah asks, her eyebrows just about at her hairline. She obviously got the wrong idea.

"Go for it, Juno," I say. "Unless you and Colton..."

Juno narrows her eyes. "How many times have I told you, we're just friends. *Best* friends."

Savannah playfully rolls her eyes at me. Juno throws a pillow at her.

"Hey!" Savannah says, throwing it back, but Juno catches it.

Told you she's got the reflexes of a cat. I bet if I pushed her off a building, she'd land on her feet.

"Back to the apartment. Joel says that—"

"Who's Joel?" I ask, running the small scissors along the seam. It's oddly therapeutic.

"Your landlord. Come on, Brooklyn." Savannah acts as though I'm a flake, as always.

Should I mention that she's currently sitting across from a sister who believes she's been born with the gift of matchmaking, but *I'm* the flake because I cure things with essential oils?

"I didn't get his name." I shrug. *Clip. Clip. Clip.* I release a cleansing breath.

"Well, he said you signed the lease, and since Jeff is nowhere to be found, that leaves you on the hook."

"Anyway..." Juno sends Savannah a look. "The hottie is your new neighbor." Juno waggles her eyebrows.

I have no idea what happened with the guy because his comment was the straw that broke me. I locked myself in the bedroom, the tears finally cresting to the surface. "Really?"

"Yeah." Savannah sips her wine.

"I have a feeling about him." Juno looks off into space for a second.

I swear, my sister. She says she predicted my oldest brother, Austin, and his girlfriend, Holly, getting together last year, but unless she shoved alcohol down their throats and stuffed them into his Jeep behind Lucky's Tavern, it wasn't her doing. They were hot news. Well, still are. They were in the town's online gossip blog for months.

"Oh God." I drop the scissors on my lap. "Buzz Wheel!" My forehead hits the coffee table.

Savannah runs her hand in small circles on my back. "I'm sure they'll be kind."

Juno huffs. "A Bailey being stood up at the altar?"

I miss the look I'm sure Savannah gives Juno.

"Maybe stay off for a few days," Savannah says.

I've always loved that site. The *Lake Starlight Buzz Wheel* is a sick obsession I've indulged in my entire life. Well, most of my life. I don't quite remember when it started, but Savannah's right. I need to stay clear of it for the next day or two. Since the site is updated with new content at midnight every day, there'll be no record of... my mind trails to what they could unfold.

"Do you think they got a picture of Jeff?" I ask, pressing my hands on the table to rise from the floor.

"No. Don't read it." Savannah's hand plants on my arm to keep me put.

"Sooner or later I'll have to face it."

Juno pulls out her phone. "I'll read it." Her thumbs run along the screen.

I move toward my phone, but Savannah doesn't let go of my arm. "Let Juno."

I nod, my ass falling back down to the floor. I pick up my scissors and get back to work unstitching the bodice from the skirt.

Juno laughs and positions her phone so we can see. "There's a wanted poster with a weasel on it."

My stomach sinks at the confirmation that my Dear Jane moment has made the Buzz Wheel. Not sure why I had a sliver of hope that I'd escaped it.

"Ready?" Juno asks, looking at me.

Savannah slides to the floor with me, clasping her hand over mine.

"Go." I nod.

Juno reads. "'Well, the news is out and unfortunately, Brooklyn Bailey has been left at the altar. After two years of preparations, the Bailey clan, with new addition, Holly Radcliffe, were ready to give away their sister, but no one was at the end of the aisle to take her. Rumor has it, she's on their honeymoon by herself. Oldest brother, Austin, is rumored to have stated, 'The guy has a death wish.' He and the other three Bailey brothers stalked out of the wedding in search of Jeff Brickle. I sure hope he's bunkered down somewhere safe tonight. All in all, it's sad news, but many men in Lake Starlight are questioning, how short of a time is too short to ask Brooklyn Bailey out?'"

Juno's thumb scrolls, and I wait for more.

"Oh, and something about Austin and Holly in the truck outside Lucky's again. Seriously, what sick fascination do they have with doing it in the back seat?" She clicks off her screen and drops her phone in her lap.

"They're still in that screwing-every-minute phase," I say in a morose voice.

Savannah shakes her head. "I can see those two never getting out of that phase."

I laugh.

A real laugh.

I jolt and look around. My sisters didn't notice, but I shouldn't be laughing right now. How can I? I should find no amusement in anything.

"You know what you need to do?" Juno pours herself another glass of wine. "Go on the honeymoon. You have the time off." She leans back in the chair.

Savannah steals the bottle to refill our glasses. "She's right. It'll clear your head."

"Yeah, walking on a beach solo when I should be there with my *husband* will be the best way to clear my mind. Good idea, girls."

Clip. Clip. Clip. Ahhh.

"I'm serious, Brookie." Juno uses the nickname she used when we were kids. "I think it's exactly what you need. Get out of here for two weeks. In the meantime, we'll figure out this whole apartment thing. I'll move in to help. Kingston's never home anyway."

I stop cutting the strings that were supposed to bind my future. "No. I'm not going on a honeymoon for one and then having my sister move in with me out of pity, leaving my brother to move back home. Plus, Holly and Austin just got the house to themselves."

"Not true. Rome is still there," Savannah adds.

In case you weren't keeping track, there are nine of us Bailey siblings. Don't worry, you'll get them all straight pretty quick.

"Not for long. He's opening that restaurant and told me there's a place above it he's moving into."

Savannah says nothing because she knows I'm right.

None of us do anything without Savannah or Austin's approval, for some reason. I guess because they held the family together after our parents died. They played pseudo-mom and dad.

"Okay, whatever. Just go on the honeymoon," Juno says. "And you should take that hottie." She points toward the door of my apartment.

"Do you live on planet Earth?" Savannah asks her.

"I'm telling you, there's something there." She chews her cheek for a second. "If he would've stuck around for more questions, I would've predicted the why and the who, but he seemed kind of touchy."

"Maybe because he got hit by a brick of a book and has a head wound. Not exactly a great welcome committee," I say.

"Yeah, Juno. He was scared that he'd walked into his own wedding when he saw Brooklyn. That's not the guy she needs in her life." Savannah is clearly unimpressed, but she's a hard one to impress.

Juno sips her wine. "I'm just saying what I'm feeling, and since I'm the one who inherited the matchmaking gene, I suggest you believe me when I say there's something about him."

Savannah shakes her head, pouring another glass of wine.

"If you let me set you up, you'd have no reason to think I'm not the real thing." Juno widens her eyes in question to Savannah.

"Never." Savannah nudges me. She seems pretty eager to change the subject. "Go on the trip. Come on. You're already packed."

True. My lonely honeymoon suitcase was the only one left in the closet.

Clip. Clip. Clip. Ahhh.

It would get me away from the pitying looks on Lake Starlight's residents' faces. Not that I wouldn't be returning to them, but it's not like I feel like going to work or sitting around in my new apartment that I can't even afford for the next two weeks.

"I'll go," I say softly, dropping the scissors. I tear apart the rest of the dress, splitting it into two halves. "That felt fantastic."

"*Yay!*" Juno jumps up. "Let's go double-check that you have everything you need."

It seems crazy, but I need some time alone to come to terms with what Jeff's done to me. I need to rid him from my body and soul. I thought I was on my way to becoming a stay-at-home mother, but since that ship has sailed for right now, I need to figure out a plan and I can't do that here. My family will design a wellness check rotation and drive me crazy in the process.

The buzzer from downstairs rings, and Juno presses the button to answer. "Who's there?" There's a note of satisfaction in her voice now that I've agreed to go on the trip.

"Let us up," Rome says, annoyance laced throughout his tone.

She presses the button. The thin walls of the apartment don't hide the sound of numerous footsteps venturing up to the third floor. Juno opens the door, and one after the other, the rest of my family files in, their eyes seeking me out.

"Pizza and beer." Rome drops two pizzas on the table and a case of beer on the counter.

"More pizza and beer." Denver drops two more pizzas and another case on the counter.

They each beeline it over to me.

"Get up," they say in unison, their hands motioning for me to stand.

Once I'm on my feet, they pull me into their arms.

"I will kill him as soon as I find him," Rome whispers.

"Not if I get to him first," Denver adds.

"Let me join in." Kingston huddles in from the other side.

"What's a brotherly hug without the eldest?" Soon Austin is on the other side and I'm suffocating from the smell of the alcohol they've already consumed.

"Drinking so early, boys?" I mumble into someone's chest.

They laugh and disperse, each pointing at the others.

Austin holds up his hands. "I was the driver."

The other three shrug.

"He was a douchebag anyway." Austin heads back to the kitchen to help Holly put the beer in the fridge.

"Sorry, Brooklyn." Sedona hugs me.

Phoenix comes in next, hugging me without saying anything. She's not one to display her emotions. Unless they're bitchy.

They both sit on the couch, their heads in their phones almost instantly.

We all party with pizza, beer, and wine, acting as though Jeff standing me up was the best thing that could happen to me. I'm sure a few of them think it is, but tell that to my heart.

Juno stands on a chair to grab everyone's attention. Surprisingly, they grant her the floor. "Guess what? Brooklyn's going on her honeymoon."

Denver raises his hand. "I call dibs on Asshole's ticket."

"No way, she loves me more." Rome slides in front of him.

"Remember that time I fixed your car for free?" Kingston joins in.

I laugh because I'm absolutely not going on my honeymoon with any of my brothers. I'm already embarrassed and ashamed enough. "I'll be going solo, thanks."

The buzzer rings again. Juno rushes over to grab it.

"It's not the hottie! Relax, Juno," Savannah screams to her around a mouthful of pizza.

My stomach is eating away at itself. The yogurt this morning wasn't enough to fill me until dinner. I probably shouldn't be hungry either.

"Sorry, party is full unless you're the hottie next door," she says into the intercom then looks back. "That almost rhymes. I'm a rapper!"

Austin raises his eyebrows, clearly concerned about how much Juno's had to drink. "Kingston, you're getting her home tonight."

"Let me up, Juno!" Grandma Dori yells through the speaker.

"Sure thing, G'ma." She presses the buzzer.

Rome heads out to go help my grandma up the three flights of stairs. Phoenix links her phone to my Bluetooth speaker and starts some music. Maybe a party is just what I need to get evicted from this place.

"Turn it up, Phoenix," I call to her.

She nods, for once listening to instruction.

After what feels like forever, Rome opens the door, but Grandma Dori is nowhere in sight.

"Where is she?" I ask.

He thumbs behind him and smirks. "She found someone better to help her up the stairs."

In she walks with my hot new neighbor attached to her arm.

FOUR

Wyatt

As we round from the second floor to the third, the guy ahead of us leers over his shoulder as if I'm trying to pick up the woman he refers to as G'ma D.

"You're so sweet. What's your name?" She pats my hand and stops at the landing with only half a staircase left.

I don't blame her for taking a breather. I run every morning, but climbing these stairs three times today tells me I'm not as in shape as I thought. "Wyatt, ma'am."

"Don't ma'am me," she says.

The guy who came down to meet her stares at us from the top step. "She's Dori."

"Yes, and not to be confused with anything blue, like that damn fish," the elderly woman snipes.

My attention falls to her.

The guy above snickers.

"Unless you're going to compliment my eyes." She widens them, batting her eyelashes at me.

"Very blue and very pretty." I refrain from mentioning that her hair only brings out a deeper shade of blue in her eyes.

"Thanks. My granddaughter Brooklyn has the same color."

Ahh. The jilted bride is her granddaughter. Should've put those two things together.

"Yeah, but she's recently sworn off all douchebags," the guy says.

I eye the guy. He's stereotyped me pretty quickly. Not that I haven't him. I'd bet we're similar in our thinking when it comes to settling down.

"I'm not looking," I confirm.

"Brook's not looking for *any* companionship." His clarification is a clear warning to stay the fuck away.

As if I'd get involved with a scorned bride. What am I, an idiot?

I nod. Message received—loud and clear.

"Stop it, Rome," she scolds then turns to me. "He's acting like a *big* brother when the truth is, he's the *little* brother."

I glance at him with a smirk, and he rolls his eyes.

"None of us really cared for the groom, truth be told. He was a fine boy, just not meant to be a part of the Baileys," she whispers.

Rome chuckles. "We don't take applications. Can we finish this trek? The pizza's getting cold."

Dori waves him off. "You go. Wyatt's got me. Don't you, dear?"

Rome's eyes laser to mine. "Cool. He's not looking for anyone anyway, right?"

He laughs, turns around, and disappears to the sound of a door in the hallway above opening and closing.

"Okay, let's go." Dori steps on the first stair. "I'm not sure I'll be visiting my granddaughter much with these stairs."

"Maybe she'll come to you."

"You'll watch out for her, won't you?" she asks.

I want to cock my head back and shoot her a "you're insane" look. Is this what a small town brings you? In New York, I could see the same person on the elevator for three years and we'd both be content with not saying one word to each other. "Well..."

She pats my hand. "Thank you. Her ex-fiancé was a jerk, but the feeling of being unwanted has to be hurting her. She'll put up a good front today because the family is here, but my Brookie keeps things in and thinks of everyone before herself. Always has."

The genuine concern on Dori's face and in her tone strips the New Yorker right out of me. "Sure. I can do that."

We finally reach the top of the stairs. I swear I could've gone up and down them ten times by now.

"You're a lifesaver. It's like fate moved you in across the hall." She smiles at me, and I step forward to nudge her toward the apartment her granddaughter lives in. "Now come have pizza."

Her grip on me grows tighter, leaving me no chance to escape. Before I can do anything, we're in the apartment with what seems like a million sets of eyes on us.

I do a double-take twice because there are two sets of twins.

And the two women from earlier are here.

As heat rushes to my cheeks, my eyes stop mid scan across the room and land on Brooklyn. She's freshly showered, the overabundance of makeup stripped to show her clean face. Her blond hair is pulled up on the top of her head in a loose messy bun, and redness tints her cheeks at finding me, a stranger, in her apartment once again. Or maybe she's still embarrassed about hitting me with a book.

"This is Wyatt," Dori says to the room then leans into me. "Sorry, I never caught your last name."

"Wh—sorry. Wyatt Moore." I almost slipped because my first name rarely goes without my last name attached to it. My dad scolded Haylee and me when we were younger for not including our last name whenever we had to introduce ourselves. He said always to have my chin up and my shoulders back when I said it—let them know I'm someone important.

"He was a dear and helped me up the stairs." Dori doesn't let go of me, walking me over to the piles of pizza boxes on the kitchen table.

Everyone else still stares, assessing the situation.

"Why don't we give Wyatt a big Bailey welcome?" Dori says.

They all snap out of their trances.

"Hey, I'm Holly." An auburn-haired woman is first to walk up to me, followed quickly by one of the guys, who places one hand on her hip and the other between us.

"I'm Austin."

I shake his hand.

Then it feels as if I'm in a wedding reception line.

"Kingston."

Shake.

"Denver."

Shake.

Wait, wasn't that Rome? With a line between my brows, I search the room, and the guy in front of me laughs.

"Twins," he says.

I nod, remembering.

"Juno, as you know." She does a cute curtsy.

"Savannah, we met earlier." The blonde's handshake is firmer than my own.

"Phoenix."

"Sedona."

When I shake their hands, they stand side by side.

"Twins," they say, in case I'm an idiot.

"And lastly, Brookie." Dori finally releases me and wraps her arms around her granddaughter's shoulders.

"A man with matching coffee mugs is a man no one loves," Dori says, eliciting an eye roll from each family member close enough to hear.

"I know. I know." Brooklyn hugs her grandma. She's surprisingly upbeat for a woman who had the unthinkable thrust upon her today.

"What are you talking about, Grandma?" Savannah asks, pouring wine into her glass. She sits down and cuts her pizza with a plastic fork and knife. God, she reminds me of my sister.

One of the brothers—I think Kingston, he looks younger than the rest—hands her a beer and holds one out for me, bearing no smile. "You're going to need this if you're staying."

"Thanks." I accept it.

He nods, grabs a slice of pizza, and heads over to the couch, where the girl set of twins are on their phones.

"Coffee mugs are an easy gift. Cute sayings, words of love, puny references. I think the first gift I ever got from your dad was an 'I love my mommy' mug. It still sits in my cupboard. A coffee mug says what people think of you."

Dori tips the beer back. I'm impressed by how large a pull she takes.

Brooklyn smiles with a slight roll of her eyes.

"What is it with this family and coffee mugs?" Austin calls, and Holly lightly smacks him in the stomach.

All eyes shoot to Savannah, who stands and takes her pizza and beer over to the couch area.

"So I've asked Wyatt here to keep an eye on you, sweetie." Dori's hand grips my upper arm. Her tone isn't forceful, but now I'll really feel like a dick if I don't look out for her granddaughter.

Wonderful. Six months of helping Brooklyn lug groceries up the steps and trying to fix stuff in her apartment. She should know I'm not a repairman.

"Oh, Grandma." Brooklyn looks at me. "I'm good. Swear."

"Well, if you need anything, just knock." I look at my watch. "I should get going."

"Nonsense," Dori says, scoffing as if that's the most absurd thing she's ever heard.

"Really. I just got into town today and I'm beat." I finish off my beer and drop the empty bottle on the table.

"Well, thanks for the help. You'd think my grandbabies could help an old lady out."

"Hello?" Rome says, raising his arms.

Everyone laughs.

"Any time. Nice meeting you all." I smile and wave, backtracking to the door.

"Welcome to Lake Starlight," Holly says with a huge smile.

"Oh, look at the newbie." Denver ruffles her hair.

"I bet you've been dying to tell someone that," Austin says, staring at Holly as if Cupid just shot him. Holly blushes, and Austin looks at me. "She's the newest resident in Lake Starlight, but we do welcome you."

"Thanks. I'm sure I'll see you guys around." I wave.

"Lucky's is the place to go. Some of us get really lucky there," Denver says, waggling his eyebrows.

Rome can't hold in his laughter and beer sprays across the room.

Obviously an inside joke.

"*Rome!*" Juno screams, touching the back of her hair.

Hey, I really am getting these names straight. Go Whitmore.

As the room shifts back into chaos, I slide out, shutting the door as quietly as I can. *Shit, I can't even imagine being a part of that family.*

I dig into the pocket of my jeans for my keys, but before I can escape into my apartment, Brooklyn's door opens.

Looking over my shoulder, my heart beats a tad faster when I see her standing there. "Should I run for cover?"

Her shoulders fall and so does her smile. Padding across the floor in her socks, she stops right in front of me, making eye contact. I don't even make eye contact like this while I'm screwing someone. Only when I'm closing a deal, which isn't often since my dad is making me earn my stripes.

She touches my arm. "I just wanted to say I'm sorry." She runs her finger over the cut on my forehead. "I hope it doesn't leave a scar."

I hate to sound like a broken record, but she is so damn beautiful. Not at all like the type of women I usually find attractive.

I've always found it ironic the way my parents raised us to have core values—to earn our money, cherish family, treat everyone with respect—then sent us to snooty private schools, had family Sunday dinners at the club, and mingled with the richest of the rich in Manhattan. Needless to say, the women I'm used to would never touch my forehead in a caring manner if they didn't know me. Brooklyn knows nothing about me. Hell, she doesn't even know my real name.

"I'm sure it won't." I'm stiff as a board as she runs her finger beside the raised cut.

"Well, I never meant to hit you. It was just a bad day." She frowns, and her eyes glisten with unshed tears.

Just a bad day? I want to scream at her that she got fucked over and it's okay to be pissed beyond belief. "Yeah. I'm sorry about... that can't be easy."

She nods, her mind not on my cut anymore as she lowers her hand and entwines them in front of her. "I'll be gone for two weeks. I've decided to take my honeymoon."

"Good for you."

She nods. "But don't listen to my grandma. You don't need to do anything special for me. She likes to pry into everyone's lives. But when I get back, if you need anything, let me know. I've lived in Lake Starlight my entire life, so treat me like Google." The cutest laugh falls out of her and she shakes her head. "Anything, just shout."

"Thanks. That's a two-way street."

She smiles, stepping backward but still looking at me. "Have a good night, Wyatt." Her hand lands on her doorknob.

"You too." I turn the key for my apartment.

She opens the door to her apartment, initiating a scattering of hoots and hollers from the Baileys inside her apartment.

"Seriously! You all need your own lives!" Brooklyn screams, shutting the door.

I step in and shut my door, finding the quiet calming. As

I head down the hall to unpack my clothes, I can't help but wonder what kind of dickhead you have to be to stand up a woman like that at the altar. Even if I'm not the marrying kind, it doesn't take a genius to figure out that any guy would be lucky to call Brooklyn Bailey his wife.

FIVE

Brooklyn

"Here you go." Savannah takes my suitcase out of the back of her SUV. She's wearing her mothering expression today. "You sure you don't want me to park and come in?"

"No. You can't get past security anyway. I'll message you when I land."

"I can if Duke is working." She gives me a smug smile, referring to the time she and Grandma Dori surprised Austin at the airport to get him to pull his head out of his ass about Holly.

"I'm fine," I insist.

She nods and inhales a deep breath. "Okay."

I swallow back the tears that want to burst out.

After a night of pizza, drinks, and laughing with my family, I woke up realizing it really did happen. I was one of those brides I've read about but never thought I'd be. I'm destined to be Brooklyn Bailey, the Bailey who got left at the altar. If it wasn't for Savannah this morning, I might've shut myself in the apartment and hid under my covers for eternity.

"You're going to have so much fun. I stuffed a book in your carry-on. Just relax and enjoy." Savannah grips my upper arms. "Be safe though. Don't trust everyone you come across. I don't want to have to fly down to Hawaii searching for you."

"I'm twenty-six."

Even though Savannah's three years older than me, sometimes it feels as if she's decades older since she had to step up when our parents died. I guess responsibility has a way of changing the dynamics.

"I know. I know." She releases my arms only to hug me tightly. "You sure you don't want someone to go with you? Rome would rush over here if you say yes."

I giggle and shake my head in the crook of her neck. "I'll be good. I need the alone time to figure out what's next."

She pulls back and shuts the back of her SUV. "Okay, well, text me before you leave Hawaii and one of us will pick you up when you get back."

She smiles and climbs into her SUV. As she drives away, I watch her as if she's my life vest in the middle of a vast ocean. When I walk through the sliding doors into the departure terminal, the airport is a zoo. It's peak vacation season.

Using the new kiosk system, I pull up my confirmation and scan my confirmation on my phone, but the screen tells me to see an attendant. I blow out a breath and grab my suitcase and carry-on to go stand in the long-ass line.

Obviously this line is used by everyone who has ticket problems, because it moves as fast as Grandma Dori did down the stairs in my apartment building last night. I think she was hoping Wyatt would come help her. He does seem like a nice guy.

After he left last night, we all speculated on what brought him to Lake Starlight, since no one asked him, which is so not like us.

I inch forward in line, smiling at the little boy in front of me. *I was hoping to have one of you in a couple of years.* Now I'll be starting over. The entire process of meeting someone, dating them... I can't even continue the thought. It sounds exhausting.

I don't know how to be single. I've been with Jeff since college. He was the one who got me out of the depression that hit hard after my parents died. The one I trusted when he said he wouldn't hurt me. Well, look at me now, Jeff. Can someone really change that much in such a short amount of time, or was I blind?

"Next," the woman at the counter says, waving me over.

I rush over, eager to get this show on the road before I chicken out. "Hi. I tried to scan my confirmation and it said to see an attendant."

She smiles and takes my phone, typing away on her keyboard. "Maui?"

"Yes." I place my hands on the counter, staring over at her, anxiously tapping my foot.

Her lips turn downward from her professional smile. "This ticket has been canceled."

My body tenses. "Well, I don't know how that would have happened."

"Oh wait." She types some more, her eyes on the screen.

Good. It was a mistake, she's figured it out. I let out a relieved breath.

She slides the phone back to me. "Did you purchase these tickets?"

I close my eyes, understanding the problem. "Well, my fian—my ex did, but this ticket is in my name."

Her demeanor and attitude soften, and a pitying look creeps into her eyes. Those damn eyes. The whole reason I'm going on this honeymoon is to escape the exact look she's giving me right now.

"The purchaser canceled the ticket," she says in a low voice.

My head snaps back as if she slapped me. "What? That's impossible."

She looks at the screen to make sure she has it right. "Jeffrey Brickle?"

"Yes, that's him."

Her gaze shifts to the right—where a corridor leads to security. "Since he purchased the ticket, he can cancel the ticket. But..." She looks down the line of desks of her coworkers helping other people and leans closer to me. "I'm sorry, he told us how you left him at the altar."

"What?"

The guy working next to her glances at me. Obviously he's familiar with Jeff as well. The man he's helping scurries away with his ticket in hand. The airline employee puts up a closed sign in front of his area and steps over beside the woman assisting me.

"Ma'am, it's none of our business. All we can really tell you is that your ticket was canceled." The look on his face says he believes the tale my ex-dipshit spun.

The woman's eyes veer down the corridor once again.

I follow her gaze, but all that's there is a sea of people heading toward security.

"The ticket was in my name!" Tears are welling, my nose is tickling. At any moment, I'm going to lose it.

"Yes, but he paid for it," she says.

I grab my phone and put it in my pocket. "So what do I do? Buy another ticket?"

"I'm sorry, but the flight is full," the man says.

I'm tempted to believe he's lying to me because he thinks I'm the one who walked out on my wedding.

"Fine. I'll take my business somewhere else." I grab my bags and turn around to find the long line of people waiting in the queue staring at me. I circle back around. "Just so you know. He left me, asshole. In a text message."

The man's face pales.

"I believe his exact words were, 'I just can't do it. Sorry Brooklyn.'"

"I knew it!" the woman says, jabbing her elbow into the man's ribs. "He's heading through security now. With the woman he used the other ticket for." She shoots me a sympathetic look.

"What?" I whisper. Clearly I didn't hear her correctly. There were no signs of Jeff cheating on me. I scoured the apartment like a drug dog.

She nods.

The color hasn't returned to the other guy's face. If I felt nice, I'd apologize and tell him not to feel bad, Jeff Brickle fooled me too. But for once, I'm not feeling nice.

"He canceled yours and re-bought the ticket in another woman's name. The two of them are going on your honeymoon." She points again. "If you hurry, you'll catch him."

I stare blankly at her. Why would I even want to catch him?

As the reality of what the woman behind the counter told

me sinks in, I grip my suitcases tightly and run down the corridor. I weave between families and accidentally spill a man's coffee. Apologies fly out of my mouth once I'm strides away because my eyes are glued to the big security checkpoint sign.

I'm trying to get oxygen in my lungs and look up right as Jeff is about to step through security. "*Jeff*!"

He looks back, his eyes widening.

"Brooklyn." The love I thought filled the syllables of my name when they came off his tongue are no longer there.

Abandoning my luggage, I zig-zag through the ropes, past passengers staring at me with intrigue and shock. "I want answers!"

"Sir," the security personnel says at the same time an arm stretches to stop me from going forward.

A small brunette peeks her head around the other end of security. I don't recognize her, but she obviously knows me.

"Just tell me," I say to Jeff. I look at the woman security officer keeping me from approaching any closer. "He left me at the altar yesterday."

Everyone within earshot gasps.

"I told you. I'm just not happy," Jeff says.

"And *she* makes you happy?" I point at the brunette.

He glances back at her then back at me and shakes his head as though I'm a petulant child. "Don't do this to yourself."

"Seriously, that's all you've got? *You* did this to *me*! *You* asked me to marry you! *You* made me plan some big, elaborate wedding, and *you* sent me a text message five minutes before our wedding ceremony was supposed to start!" I point at him, my body bending forward as far as the security woman will let me go.

He abandons his spot, and I catch a more professional-looking guard coming from down the hall. He's obviously been notified of the disturbance I've caused.

"I'm sorry. I should have said something earlier," Jeff says.

"And now you're taking her on our honeymoon?" My throat clogs with emotion.

"I figured you wouldn't want to go."

As I stand there wanting answers, I realize there's one simple reason for all this. It's me. Plain and simple.

"Tell me," I demand. "Say the words."

"What?" he asks, putting his arms out to the sides like he does when he's trying to avoid answering a question.

"Tell me. Say it, you fucking coward," I say between gritted teeth.

He looks back at the brunette and returns his attention to me.

The security guy is getting closer, his eyes focused on me.

"Things between us changed at some point. It's not you."

"Jeff!" I yell, inching forward. The security lady is giving me a little more leeway.

"What do you want from me?" he asks. "I just don't love you."

I push past the security woman, and the crowd between us disperses, leaving an opening for me. "Fuck you!" I slap him across his face. "You don't love me? Shame on you for stringing me along all this time." I lean around his shoulder to glare at the brunette. "Good luck."

She sneers, her cheeks red.

Jeff holds his cheek as I stare at the man I'd thought would be my husband. "My family is right. You're not even close to being good enough for me, you weak bastard."

I turn on my heel, the passengers leaving room for me to get by.

"Thank you," I whisper to the security lady.

"Gladly," she replies.

I zig-zag back through the ropes, pick up my bags, and follow the signs to the rental car area because the last thing I want to do right now is call my family.

SIX

Wyatt

I swear every minute in Lake Starlight drags on longer than in New York. It's Sunday morning and I've already gone for my run, eaten breakfast, and read the *Wall Street Journal* on my iPad.

Needing to get familiar with this town, I head down the stairs of my apartment complex—only to see Brooklyn standing on the other side of the door. My heart sinks when I notice her red-rimmed eyes, the sadness tattooed on her face as though it's permanent. What a shame it would be if this ruined her for some guy who actually deserves her. I've seen it with my friends. One heartbreak and they're done, never to trust anyone again.

She fiddles with her keys, drops them, and bends to pick them up. Instead, she ends up sitting on the concrete alongside a pair of suitcases, head in her hands, obviously devastated.

I open the door and squat beside her. "Are you okay?"

She peeks at me through her laced fingers then wipes away tears before standing. Grabbing her keys and her bags, she steps forward.

"Whoa." I place my hand on her shoulder. "Slow down."

She shakes her head frantically and slides past me. "Thanks for opening the door."

"Brooklyn," I say, following her up the stairs.

"Don't worry, I won't tell Dori you saw me like this. Actually, my entire family will never know I didn't go." She drags her bags up the first flight of stairs as if demons from hell are chasing her.

"Will you stop? I know we don't know each other, but—"

She stops on the second landing, a fresh stream of tears falling. "I'm not your problem, but thank you for trying."

Her hand presses on my forearm, and even though my long-sleeved T-shirt blocks any skin-to-skin contact, her warmth is there. It's in her.

"You obviously need someone. If you're not going to tell your family whatever's going on..." I follow her up the next flight of stairs.

"I'll be fine. I just need to decompress." She reaches her door and fumbles with her keys, putting in the front door one before realizing it doesn't actually unlock this door.

This is why key codes are so much simpler. I take the keys hanging out of the doorknob, swap them out, and open her door.

She pulls her bags in, stopping and turning around before I can follow her. "Thank you." She slams the door in my face, even though I still hold her keys.

I swear this town. Or maybe it's just this building. Maybe it's just the Baileys.

I knock lightly.

No answer.

I knock again and lean my ear to the door.

Not one peep.

Shit.

I clutch the doorknob and it turns.

Simple enough. I'll crack it open, fling the keys in, and lock it from the other side before I shut it again. My mom would kill me if I left a girl in an apartment with an unlocked door.

Then again, I'm not in New York. I'm in Lake Starlight, with what feels like a population of one hundred so far.

The knob clicks and I open the door just enough to throw the keys in and reach my arm around the door to lock the bottom lock. I can't help but look through the crack in the opening.

I don't see Brooklyn anywhere. She must be in her bedroom.

My fingers blindly fiddle with the lock. I'm about to let the door shut when my gaze flickers to movement on the right. Forgetting the lock, I push the door open.

She wouldn't notice anyone if they busted down the door. She's curled into a ball on the couch, clutching a pillow to her chest, tears streaming down her face.

Fuck.

Why can't I mind my own business? She's not my business. The last thing I want is to sit around all day and listen to her carry on and on about some dipshit who didn't give a crap about her. How the hell do I know what to do with a broken-hearted girl? Do I look like Dr. Phil?

My mom wonders why I don't want to settle down?

Look at this girl. Some guy promised her the moon and the stars then left her at the altar. Do you ever really know someone?

"Hey." I slowly step into the room. "Brooklyn?"

She doesn't look up, so I continue to her small living room. When I sit at the far end of the couch, she never even glances my way.

"Are you okay?"

What a stupid question. Of course she isn't. Her life as she knows it is over. Not that I've ever experienced heartache from a romantic relationship. But the mess of emotions she's feeling is the exact reason I shy away from them.

"I'm the stupidest woman in the world," she murmurs, her head on the pillow as she stares out her patio door at the lake.

"No, you're not." I clench my fists to stop myself from touching her. "You're not the first woman to be fooled by a guy or vice versa."

Her eyes flicker to me. "He stole our honeymoon too. Canceled my ticket and bought one for some slutty brunette." She winces. "I shouldn't say that. I don't even know her."

I huff. This guy is in the running for asshole of the year.

"I'm sorry," I say like a pure schmuck. I should have some words of wisdom, but I've got nothing.

"You don't need to be sorry, you didn't desert me." She sits up, looking straight ahead still. "You know what gets me?" Her ass wiggles into the couch like she's a dog finding her most comfortable position. "The fact he let it go that long. I mean, I'm sure we were caught up in the wedding planning and everything, but he wanted that. If it was my decision, I would've been married out by the lake at my parents' house. Had a tent put up and invited only our closest friends and family. But he wanted the big to-do." She stretches her arms out on either side. "Do you think it's because I'm a Bailey? Like he just wanted to marry one and he thought 'well, I'll take that one,' and like a dummy, I let him take advantage of me?"

There they go again. They act like the name Bailey in Lake Starlight is akin to a Kennedy in Washington.

"I'm sure he loved you for you." I clamp my hands between my legs, sitting on the edge of the couch so I can make my escape as soon as she seems like she has it together.

"If he loved me, he wouldn't have done what he did."

"I can't say I disagree."

"Listen." She puts the pillow between her legs, wiggles again, and stares me down. "I'm not going to tell my family what happened. At least not yet." Her eyes drift to the window. "I just need some time to myself. So can we pretend you didn't run into me?"

"I don't know your family."

"Well, the more you're in Lake Starlight, the more you'll realize that everyone knows my family, and I guarantee you'll run into them. I don't want to put you in a bad situation, but they'll suffocate me until I beg for mercy." She giggles.

That's a good sign, right?

"My lips are sealed." I stand, relieved that this won't take up my whole afternoon.

"Thank you. I promise I'll repay you for all the shit you've dealt with in the short time you've been here." A small smile creases her lips.

Her ex truly is an idiot. I'm not comfortable sitting here with a crying female, but it's clear to see that on a good day, you'd be lucky to spend time with Brooklyn. "Not necessary."

"This is Lake Starlight. Paybacks are a must. Besides, it's neighborly."

I rock back on my heels. "I'm starting to notice the small-town mentality."

Her eyes focus out the window again, her mind somewhere other than me. I'm not used to that.

"If you need anything, I'm across the hall."

She turns her head, and again, a small smile plays on her lips. "Thanks."

"I'll lock up."

She says nothing, sliding down the sofa and falling into the same position I found her in.

I shut the door. Though a feeling of relief should envelop me, it doesn't. For some weird reason, I still feel pulled to the other side of the door. I shake my head as I walk over to the stairway.

My focus needs to be on Glacier Point Resort and making it the hotel in Alaska that everyone wants to visit so that I can hightail it back to New York, where people stick to themselves.

## SEVEN

Wyatt

I enter the hotel on Monday morning wearing my lucky suit. These people need to know that even though I'll be acting as the bellhop for the next couple of weeks, I *am* their new manager. No matter what my dad says.

The heads at the front desk turn and clock me the minute I circle through the revolving door into the lobby.

So it's better than a three-star hotel. Maybe a three and a half. The lobby is a good size, with decent furniture and a few plants sprinkled throughout.

A young kid comes up and greets me. "Hello, sir."

My assumption is that this pimple-faced boy is my new boss for the foreseeable future. *Thanks, Dad.*

"Hi, I'm Wyatt Moore." I hold out my hand, thankful that I didn't stumble over my last name.

Practice makes perfect.

The kid's eyes widen. "Hello. I'm Mac."

I shake his limp hand. Note to self—teach this guy how to be confident if he's going to be our frontline connection to customers. "Nice to meet you. I'm going to situate some things with Mr. Clayton, then I'm all yours."

Mac smiles nervously and nods.

The heels of my loafers click on the tile floor, announcing my arrival to the front desk the entire way. A woman and a man there smile at me. They know who I am. Well, not really. They think they do though.

"Mr. Moore?" the woman asks, holding out her hand.

"Wyatt," I say. One way I'm not like my father is having to be called Mr. Whitmore all the time. Not to mention, I probably wouldn't answer to Mr. Moore since it's not my name.

"Nice to meet you. I'm Noelle, and this is Neil." She tilts her head toward the man next to her.

He smiles, and I shake his hand.

"Should be easy to remember you two. Noelle and Neil. The two Ns."

They laugh nervously, though I'm trying to put them at ease. I don't believe in managing by fear.

"Is Mr. Clayton in?" I ask. My father bought the hotel from Mr. Clayton, but he agreed to stay on during this whole transition/experiment of my father's.

Noelle's eyes shift to Neil. "Not yet. He usually comes in sometime within the next hour or so."

"Oh."

"I do have your bellhop outfit all dry-cleaned and ready to go," Noelle says.

I forgot about that. "Great. I'll get started and maybe catch Mr. Clayton on my lunch."

"Right this way. Come on through that door." She

points toward the door next to the front desk marked "Employees Only."

There hangs my polyester uniform. Red jacket with gold trim and buttons. Wonderful.

I'm doing this for an entire chain of hotels. I have a feeling I'll need that reminder over the next couple of weeks.

"Thanks, Noelle." I pick up the wire hanger off the hook and follow the signs to the employee locker room.

Ten minutes later, my eight-thousand-dollar suit hangs on the hanger formerly occupied by the fifty-dollar uniform that's so durable it would probably survive long after I did if I lit it on fire.

I walk out of the employee locker room and to the main lobby. Mac is standing near the small desk by the rotating doors, his eyes meeting mine.

"All right, Mac, teach me everything I need to know. Fast." I laugh.

He laughs. "Well, it's Monday, so we have more departures than arrivals."

That's typical of most hotels geared toward vacations. It's not like this is a city hotel where business people are coming and going all week.

I follow Mac around, carrying luggage from carts to the trunks of their owners, and by lunchtime, I have a good stack of tips. Mac returns from his lunch, so I take mine.

I really hate first days on the job. They suck.

Mr. Clayton stopped by earlier when we had three guest rooms checking out. One with so many kids, I looked around after they drove away, thinking they had to have missed one. Since I obviously didn't have time to talk to him then, I told him I would meet him while I was on lunch.

"Hey, Noelle."

She smiles.

"Mr. Clayton around?"

She nods and picks up her phone, informing him that I'm hoping for a word. "Go ahead."

Before I can actually step into his office, he appears and signals for us to head to the bar restaurant that overlooks Glacier Point, hence the reason for the resort's name.

"Sorry I wasn't here this morning, but you're aware of"—he looks around to be sure we're alone—"our reason for selling."

I nod.

It's a sad story really. Mr. Clayton's wife was diagnosed with fibromyalgia, and they've decided to head to Arizona where the warm weather will help with her condition. His words were life is too short and he's too old. If warm weather will help her, then he'll move.

"She's having a rough morning." He waves at the bartender and a young waitress, situating us in the farthest corner he can.

"I'm sorry to hear that."

"The nice thing is we'll be gone before winter hits. I've already lined up a house for us with a pool. She's excited, and as you can imagine, there's nothing better than seeing the woman you love happy. It's like a shot of Jack. Numbs whatever shit is going on in your reality for a while."

I smile although I don't know what he's talking about.

"So Mac seems good." I settle in the booth. Booths that will be replaced once Whitmore Hotels renovates. Booths take up too much room and the upkeep is unreal.

"He's eager to succeed. A little intimidated by our older guests, but always polite."

A waitress comes over. She can't be more than twenty. Blond hair strung up in a ponytail, natural-looking makeup, her polyester uniform wrinkle-free. There are advantages to polyester, but these uniforms are right out of 1976.

"This is Molly. Molly, this is Wyatt W—Moore. He'll be the new manager, but right now, he's learning the ropes per their company policy."

She smiles at me. "Nice to meet you."

I hold out my hand and she daintily shakes it. "You too."

"I'll have a coffee," Mr. Clayton says.

"I'll have a Ja—" I shouldn't have alcohol. "I'll have a diet whatever you have."

She nods and heads to the bar, where she must tell the bartender who I am because her gaze lands on me.

"She's sweet too. She has a one-year-old. Sadly, the father was here for fishing one weekend and hasn't been back since. So it's just her and the baby."

"But she gets to work on time okay? Any issues with tardiness or sick days?"

Mr. Clayton's face twists into displeasure for a moment, but he masks it. "No. Her parents help her as much as they can."

"That's good news."

Molly brings us our drinks. "Are you eating as well?"

I glance at my watch. According to Mr. Clayton, everyone gets an hour lunch, which is absurd. A half hour is plenty.

"Sure. Can you bring me whatever the most popular dish is?" I ask.

Her eyes fall to Mr. Clayton for guidance on my question.

"Bring him the bison burger with the twisted fries."

She smiles and nods, her hand touching his shoulder. "Anything for you, Mr. Clayton?"

"I'll take a bowl of chowder with—"

"Oyster crackers." She giggles. "I know."

The interaction tells me Molly has Mr. Clayton wrapped around her little finger.

Note to self—check Molly's time cards.

"Anything else I need to know?" I ask once Molly's gone.

"No. I imagine Lake Starlight is a big change from New York City. How are you adjusting?"

I think about my time so far and only one name comes to mind, but I keep that to myself. "Let me ask you a question. Have you ever heard of the Baileys?"

He smiles, followed by a frown. "I'm guessing you heard the gossip about Brooklyn Bailey. Sad really. Jeff used to surprise her here with flowers and candy." His eyes shoot out to the clear blue lake out the large window. He points at the arced overpass that I thought would be great to host wedding ceremonies under the first time my dad showed me pictures of this place. "He proposed there."

"Why here?" I ask.

Mr. Clayton tilts his head. "Have you read the list I sent with everyone who works here and a little of their background?"

I started to but got bored after two pages. I don't need to know how many kids these people have, who married their high school sweetheart, and whether or not they usually attend the Christmas party. I just need to know if they can do their damn job.

He realizes my answer without me responding. "Brooklyn Bailey works in housekeeping for us—well, for you now. She's a sweet girl. Worked here ever since college. I was surprised that a Bailey would work here. I think it was meant to be temporary, but after Jeff proposed and him being so tech savvy..."

Here he goes again, telling me information I don't care about.

Okay, I care a little bit.

"Why does everyone act like the Baileys are royalty?"

He tilts his head. "You need to do some more research."

I refrain from rolling my eyes.

"The Baileys employ most of this town. They came here and saved it from disappearing off the map decades ago. Bailey Timber Corp is the reason Lake Starlight is what it is today. But everyone took to them even more after their parents died."

That explains why there weren't any parents at her place the other night.

"They died nine... no, ten years ago. The anniversary is this winter. There's nine of them. Brooklyn is in the middle. The eldest, Austin, returned to town to raise the younger kids back when it happened, and Savannah, the second eldest, took over Bailey Timber Corp, along with their grandmother, Doris Bailey. It shocked and stunned most of Lake Starlight. I think everyone just knows them now and has a vested interest in their happiness."

I lean back and sip my drink, scanning the area.

"Anyway, I'm guessing you heard Brooklyn's wedding didn't happen and she's off for two weeks. I heard she went on her honeymoon anyway. I really hope that's the case. The girl works so hard, she deserves the time off."

I nod, knowing full well where she is and it's not on a beach unless she poured sand in the apartment and started putting umbrellas in her drinks. "I vaguely heard about it. It's amazing how small this town feels."

"Yeah, well, most people in this town are lifers." He shrugs.

Molly brings over our plates and leaves ketchup, mayo,

and mustard bottles on the table as though we're at a discount diner.

Another note to self.

"Anyone else you want to know about?" he asks.

"Which employee has missed the most time?" I ask before I bite down on my burger.

His face distorts again but recovers quickly. "We have one maid who's missed some time, but—"

"I just need her name." I take another swig of my drink.

His shoulders deflate and he rests his spoon next to his bowl. "Can I offer some advice?"

I'd like to say no. That his way of doing things ran this hotel into the ground. Now whether that was because of his wife's health or not, I don't know, but the fact remains, Whitmore Hotels is famous for a reason. So I don't really need him to advise me on what we should be doing.

But I'm polite until someone gives me a reason not to be, and there's no sense getting this off to a bad start. He can offer his advice, but I don't have to take it. "Sure."

"Get to know the employees. Don't treat them as numbers, view them as people. People like you. After all, we all put our pants on one leg at a time."

His insult doesn't go unregistered. I don't think I'm better than these people because I grew up with money. I simply think there are those with a work ethic and those without. And part of managing a successful enterprise means making tough decisions. I'm not doing anyone any favors if this place doesn't turn a profit and my dad decides to close it. Then everyone's out of a job instead of just the dead weight.

"Thank you." I wash down what was a pretty amazing burger with my Diet Coke and wipe my mouth with my paper napkin. "I'll consider it."

After my shift, I can't wait to get into some more comfortable clothes that aren't made of polyester. I trudge up my stairs with the paperwork Mr. Clayton gave me at the end of the day—everyone's attendance records since they started. When I reach the third floor, my gaze shoots to Brooklyn's door.

I wasn't considering screwing her, but the fact that she's my employee takes the option off the table completely.

Like some creep, I press my ear to the door. What? I'm only doing what I promised her grandma I would. But all seems quiet behind the door, so I walk across the hall to my own door, hoping she's finding the peace she needs.

EIGHT

Brooklyn

My phone dings next to my bed.

I've had it plastered next to me in case my family gets the urge to call me.

I turn it over and see the string of messages my friend Reagan left me on Doomsday and every day since.

Reagan: *Call me.*

Reagan: *I knew he was an asshole.*

Reagan: *I hope you're okay.*

Reagan: *Talked to Juno, if you need me, you know where I am.*

Reagan: *Juno says you're going on your honeymoon.*

Reagan: *Have fun and call me when you get back.*

Reagan: *Oh shit, you should see the new bellhop. Damn girl.*

Reagan: *Oh, I just found out, he's the new manager from that swanky hotel chain that bought us.*

Reagan: *He has to learn every position in the company.*

Reagan: *I might end up getting him tangled in the sheets when I show him how to make a bed. ;)*

Reagan: *I miss you.*

Reagan: *My days are boring without you.*

Reagan: *Call me as soon as you get this.*

The guilt piles on as I read her texts. Even if the last six were sent within the last minute. The girl has a unique way of texting her thoughts one after the other instead of in one message.

I pull the comforter over my head.

Darkness is my serenity.

NINE

Wyatt

It's been five days and I haven't seen or heard anything from Brooklyn. There's been no noise from her apartment. I haven't heard the door open or shut.

I should check on her.

I open my door, staring across the empty hallway at her door.

It's none of my business.

That's not true. Her grandma literally made me promise to check on her.

Her happiness is none of my business. There's nothing I can do that will make her feel better.

That's true.

I shut my door.

TEN

Brooklyn

y body is sore from stagnation. I didn't even know
that was possible. Even so, I force myself to pick up
my phone and text my family pictures of sunsets that
someone else took on *their* honeymoon.

Juno responds with a smiley face and words about how
beautiful the pictures are.

Savannah: *Have you thought any more about what you
want to do when you get back?*

Leave it to my eldest sister to make sure I have a plan in
place.

I sit up in bed, consider getting up for all of five seconds,
then plop back down. A knock hits my door and I startle,
my eyes wide and my muscles tight while I lie there, not
moving a muscle.

Another knock sounds.

I climb out of bed and tiptoe to the door, praying whoever it is can't hear me. Another knock hits the metal right when I look through the peephole.

"Brooklyn!" a deep voice yells.

Two bright blue eyes look back at me through the peephole.

"I've given you a week."

I jolt back. Why does my new hot neighbor care how I'm doing? Then again, he's the only one who knows I'm in hiding.

"I'm busy," I say through the door.

"No, you're not."

I scrunch my forehead. "How do you know?" I yell and step back from the door, surprising myself.

I don't yell.

Ever.

Well... rarely.

"Because your apartment has been as quiet as a monastery."

I lean closer to the door. "I appreciate your concern, but I'm fine, thank you." I step back again.

"I didn't ask how you were. I knocked, and I'm pretty sure the same rules apply in this town as they do everywhere else in the world—you open the door and we say hello face to face. Good job using the peephole, but let's be real here—I don't think *you* need to fear *me*. I have the scar to prove it."

I set my hand on the doorknob. "I apologized."

"And you also said you'd repay me sometime. That time is now."

"You told me I didn't have to." I drop my forehead to the door.

"Fucking hell, just open the door. I haven't worked this hard to feed a woman since I was fifteen and the first girl I asked out on a date had more dietary restrictions than my ninety-year-old grandma."

I lift up on the balls of my feet and glance out the peephole one more time. He's standing farther back now, a brown paper bag in his hands.

Wok For U.

My mouth salivates. "I look like shit," I grumble.

"I don't care."

"Orange chicken?"

"You have to open the door to see, but you should be thankful this town is small and they like to plaster pictures of its people proudly on the wall."

"What?" I spring open the door.

His gaze travels down my body. I pull the edges of my cardigan sweater closed, and Wyatt's eyes spring back up to mine.

"I didn't realize that you're kind of a celebrity around here." He steps in, places the brown bag on the kitchen table, and opens drawer after drawer in my kitchen.

"Buzz Wheel? Did they figure it out?" Fuck. If they know I'm not on my honeymoon, that means my family will be here in minutes.

"Buzz Wheel?" He looks skeptically over his shoulder and grabs two forks out of the drawer. "You won some kind of eating championship at Wok For U five years ago for eating orange chicken."

The tension racking my body loosens and I can breathe again. Thank God. I'm not ready to handle all my siblings yet. "Right. Well, it wasn't a huge thing."

"Well, the picture of you with your bib and all the sauce smeared on your face was enough to tip me off that you're a fan of orange chicken." He picks up the bag off the kitchen table and heads to the family room. "Come on."

"Thank you for the food, but—"

"I get that you ate your weight in orange chicken five years ago, but I'm still a growing boy—I need my food."

"You're planning on staying?" I double blink.

He rounds the couch, deserting the food, and grabs two waters from the fridge. He stares into the fridge for a minute then makes his way back to the family room. "Looks like someone needs more food since they're in hiding. Oh, and I figure you could use a little interaction with an actual human being. I won't stay long."

"Okay. Maybe I should get presentable." I walk toward the bathroom, but his long arm reaches over the edge of the couch and he grabs my wrist.

"You need to eat before I can blow you over with one breath."

I look down at myself. No bra. No panties. Pajama pants, a cami with a great big sweater, and a pair of socks with dogs on the backs. *Lame, Brooklyn.*

When I decided to strip myself of anything that reminded me of the wedding or Jeff, I took off the nail polish from the pedicure I got before the wedding. Now I just need hair to grow back between my legs so I can return to having a small patch instead of being completely bare. Then I'll feel like myself again.

I feel like a fool sitting here as such a hot mess when he's all... perfect and put together. It's not like I'm trying to date the guy, but after what happened, it would be nice to have some pride left.

"Come on. Stop fighting me." He pulls out the containers, leaving them on the coffee table.

The one thing having to do with the wedding that I

couldn't get rid of because I know Holly put a lot of work into refinishing it.

"Okay." I sit down next to him. "Do you want plates?"

He glances at me from the side of his eye. "No one eats Chinese with plates unless it's a business meeting. It's meant to be eaten out of the container. I promise I don't have cooties." He winks.

My stomach flips. I cover my belly with my hand. We do not flip over some charismatic man. We hate men. Remember?

Wyatt clicks on the television and scrolls through the channels. "Since it's your house, you get first pick."

"I thought you weren't staying long?"

He smiles. "I feel a little offended right now. I bring you orange chicken. I grab the silverware and drinks. For someone usually so polite, you act like you can't stand me." He's teasing me, that million-watt grin shining, and for a moment, my problems fade into the background.

"Fine." I snatch the remote. "If you're staying, I'm going to torment you." I click through a few channels until it lands on *Sex and the City*.

He grabs the remote. "I'm vetoing that."

"You can't veto." I reach to grab the remote from his hand, but he raises it up over his head. "That's not fair. I'm not as tall as you."

"First of all, everyone gets one veto. I'm not going to sit here with you and watch an entire television show about women trying to find the love of their life."

"You have no idea what *Sex and the City* is really about. It's about female empowerment and the relationship you have with yourself and other women. So there." I lean back into the couch, surprised by my lashing out.

"You're a lot sassier than I thought."

"I'm n—"

He raises his hand to my lips. "It was a compliment."

"Oh."

His hand falls and he changes the channel on the remote. "Regardless of whether it's about female empowerment or not, it has a hell of a lot about relationships in it. Let's watch *Paradise Lost*."

"I'm not watching that."

Three men's mug shots show up on screen.

"It's true crime." He presses Play and opens the orange chicken, then tosses in a fork and hands the box to me. "Do you scare easily?"

"No." My tone makes it sound as if I have a point to prove, but it's true. I don't scare at all usually. Except now I'm scared of any man I might have feelings for. I'm scared that my internal compass will point me toward another snake.

"Great. Then eat your chicken and settle in. It's a three-part series."

"You're staying for the entire three parts?"

"Do you have better plans?"

I stick out my tongue like a toddler and pick up my fork, stabbing a piece of chicken and wishing it was Jeff's dick. I guess I haven't worked through the whole anger stage yet.

ELEVEN

Wyatt

I should note that yes, Brooklyn does, in fact, scare easy.

The only reason I put on a true crime story about three sickos was because I've helped my sister, Haylee, through enough heartbreaks to know that any show or movie about love isn't a good idea right now.

Now, I stare down at Brooklyn's head on my shoulder and wonder if some sick part of me wants her. She's suffering, and the only thing that pops into my head is the fact that her left breast is pressed against my forearm and her lips are so close to mine, it wouldn't take much for me to kiss her.

I blink.

I need to get the fuck out of here before I do something I regret. Something that makes me the dickwad in her life rather than her ex-fiancé.

Sliding out from under her, I guide her head to the

pillow then lay the blanket over her body. I pick up all the Chinese food containers, close them, and put them in the fridge. On my way to the front door, I peek over the edge of the couch to find her fast asleep with her hands tucked under her cheek.

It's a shame really. We might've been a good fit, because no woman I know would ever let me convince her to eat Chinese food without a plate and watch a true crime story. But she's heartbroken, I'm essentially her boss, and I won't be in Lake Starlight long. Three strikes and I'm out.

I flick the lock on her door and slowly start to shut it behind me.

"What the hell?"

I spin around and jolt back against the partially open door. *Fuck.* Is this Rome or Denver?

"Shit. I really don't want to know." He shakes his head, glancing at the blonde hanging off him.

I'm pretty sure this is Rome.

"Brooklyn asked me to water her plants." I block the door as casually as I can so I don't alarm him.

"Her and all that herb shit." Rome holds up a key. "You should see her garden at the family home."

At least my lie holds some weight.

"What are you doing here?" I ask.

He checks out the woman again. "What does it look like? I figure Brooklyn is gone, so I might as well use her place." He shrugs.

"How did you get a key?"

"Okay, Sherlock Holmes, step aside." He motions with his hand, inching closer.

I stand my ground. "No. I mean... there's a bug problem in her apartment."

"*Ew!*" the blonde says.

Rome inhales a deep breath through his nose and stares at me as though he's about to rip off my head. Just when I expect them to leave, he turns to the blonde. "Stay here for a second." He kisses her cheek and whispers something in her ear that has her giggling and losing her balance.

He motions with his hand for me to move again, and I really don't have a choice.

I'm sorry, Brooklyn.

"How did you get a key?" I ask.

The devil's glint shines in his eyes. "I have my magic ways."

The woman makes an audible sound as though she agrees.

"Joel said not to go in. That it's really bad," I say in a last-ditch effort to get him to leave.

He glares at me while opening the door. "You were just in there."

He steps inside and peers into the small kitchen before heading to the living room. I watch from the doorway as his shoulders fall and his eyes close when he sees his sister tucked in, asleep on the couch.

I like to think Haylee and I are close. I mean, she's a little more high society than me, but if I was in Rome's position, I'd be putting up a Want ad with the bastard's picture on it. Even though I know nothing about Rome, the heartbreak on his face is evident. He's hurting because she is.

He turns and looks at me, points toward the hallway, and walks out. I lock the door from the inside again and turn to face him.

Rome turns his attention to the woman. "Sorry, babe, another night. Something's come up."

"But you said—"

His hand molds to her hip and I look away, not interested in playing the role of Peeping Tom.

"Sorry," he says again.

She huffs and walks down the stairs. Rome bites his fist as he watches her go. Once she's out of view, he snaps his fingers and points at my door. I'm not about to argue, since he probably thinks the worst of me already. I'm sneaking out of his heartbroken sister's apartment and he knows I lied to him about her being there.

"What's going on?" Rome blurts the minute my door shuts. He crosses his arms and presses his lips into a thin line.

"You have the wrong idea. I was just making sure she ate, and I tried to help keep her mind off what happened."

He huffs. "I'm a red-blooded male too. Don't bullshit a bullshitter."

I raise my hands. "Like I said, you're seeing this all wrong."

"Then enlighten me, because right now, I see a scumbag taking advantage of my sister who just had her heart shattered."

At my fridge, I grab a beer and offer one to Rome. He shakes his head.

"I found her in shambles at the front door of the apartment complex last week. She was crying, devastated."

"She's supposed to be in Hawaii. She's been messaging my sisters." He hasn't moved yet, his arms still crossed, showcasing just how much muscle will be behind a punch if he decides to go that route.

"She's lying. She's been here the entire time. She said she needed the two weeks to herself." I take a pull from my beer.

He shakes his head and stuffs his hands into his pockets. "Fucking shit. Why wouldn't she come to us?"

I say nothing because if roles were reversed, I wouldn't give one shit what some guy who knows nothing about my sister thinks.

"Why didn't she take the honeymoon? Do you know?" His eyes narrow on me.

Fuck. Having a sister means I also know what Rome's going to do when I tell him this next bit. How did I find myself in the middle of this family's drama? "*He* went on the honeymoon. Canceled her ticket and..."

"What?" Rome steps forward, eyes narrowed.

"Took another woman with him. He essentially traded Brooklyn's ticket for another woman's."

Rome's mouth hangs open.

Okay, this isn't bad. I thought for sure I'd be handing over my security deposit to Joel because of smashed drywall and broken glass.

"That son of a bitch," he whispers.

The longer the silence carries on in my apartment, the redder his face grows, hands clenched at his sides.

"Let's go." He stomps over to my apartment door and opens it.

"Uh, where?"

"We're going to Lucky's."

"Listen, I shouldn't have told you. Don't tell her I said anything."

He picks up my jacket off the hook near the front door and tosses it to me. "Probably not because I might get arrested when I fly to Hawaii and beat the shit out of him."

"Don't do anything hasty."

"Hasty?" He scoffs and steps out into the hall.

I lock up my apartment and follow him down the stairs.

"Don't worry, I keep a shitload of secrets in this family. Hell, I knew Austin was fucking Holly forever before anyone else."

We take the stairs two at a time, and he pushes open the main door of the building. I follow him down the pathway into the parking lot.

"Do you have a sister?" he asks as we climb into his Bronco.

"I do." I buckle my seat belt while he throws the car into reverse.

"Then you know how hot my blood is right now." The tires squeal out of the parking lot as "The Phoenix" by Fall Out Boy streams from his speakers.

He's got good taste in music. Not sure this is the right song for this moment, but the hell if I'll say anything.

"I can imagine." If Bradley stood Haylee up at the altar, I'm not sure what I would do.

We arrive at Lucky's Tavern quickly, thanks to Rome's driving. He appears to be on a mission as he slams his door and heads into the bar without waiting for me.

What the hell did I get myself into?

Following Rome, I enter the tavern, which turns out to be exactly what I would picture an Alaskan bar looking like. Lacquered wood is everywhere, but it's more welcoming than the dark clubs I usually go to in New York. Rome waves me over to where he's talking to his twin, Denver, and some other guy at a table, then he signals to the bartender with two fingers in the air.

"So this is Wyatt," Rome says to the other two.

Denver holds out his hand. "G'ma D's eye candy." He squeezes hard like I assumed he would.

I take the dig. I just hope he can take it back when I send one his way.

"Thank fuck, someone took my spot with Dori." The bigger guy with a sleeve of tats on both arms and a scruffy beard, sticks his hand out toward me. "Liam."

I shake his hand.

Rome sits in one of the empty chairs, so I sit in the other. A few seconds later, the waiter sets a beer in front of each of us.

"Thanks, Nate."

"No problem." He nods and heads back to his post behind the bar.

"I thought you were with Sasha or Cindy or whatever her name is." Denver tips back his beer, smirking.

"I was."

"Then you realized you had to take her to your child-hood bedroom with Austin and Holly down the hallway?" Liam laughs and Denver joins in.

"No, idiot. I went to Brooklyn's."

Denver tilts his head. "You weaseled a key out of her landlord, didn't you?"

Rome smiles, holding the top of the beer bottle to his lips.

I guess it's true that twins share a brain.

"I told you that you can use my place any time," Liam says. "Hell, I even offered for you to move in."

"Yeah, he's sitting in a four-bedroom house like some suburbanite dad," Denver says and clamps his hand on Liam's shoulder, laughing.

Liam narrows his eyes at his friend.

I feel as though I'm peering through a window into their life. A life that doesn't resemble mine in the slightest, but their friendship... I hate to admit it, but I'm slightly jealous.

Not that I don't have friends in New York, I do, but what these guys have is different, less superficial.

"I'm good, man." Rome sips his beer. "Anyway, you'll never guess what good ol' Wyatt told me."

Denver must sense something in Rome's tone because he puts all four chair legs on the floor and leans forward on the table. Liam does the same. The lighthearted vibe vanishes as though a big wind came through and swept it out the back door.

"Jeff went on their honeymoon."

Denver's fist slams on the table.

"With another woman."

Denver raises his hand as though he's going to throw the beer bottle, but Liam clamps his hand around Denver's wrist.

"I know. I know." Rome waves off his brother's temper. "We have to be smart about this." He leans forward, lowering his voice. "He's in Hawaii for another week, for which he should be thanking his lucky fucking sac of balls because I'm pretty sure we'd kill him if he was reachable today."

I lean back in my chair, not interested in having any part of this conversation. I'm in this town with a fake name as it is. I definitely don't need to draw attention to myself, and an assault arrest would definitely do that.

"Truth," Denver says, clicking his beer bottle to Rome's.

As they make an elaborate plan for payback, I sit there feeling as though I'm in some mafia movie. And though I'm trying to figure out a way to extricate myself from this situation, I have to wonder if I really want to.

TWELVE

Brooklyn

I'm not sure if it's the morning light or the fact I ate an actual meal last night thanks to Wyatt, but regardless, I wake up a little less depressed and with a little more energy.

After some coffee, I pull out my phone and dial Reagan's number. It's time I spoke to my bestie.

She answers on the first ring. "Okay, we really need to discuss where I fit in your life."

A sad chuckle leaves my lips. "Are you at work?"

"No. I'm at the nursing home. Mom's becoming combative."

I sit on the couch. "I'm sorry."

"I know you are. I just hope I don't get fired. I mean, Mr. Clayton always understood, but he's from Lake Starlight and knows Mom. This new guy, although he's so cute I could eat him up with a spoon, he seems stricter. He's constantly jotting down notes in his phone."

"Anyone would understand what you're going through."

At least anyone in Lake Starlight would. When Reagan's mom was diagnosed with early dementia, it was a shock to everyone. Eventually Reagan had to put her in a nursing home, but she's still getting used to the new surroundings. Reagan gets called there all the time, which means she misses time at work. The rest of our staff covers for her as much as we can, but with a new boss in the mix, it might change things.

"Well, we'll see. I can't afford to lose my job. I'm barely surviving now with all the missed hours."

Silence commences, as it usually does when we talk about this. I wish I had a magic potion to fix the entire situation for her. I listen and offer advice when I can, but I have no idea what she's going through. Not really. My parents were here one day and gone the next after a snowmobile accident. So I do what any friend would—clean her rooms when she has to miss work and sneak money into her purse when she's not looking.

"Forget me. Brook, I'm so sorry. I thought Jeff was the real deal."

I laugh. "No, you didn't."

She doesn't deny it.

We both know the truth. When I dissect my relationship with Jeff, I realize no one really cared for him.

"I'm still sorry he did what he did. And FYI, your family is like the Secret Service. I couldn't have gotten to you if I'd tried."

It bothered me that I couldn't ask her to stand up in my wedding, but with four sisters and Jeff scraping the bottom of his barrel for groomsmen, I had no choice but to tell her I would if I could.

I lean forward, picking pieces of dried fried rice off the

coffee table. For the first time in a week, my mind isn't solely on Jeff. Wyatt seems like a good guy. I mean, he doesn't even know me, and he brought me dinner out of concern.

"Hello?"

"Sorry." I shake away the memory of the feeling of his strong shoulder on my cheek last night. *You're a week off being dumped, the last thing you need is a rebound.* "What were you saying?"

"Nothing. I almost gut-punched Colton for not telling me what was going on, but Father Steve interrupted us."

"Probably a good thing."

She laughs. "For Colton's sake."

"It wasn't his fault. I'm sure Savannah directed everyone to their jobs and..." I let the topic trail off because I don't want to talk about it. I want to forget it ever happened. "How is work? I kind of miss it."

"You're insane. It's okay. Like I said, the bellhop, a.k.a. manager guy, is nice to look at, but other than him, everything else is the same. Oh, there is one thing though."

"What?"

She blows out a breath like it's depleting all her energy to tell me. "Devon asked me out."

"That's great news! Why do you sound like your cat died?" My forehead scrunches.

"Because this could not come at a worse time. Hello, my mom has dementia and threatens her nurses with a comb she thinks is a switchblade on the daily, I barely have enough money for Frosted Flakes, and if I did happen to get lucky, there's no sexy lingerie waiting under my ripped jeans and T-shirt."

"Slight exaggeration," I say, the truest smile I've had in days on my face.

Reagan has a way about her—she can bring humor out on the worst of days.

"Still. I don't have the energy for a relationship right now. The thought of dressing to impress is exhausting. And trying to decipher all the man code shit he's inevitably going to say sounds less than thrilling."

"It would be a good distraction from all those things you just mentioned."

She sighs. "True, but... I don't know."

"What did you tell him?" God, it feels so good to talk about someone else's issues. *Thank you, Reagan.*

"I told him that I'd think about it."

"And he said?"

"He said he's got the rest of his life."

I smile and look through my patio door at the lake. "Cute."

"I don't like lines, but the pink tint of his cheeks has me thinking he meant it."

"Of course he did."

"Again, you keep twisting this conversation back my way. I want to talk about you."

I stand from the couch, walk over to the balcony door, open it, and step outside. The fresh air feels amazing in my lungs after inhaling the stale oxygen of my apartment for the last week. "I'm healing. He went on our honeymoon with someone else, but I don't want to talk about it or him or anything regarding him. I want to forget him and move on. Dwelling on it isn't going to do any good."

"You need to grieve, Brook."

Surely I can tell Reagan... "I'll let you in on a secret—I've holed myself up in the apartment for the last week. I'm done grieving."

"Why didn't you tell me? I would've brought over wine and junk food."

"The only person who knows is my neighbor."

"I completely forgot you moved. So are you staying there?"

"Yeah. I can't get out of my lease. Even Sav tried and failed."

"Wow. How will you afford it?"

I shouldn't be surprised she's asking. We make the same hourly wage. The apartment is pricier because it's on the lake, and newly renovated. "I haven't figured that part out yet. I'm thinking about starting a side business with all the oils I make."

"Oh. My. God. You just reminded me of something. There was this woman who was staying in the penthouse. We all had bets on who she was. Mac swore she was a celebrity. Neil said he saw her on a reality show. Anyway, she kept asking everyone who made the lavender oil that was in her room. She said she's never slept so soundly before."

"That's nice."

"Nice? Brooklyn, you're thinking of starting a company and here's this super rich lady who loves it. This should be your 'take the bull by the horns' or 'the horn of the bulls.' Agh. Whatever. You know everyone raves about your stuff. Heck, your tea tree shoe deodorizer helped Mac out. When you gave me the orange for my cramps last month, it made a huge difference."

I glance back at the hallway that leads to the closet where Jeff insisted I put all my herbal stuff because he said they weren't an everyday item. He always hated going to the garden behind my family home where I grow my lavender and chamomile. Always complained about the bugs or the smell of all the plants.

"I think it's a great idea. Go for it, girl. Take the plunge."

"Would you?" I ask.

Lots of people think that because I have the Bailey name, I must have the Bailey money, but I don't. Yes, we all had money set aside for college, but Savannah and Austin won't bail me out if I fail. Sure, the family home is always open, but I'm twenty-six now. I alone have to make a future for myself.

"If I had your talent? Yes. At some point in your life, you have to take a chance."

A woman's scream rings through the receiver.

"Sorry, Brook, Mom woke up. I'll call you later."

The line dies and I hang up, my heart sinking for what Reagan is going through. I need to volunteer to be on call for her mom and make sure she goes on that date with Devon. Her sanity needs it and he's liked her for so long. He'll be good to her.

I go back inside the apartment and open the closet door. The box marked *Brooklyn's oils and stuff* sits at the bottom, shoved behind our coats. This is the only place I never checked when I was cleansing Jeff from my space.

There sits his parka and his ski gear. His boots and hats and gloves.

Shoving them aside, I sit on the hardwood and pull out the box. The mixture of smells pulls a smile from deep within me. I open the cardboard box and see the evidence of the one thing I've always been good at—creating mixes to benefit people.

Wyatt's good deed from last night comes to my mind again.

I need to thank him, and I know just how to do it.

THIRTEEN

Wyatt

Finally, I got to turn in the damn bellhop uniform. Not that exchanging it for a housekeeping uniform is much better. Especially since it's made from the same material as the bellhop's. Polyester is my new existence. I have to say it's durable. When a guest spilled her coffee on me two days ago, I barely had to wipe it clean.

My phone rings over my Bluetooth. Seeing it's my mom, I'd better answer now rather than let it go to voicemail. "Hey, Mom."

"Two weeks and no calls. I had to follow your Instagram after Haylee told me how beautiful Alaska looks."

Cue my mom's melodrama.

"Well, I am working, and besides, all you like to talk about lately is my future never-going-to-be wife." I turn down Main Street and spot Liam hanging up a sign outside one of the shops. He must own the tattoo shop, Smokin' Guns. Of course he does. That shouldn't surprise me.

"I'm just trying to make sure you're happy."

"I am."

"You're really not. A mother knows."

And she wonders why I dodge her calls.

"What else is going on?" I ask. "Haylee good?"

"We're at the four-month mark, so things are getting busy. Flowers, cake, groom's cake, menu tastings, dress fittings. It just brings happiness to everyone. Except your dad, who keeps grumbling about the money." Her nervous laugh rings over the phone.

"Because twenty-thousand dollars on flowers that will die the next day is ludicrous."

Great, I'm on speakerphone. "Hey, Dad."

"I hope that's not how you talk to the guests. 'Hey' should be stripped from your vocabulary." I hear ice cubes being dropped into a glass. I still forget the time difference sometimes between here and New York.

"Haylee only deserves the best." My mom's sweet tone suggests this is a regular topic of conversation in the house.

"How are things there?" my dad asks. "You've yet to send me the numbers I asked for." More ice clinks into a glass.

"I'm close," I say.

"It doesn't help that Bradley's parents are demanding so many guests, but I guess this is what you get when your daughter is marrying a future congressman." My mother continues with her attempt to remove work from the conversation, as usual.

"I suppose so," I say.

Funny thing is, Bradley was my closest friend through

high school. I've taken a back seat to his politician friends though. In truth, we've drifted apart.

"Maybe his family should open their billfold. This isn't some big affair."

"Your daughter is getting married. It is. Which brings up the topic, Wyatt, any date prospects?"

I roll my eyes. "Mom." I turn into the parking lot of my apartment complex.

"It's a simple question. I'm not trying to pry."

"That's exactly what you're trying to do."

"If he knew what was good for him, he'd be calling Veronica Adley," my dad grumbles.

I blow out a breath.

"I heard that," he quips. "She's a perfect fit for you."

"Now, Abe, he should get to pick his own wife."

"Wife?" I choke on my own saliva. "Slow down. Veronica is nice—if I'm comparing her to a mountain lion."

It's the typical story. Our dads are friends. Well, as close as two alpha dogs can get. I escorted Veronica to her debutante ball, and after she flipped out on a waiter for spilling a drop of champagne on her white dress, that was it for me.

"Okay, fine, how is the hotel doing? The picture of the lake that you posted on Instagram was gorgeous, honey," my mom says with a wistful quality to her voice.

What is it about knowing your mom is stalking your Instagram page that makes you want to stop posting on it?

"You have time to post to Instagram but not get me the numbers?" my dad adds.

I really wish she'd take me off speakerphone now. "It's good. Definitely needs some changes implemented. The previous owner let his employees walk all over him." I park and sit idling in the lot, my gaze fixated on an apartment they shouldn't be.

Her blinds are open. That shouldn't make me happy, but it does.

"It's a small town. Employee and bosses tend to be closer in a small town," my mom says.

My dad chuckles. "That's why your mother heads up charity functions and doesn't run million-dollar businesses."

There's silence on the line. My mom says nothing in rebuttal, and I have no idea why she bites her tongue when he insults her like that. But I'm happy to use this as my opportunity to get off the line.

"Okay, I need to run. Love you." I click the phone off, thankful to escape that conversation. I'm sure my mom understands.

I head through the parking lot to the front door of the building. The day runs through my mind while I make the trek up the three flights of stairs that grow easier to climb each day. I need to make a list of what to conquer first. In four months, I'll be sitting in front of my dad at Haylee's wedding and he'll want a full report, if not sooner.

Stepping onto the third floor, I look at Brooklyn's door, but I shake my head. I intruded yesterday. Nothing good can come of me doing it two days in a row.

I turn to my door, finding a small basket filled with little glass bottles and a big plastic one. I pick up the basket and see a small note stuck between two of the bottles. Opening the card, the girly script tells me it can only be from one person, unless I have a secret admirer.

WYATT,

Thank you for dinner and the company last night. Look on the back for directions.

Brooklyn

. . .

I FLIP THE CARD OVER TO SEE A LIST OF SCENTS AND the ailments they can cure. Lavender for sleep, eucalyptus for headaches and sore muscles, sandalwood to heal dry skin, peppermint with almond for colds, lemon and orange body wash to invigorate.

I huff, tuck the basket under my arm, and open my apartment. Once inside, I dig through the basket and test each scent. None of them are too flowery. Since my head has felt as though there's a beating drum in there since lunch, I pull out the eucalyptus oil and place some on my temples as instructed. After that, I go through my mail, change out of my clothes, and stare into my fridge, realizing I have nothing to eat. At least nothing I want to.

It's not twenty minutes later that I realize my headache is gone. No way it could've been the oil I used. Not after four aspirin earlier in the day didn't work. I pick up a bottle and her card to read the directions over again. She must believe in this shit.

Screw it.

I leave my apartment and knock on her door. "It's me," I announce, since she's probably fearful it's her family.

I'm crossing my fingers Rome, Denver, and Liam can keep a secret. Otherwise, this newfound friendship with Brooklyn will die a quick death before it ever begins. Then I'll have a neighbor *and* an employee who hates me.

She opens the door, looking as cute as ever with her hair pulled up in a high messy bun, a frilly apron wrapped around her body, and color back in her cheeks.

"Come in." She turns to head into the kitchen, and I notice those damn dog socks again.

"How many pairs of dog socks do you have? And if you love dogs, why don't you own one?" I ask, shutting the door.

She stirs a pot at the stove using a wooden spoon. "Jeff was allergic, so this is the best I got."

There's no frown on her face at the mention of her ex-fiancé, which I'll take as a good sign.

"I just wanted to say thank you." I walk into her kitchen to see bottles of oils placed along the counter. "I had a killer headache and it's gone after your eucalyptus sorcery. I have to admit, I was skeptical."

She laughs and places the spoon on the counter. "Yeah, most people are."

"So tell me, is this your passion, hobby, or what?" I lean against her cabinet, watching her measure out ingredients.

She glances at me. "It's been a hobby and I'm passionate about it, but now that I'm single and I have to afford this place, I'm thinking about doing something more with my love."

Shit. This is why I should have kept my ass in my apartment. I'm her boss and she doesn't even know it. "So I was at work today…"

She glances over again. "I'm such an idiot, I never asked you where you work. What do you do in Lake Starlight? Sorry, I've been in my own head for too long."

"I don't blame you. But you should know something."

She stops measuring and sets everything on the counter, turning in my direction. "What is it?"

"I'm the new manager of Glacier Point Resort." I chew my lip. "Your new boss."

She stares, her eyes wide as though we're having a staring contest and whoever blinks loses. I wave my hand in front of her face. She blinks.

"Well, great. Now I just told my new boss that I'm

thinking about starting a business which would mean that if it's successful, I'll quit, and you're probably trying to see where you can cut back, so it's like I waved my hand in the air and said, 'Pick me.' Excuse me while I bury my head under the covers for another two weeks." Her face falls in her hands.

Usually, finding out an employee is going to leave would make my job easier. Cut the one looking to move on because usually those people aren't working as hard as they could and they've got one foot out the door anyway. But I don't think that with Brooklyn. If anything, I want to encourage her. Especially since whatever this stuff is, it got rid of the headache I've been fighting all day. "No. Relax. It's fine."

She peeks through her fingers. "It is?"

"Yeah." *Because I won't be here forever*, I think to myself. "But also, FYI, we'll be working side by side for the next two weeks."

She laughs. "Your bellhop duties are done?"

I tilt my head. "You knew?"

"No. But I have friends who messaged me about the new boss."

Intriguing. "What did they say about the new boss?"

She narrows her eyes and shrugs. "Nothing major."

"Nothing?"

"Just that you're always writing notes in your phone."

I chuckle. "Yeah, that's true. Anything else?"

Her cheeks flush, matching the color of the dried rose petals next to her. "Nope."

I slide closer and bend my head so our eyes meet. "I don't believe you."

"Some people might have thought that you're kind of good-looking."

My cheeks hurt from how hard I'm smiling. "Really?"

She gently shoves me. "Like you didn't already know."

I catch my footing. "And what about you?"

She stills and looks at me. Electricity crackles in the air. A different time and circumstance and I'd break this distance and kiss her. Say screw everything—her ex-fiancé, the fact that I'm her boss, that we don't really know one another. My body yearns for her to be underneath me. To make her moan and whimper, softly call my name in praise and show me what she likes until we're both a sweaty mess. Feel her clench around me when I push inside her...

"You're all right." She shrugs.

Well, the daydream was good while it lasted.

"Yeah, you too." I slide up on the counter, wishing I never asked her because now I'm staring at the curve of her neck.

Her long thin fingers run the length of the herbs, and the thought of what they'd look like gripping my dick pops into my head. I swallow, pushing all sexual thoughts out of my mind. She's literally two weeks off a broken engagement. Then again, I'm not looking for forever, just a little fun, and she seems like she could use it.

"So tell me. If you could do or be anything, what would it be?"

She glares at me as if asking me what my end game is.

I hold up my hands. "You will not lose your job at the resort because of what you tell me. Promise. What happens here, stays here. Like Vegas." I grin, but her demeanor doesn't change. "I'm off the clock."

She picks up the wooden spoon again. "I'd love to sell these and make a business out of it."

I lean my arms back on her counter. "Then you're in luck. I happen to be a business graduate and I have a lot of connections."

The words are out of my mouth before I can stop myself. Let's not forget, I'm lying to her about who I am. I can't very well say I went to Columbia for undergrad and graduate school. That I've been mentoring under my dad for years. That I have the education and the experience. Now, I've never tried to market a product like this—essential oils for health benefits—but I know people. People who know me as a Whitmore. People who hear my last name and take my calls.

But all that will cause problems for me if she finds out.

"That's okay. I'm going to sell some at the farmer's market and start small."

Thank goodness she's the rational one here, because I would've put myself at risk for what? A woman I have no hope of ever sleeping with and definitely zero longevity? I need to get laid before I ruin my opportunity to own a chain of hotels before I'm thirty.

"I'm sure you'll do great." I hop off the counter, determined not to let this budding friendship grow into a full-blown bloom. "I'll leave you to it."

"Oh, you don't have to go. I mean... I didn't offend you, I hope?"

I turn back to face her when I reach the door. "You worry too much. We're good."

I leave, thankful for the distance. Brooklyn Bailey doesn't look like trouble, with her innocent demeanor and beautiful smile, but my gut is telling me that's exactly what she'll be for me.

FOURTEEN

Brooklyn

I inhale a deep breath and circle through the revolving doors of Glacier Point Resort. *Here goes nothing.*

"Hi, Brooklyn." Mac smiles, looking up from helping a guest with her bags.

"Good morning, Mac."

I beeline across the lobby, ignoring Neil and Noelle, wanting to start work and forget all the sad and depressing looks from my coworkers who were guests at the wedding. I spent the entire weekend making new oils with ingredients I already had because I couldn't very well go to my garden at my family house. I lied and told Savannah that I got a ride from the airport, which she was pissed about but she'll get over.

As far as my family is concerned, I got in late last night. I fully expect some calls after work today.

I open the door to the employee lounge, and streamers fly above my head as a loud horn rings in my ears.

"Welcome back!" Reagan screams, tossing confetti.

I laugh at my crazy co-worker who knows me better than I thought. "Thank you."

"I'm ecstatic that you're back." She swings her arm around my shoulders. "And I forgot to text you because this weekend was..." She waves me off as though she doesn't want to get into it. She leads me to our side-by-side lockers. "We get to work with hottie today."

"Funny story there."

We both open our lockers.

"About hot boss?" She frowns.

"Turns out he's my new neighbor."

She pushes me in the shoulder and I'm not ready for it because I've been away from her for two full weeks, so I fall to my ass. She offers a hand and helps me up. "Seriously?"

"Across the hall and..." I look around. "He didn't tell me until last night *after* I told him about starting my side business."

She laughs and covers her mouth. "Only you."

"Only me is right, but he was cool about it."

"Well, rumors here say he's a dick."

I shut my locker and wait for her to say she's joking. But she shuts her locker and sits down to tie her shoes, saying nothing more.

"Are you sure?"

She shrugs. "Mac says he's cool, but Neil said he overheard him talking to Mr. Clayton, telling him that he should be tougher on us. That he wants absentees written up with three warnings before being fired."

I sit next to her on the bench. The man I met doesn't

come close to the person she's describing. Then again, I'm not a very good judge of character. "Well..."

I don't even know what to say. That suggestion isn't unreasonable, but people like Reagan, who are going through a hard time right now, would be affected. When Molly's daughter had the flu, which resulted in her getting the flu, she was out for over a week. But she's always here otherwise.

"I'm sure he's just trying to puff out his feathers," I say.

"He's not a peacock."

I wrap my arm around Reagan's shoulders. "Well, the male peacock is the one with all the pretty colors."

She giggles. "Did you just compare him to a peacock?"

I rest my head against hers. "Well, he is the best-looking man I've ever seen."

"Why are the male peacocks the beautiful ones?" Reagan grumbles.

"I know. As if they don't get enough in this world."

The door opens, and Wyatt stops and stares at us before continuing to the locker area.

"Men suck," I say.

"We do." He lets the insult roll off his back as he unlocks his locker across from mine. "What did we do now?"

"Just the fact that the male peacock is the pretty one," I remark.

Reagan's eyes shift between the two of us.

"Better add the mallard duck to that list too." He pulls out one of my glass bottles and dabs his finger to his temples.

He's behind Reagan so she doesn't see it, but we share a smile. My stomach flips at the fact he's enjoying my thank you gift.

"True. Most birds actually. Name one species where the female is more beautiful," I say.

He shuts his locker door and meets my gaze. "Human beings."

My throat constricts for a second, but I manage to force out some words. "Not always. Men become distinguished as they grow older and woman are viewed as old maids."

He chuckles and rocks back on his heels. His uniform is a striking difference from seeing him in street clothes. If Reagan thinks he's hot here, she should see him outside of this place. "Not always true. Plus, you guys get the whole childbirth thing."

Reagan rolls her eyes and stands. "I'll gladly give that up."

"I know, it's a shame you can't though."

Reagan laughs with him, pointing. "I think we're going to have a lot of fun these next two weeks."

Wyatt's eyes shoot to me. "I think so too." His vision dips to my chest and back up.

It's just my body's response. It means nothing that right now, I'd love nothing more than to shove Reagan out of the locker room and pounce on Wyatt.

Hello, two weeks from almost getting married!

As if my best friend can read my mind, she says, "I'll see you two up there."

"Wait!" I yell.

Reagan circles back around with wide eyes as though I'm a lunatic.

"Reagan, this is Wyatt. Wyatt, this is Reagan." I gesture between them.

Reagan comes up beside me and places her hand on my arm. "Sweetie, you were the one gone for two weeks. We've already been working together."

"Oh, yeah. Okay. Never mind then."

Reagan pats my arm and grins. "Brooklyn gets a little overzealous 'cause she loves her job so much."

She disappears, and I hear the door shut behind her. The energy in here is stifling, like a summer day right before a big storm, when you can feel the charge in the air. All I can think of is Wyatt's hands running up my skirt. I guess this ridiculous maid's uniform from 1983 would be good for something.

His eyes are trained on me. "She's interesting."

"She's nice. I have a feeling you'll enjoy her sense of humor." I need to get out of this room right now if I want to avoid adding town whore to my moniker of jilted bride.

"Well, let's get started. You're the boss today." He motions with his head for me to exit first.

Great, he gets a view of my ass in a polyester skirt as long as the ones Grandma Dori's friends wear to church on Sunday. I shouldn't care, but I do.

This must be what being on the rebound feels like.

FIFTEEN

Wyatt

A man could get used to following directions from Brooklyn Bailey all day.

Mostly because I've been within one inch of her lips about fifty times today. I've struggled with making the bed exactly how she likes it, so she's showed me how to perfectly tuck the sheets in every room. I've excelled at sheet removal though. We won't go into the whys of that one.

It's almost lunch. I desperately want to ask her to join me in the restaurant, but that would be against corporate policy. The employee handbook is pretty clear, and that's without my dad's lectures about never getting involved with someone who works for us. Though I think he was probably referring to the higher-ups at our corporate level.

"Put these in the bathroom." Brooklyn hands me an armful of shampoo, conditioner, and body wash. We're in the presidential suite, so we have the bubble bath for the tub as well. "Thanks."

She busies herself with the bed, placing chocolates on the pillows. We already have a routine on our first day, which I'm hoping means the next two weeks will be easy. I walk out of the bathroom while she reaches over the bed, her ass on display and tempting me like the color red to a bull.

"We done here?" I ask.

She positions some bottles on the nightstand. "Now we are."

She steps back toward the hall, and my eyes flicker to the same small glass bottles she gifted me last Friday. There's a handwritten note that says, "Dab some of me on your wrists and sweet dreams."

"What's this?" I point at the bottles.

Her face reddens as though she got nailed for something. "Um. Shit. I forgot you're my boss." She smiles innocently, and I'm glad our relationship is so easy that she forgot, but I still need answers. She fiddles with her fingers, shifting her weight from one leg to the other. "I leave them in the suites. I'm not getting anything from it. It's a little bonus, that's all."

"Mr. Clayton doesn't pay you?"

She shakes her head.

"So then why?"

She shrugs. "I don't know. The suites cost a lot and it's like a little perk. I'd do it for every room if I could afford it."

The urge to run over to her and swallow up her goodness overcomes me. How can someone be this sweet and this unwanting of anything in return? I've never in my life met someone like her.

"Maybe we should talk to the new owner about incorporating them?" He's only one phone call away, though I'm sure his answer would be no.

My mind shifts into business mode. She's got something here. Last night when I left, I kept thinking about how she could ever make a business like this successful. I mean, health and beauty are nearly impossible to gain traction in without large sums of money. But she could begin in hotels and I'm able to make the connections for her.

"No. I don't want anything to jeopardize my job." She leaves me in the room as she heads to the cart.

I grab her wrist before she can escape. "It's incredibly thoughtful of you. It's just... where I'm from, people don't do good deeds unless it will benefit them somehow."

"Where are you from anyway?" she asks, shutting the door and pushing the cart to the next room.

"New York," I answer, being honest with her for once.

"And they had you come here?"

Maybe I should've lied. What's another lie in the bucket after all? "Yeah, just some program they're initiating."

"I heard that Whitmore Hotels is going to come in and change everything people love about this resort."

My eyes scour the old carpet, the wood railings, the overall outdated vibe. "They'll probably revamp everything and make it more fitting of their brand, but this place will still have the location and the staff."

She stops mid-step. "So they won't be firing anyone? People are scared."

Luckily, she doesn't look at me point blank. I have a feeling she'd be able to tell I wasn't being completely forthcoming.

"That's not in the immediate plans, no." My stomach

twists. It's the truth—technically. It's not in the *immediate* plans, but it's not off the table.

She sighs in relief. "Oh good. People thought you were going to slash the staff." She walks into the next room. "What did they do in here, have an orgy?"

I'm thankful there's a huge mess to distract from any more questions about the future of Glacier Point Resort. I'm not sure why, because a lie by omission is still a lie.

SIXTEEN

Brooklyn

Thankfully the two-week test of my libido to see if I could keep Wyatt tucked in the "Do Not Touch" box has ended with him still in the box. I mentally pat myself on the back for a job well done.

It's been a month since I was supposed to get married, and I'm slowly finding my groove again. My family is giving me some space, and with Jeff not returning to Lake Starlight, trying to move on has been a little easier than I expected. I have no idea where he is or what he's doing, and I try not to care. Everyone seems to be slowly forgetting that I was left at the altar, or at least they're pretending to.

I've run out of supplies to make oils at my apartment, so I have to head to the family home to grab more lilac and plant some more herbs. I'm growing small batches on my balcony, but it's not enough if I want to be prepared for the farmer's market in three weeks.

After parking my car behind Austin's Jeep, I round the side of the house to my garden. Austin and Holly live here together now. I'm sure they'll eventually have a family, so all of us have to respect that it's their space and not our childhood home anymore. Which means, no barging in unannounced. Thankfully, my garden is far enough back from the house that I don't feel as though I'm disturbing them.

I grab my digging tools and seeds. I'll do my planting before I clip off some lavender.

"Hey, I didn't know you were coming by." Austin steps out of the back door, Myles barreling by him and running right to me.

The big husky licks my face, his tail wagging a mile a minute. He's not even fully grown, but he knocks me over onto my back.

"Myles!" Austin yells and snaps his fingers, but the dog doesn't listen.

"Hey, Myles." I pet behind his ears, which only spurs his excitement to see me.

"Myles, get off her." Austin grabs the dog's collar, guiding him off me. "Go to the bathroom."

Myles runs to the other side of the yard, but I think he's chasing a squirrel, not obliging Austin by following his orders.

"I see the dog training is working." I laugh.

Austin sits next to me. He's in shorts and his Lake Starlight High School Baseball T-shirt. It's faded and has been washed a million times. That's my older brother—cool, casual, and easygoing.

"They say they're smart dogs, but I think we got the lemon." He laughs.

Myles runs over, falls down, and runs his head under Austin's hand.

"I don't know. I'd say he's pretty smart."

Austin nods and rolls his eyes. "You think he's got me, you should see him with Holly."

"Where is she anyway?"

"School board meeting." He pets Myles, his gaze not meeting mine, so I dig spots in the ground to plant. "I'm glad you stopped by. How are things?"

Focusing on my task, I put seeds in the hole. "They're good."

"If you need anything... money, an ear, whatever, you know I'm here, right?"

I nod, although I don't look at him for fear I'll cry. Austin might be my older brother, but he took on the role of father after our parents died. Some people would be surprised to find out he's got the father role down pat. Even down to the hugs. One hug and the waterworks will start.

He's quiet for a minute, watching me work, then he inhales a deep breath. "I'm glad you stopped by. I hate to bring this up, but I wanted to talk to you about something..."

"What is it?" I dig another hole, concentrating on my task. When will my life become normal again, where people aren't afraid to talk to me or upset me?

That's the one nice thing about Wyatt. He didn't know the pre-jilted Brooklyn, and he doesn't treat me with kid gloves.

"I'm going to ask Holly to marry me."

My hands pause as though I hit a rock. It's not that I didn't know this was coming. They've been together for, like, a year and they already live together. It's the natural next step.

"Here, let me." He rises on his knees to take the trowel.

"It's fine. I have it." I keep digging and digging.

"You're going to strike oil."

I sit down, abandoning the trowel and the seeds. Tears are building in the corners of my eyes and my nose tickles, my throat closing.

"Oh shit. I shouldn't have said anything. I'll wait. We can wait. I'm probably asking too soon anyway."

I smile, shaking my head, wiping my tears. "No. It's not that."

"What is it?" He puts the seeds in the hole, and I don't stop him this time.

"I'm happy for you guys. I am. I'm not crying because you're going to marry Holly."

"She has to say yes still."

I stare at him long and hard until he looks over his shoulder. "She's going to say yes. She loves you."

"I don't want to make it hard on you." He digs another hole.

"I have to move on with my life. I can't avoid attending weddings from now until eternity. And Holly is a great addition to our family. I see how happy she makes you." All my words are true, and still, I can't pinpoint the reason for my tears.

"She does. But I meant what I said. If you want me to wait, I will."

I wipe more tears from my eyes. "Not at all. Ask her."

He drops the trowel, resting his forearms on his raised knees. "Thanks, Brookie."

I nod. "You didn't need my permission."

He nods. "I did."

"You're the best big brother ever."

I stand, and he follows suit. He bats his eyelashes and his eyes roll back. "Keep saying it."

We laugh, and I bend over to grab the scissors to clip the lavender.

"Making more potions, huh?" He changes the topic. Thankfully.

"Yeah, I'm thinking about starting a little business. Selling stuff at the farmer's market."

"That's awesome. Holly loves the rosemary you gave her for the bath."

"Oh, I can make her more. In fact, I'll make her an entire bridal bundle."

Austin smiles at me then wraps his arms around me. "I have the best sister ever."

I blink back the tears.

"You were always way too good for that douchebag," he whispers.

I nod into his chest. Just when I thought all my tears had dried up.

SEVENTEEN

Wyatt

"Mom, I'm not going to answer your phone calls anymore," I say, walking into my apartment and straight toward the fridge.

"Sweetie, we're down to almost three months. You know everyone's social calendar fills up," she says through speakerphone since I just finished my run and I'm sweaty and starving.

Wealthy people's social calendars fill up. I don't think the average Joe is buying charity dinner tables and theater tickets or planning for art gallery openings.

"I told you, I'm coming alone." I open my fridge. Nothing substantial. I really need to take a cooking class.

A knock sounds on the door of my apartment and then it opens behind me.

"Alone? You need a date. It's your sister's wedding!" My mom's voice carries through the entire apartment.

I look over my shoulder to find Brooklyn's eyes wide. I stand frozen.

As my mom is carrying on and on about expectations and what she'll have to tell her friends, I hold Brooklyn's gaze until her vision dips to my bare chest.

Damn it. My dick hardens and there will be no hiding a fucking hard-on in these shorts.

"Mom, I gotta go." I reach for my phone.

"No, you don't. Listen to me. You are going to live a lonely life as you get older. You think it's all fun now, having hot girls traipsing in and out of your condo, but one day you're going to be sitting in a wheelchair all alone and looking back on what you missed out on in life."

"Thanks for the life lesson. I'll call you back."

"Wyatt Jacob—"

I hit End right before she gets to my last name. I can't explain why she's so hell-bent on me having a date to my sister's wedding. Then I stop to think for a second. No, she'd tell me for sure if... I shake the horrible thought from my head, instead focusing on the hot woman with desire in her eyes, standing in my apartment.

"Do you barge into everyone's apartment or am I special?" I grab a water to cool my body down.

"Guess what?" She's ignoring my mom's call? Best thing to happen to me all day.

"What?"

"I just had this idea. I know it's crazy, but what if I did specialty packages? Like a bride's set, a groom's set, a sleep set, a health set."

We've grown closer from working side by side the past couple of weeks. I find I like that she welcomes herself into my apartment, sliding into a kitchen chair as though she's done it a million times.

"Those are great ideas. I was thinking about it too. You need to figure out a company name, get a logo, website, a social media presence so you can brand yourself. You probably need to look into where you can buy your packaging in bulk to get your margin up. Not to mention you need to look at the tax implications. Decide what type of business structure will benefit you the most. You need to start off on the right foot, otherwise you're going to be walking up a steep hill." She stares at me as though I just let go of the string on her helium balloon. "Sorry. I don't mean to overstep."

"No," she says, looking at the table. "You're right. I have no idea how to go about all that stuff."

We sit in silence for a second.

"Do you want something to drink?" I ask.

She straightens her back, a determined glint in her eyes. "I have a deal to strike," she says, as though she didn't even hear me.

I settle down in the seat across from her. "A deal?"

"I know that if you're managing the hotel, you have business experience. Judging by everything you just said, you know all the stuff I should do, but I can't afford to pay you to help me. What if..."

Some sick, horny, adolescent part of me hopes she's going to suggest a sexual relationship. I'll seal that deal with her over my shoulder on the way to my bedroom.

"You help me with the business stuff, and I'll be your date to the wedding." She looks me right in the eye, like she did that night in the hallway when she reached up and touched my cut.

It's that look that has me feeling off-kilter. "I'll totally help you without you having to come with me."

She sinks back in her chair, her smile turning downward. "I can't let you do that." She moves to slide out of the chair. "Never mind. It was a stupid idea anyway."

"No, it wasn't. I just meant I can help you." I stand. Now I feel as if I released the string on her balloon *and* ran over her puppy, based on the look on her face.

"I can't in good faith let you help me and not do something in return." She's already at the door. The last thing I want is for her to leave.

"Wouldn't it be hard for you to be at a wedding?"

She chews on her bottom lip. "My brother is proposing to Holly, so I'll have to go to one eventually. I might as well practice at one where I don't know anyone."

I chuckle. "So my mom can ask why my beautiful date is crying in the pew?"

"You can tell her I'm a romantic. Which I am, so you wouldn't be lying."

I step forward slowly. "You really would go to my sister's wedding with me?"

"I get that you might not want me to. It's okay."

Truth is, she'd stand out, but in the best possible way.

"I just don't want you to be upset." I step closer, my hand itching to touch her. To cradle her face and tilt it up to mine. To see her eyes wanting what I do in this moment. But she's not ready, and she's not the type to sleep with me without expectations. Never mind all the other reasons it's a bad idea.

"I really want to get this business going, but with everything I need to do, I already feel like I'm drowning," she said. "You obviously need someone to take, and for whatever reason, you don't want to ask anyone. We can go as friends, no expectations between us, and you'll make your mother happy."

Her eyes plead with me, and I find the answer falling out of my mouth before I can stop myself. "Deal."

She smiles, and my heart warms at the happy expression on her beautiful face.

"Yay!" She jumps into my arms.

Her hair is tickling my bare shoulder, and her slender body slides along mine. Then I feel my dick growing as excited as Brooklyn is and I put her back down before I'm as embarrassed as a thirteen-year-old at his first boy/girl dance.

"Okay, I'm going to grab a pad of paper so we can compile a list. Are you hungry? We can order in or something." She's out the door before I can even answer.

Then it dawns on me. If she comes with me, I'll have to tell her who I am. And my father's biggest rule before I came here was that no one is to know who I really am.

Shit. How did I get myself in this situation?

I look at my dick and point. "You did this."

EIGHTEEN

Brooklyn

I've spent the last week with Wyatt filing business paperwork and talking about branding and logos and web designs. Pretty much all boring crap. I yearn to be in the kitchen, coming up with different oil combinations and experimenting with different soaps, lotions, lip balms, and other stuff, but Wyatt assured me this is where we need to concentrate our efforts. He called in a favor to a friend who designed a kick-ass logo for me. I have one week to have all my products ready for the farmer's market.

Working alongside him is hard at times—our hands brush and shivers run through me, or when I'm so excited that I hug him, I can sometimes feel his own excitement pressed against me. I ignore it. Body reflexes and all that. Technically I'm single, but I can't stop the feeling that if I did anything with Wyatt, I'd be cheating. I have to mourn my relationship with Jeff before treading into new territory.

Not that any of that matters, because the fact is he's my boss and we're just friends.

I put my iPad on the coffee table and relax back into the couch.

"So I was in Mr. Clayton's office, and he was talking about this Buzz Wheel thing." Wyatt leans back beside me, his ankles crossed on the table.

How can bare feet be sexy? I don't remember ever being attracted to bare feet.

"I haven't read it in a few weeks. I stopped after I came back from my 'honeymoon'"—I use air quotes before and after honeymoon—"and people were doing the 'I spotted Brooklyn' crap."

"What is it exactly?" He sips his beer.

"It's an online blog. People send information to whoever writes Buzz Wheel and they publish it, sometimes with photos. It's Lake Starlight's own *Gossip Girl*."

He glances my way, closes his computer, and puts it on the table. "Is that why you've been keeping me inside? You don't want people to see us together?"

I crinkle my eyes. "I don't fear the Buzz Wheel. Well, I did after the wedding, but if I'm doing something good enough to report, hopefully it means I'm having fun."

He chuckles. "Look at you, little hell-raiser."

I laugh, tossing a pillow at him.

He dodges the pillow and grabs his tablet. "What's the web address?"

I blow out a breath. "Really? You want to read it?"

"Yeah, I'm intrigued." His eyes set on me, waiting for instruction.

"lakestarlightbuzzwheel.com."

His thumbs move with ease over the screen. Why does my libido think that's attractive? It's not. He's literally just typing like everyone else does. I guess the differ-ence is that I don't think about how other people's fingers are long enough to hit my G-spot, but right now as I watch Wyatt, that's all I'm thinking. I shake the dirty thoughts from my mind. He's my boss. I'm fresh from being stood up at the altar. I'm not going to start hooking up with people now.

"Shit," he mumbles and clicks it shut.

I straighten up in my seat. "What? Is there something about me?"

He slides the iPad between his thigh and the couch. "No. It was just about the hotel. Bad review."

I reach across his lap and his hand lands on the iPad. "They don't review things. What does it say about me?"

His eyes meet mine. We're so close it would take no effort for either of us to cross the line. His gaze falls to my lips, and I lick them without thinking. Suddenly, Buzz Wheel isn't on my mind.

He clears his throat and shifts his vision. "It's not about you."

"Then what?" I ask, my hand clasped on one edge of the tablet and his on the other.

"It's about Jeff."

He might as well have said there's chocolate cake on the counter but I can't have any. He's nuts if he thinks I'm letting this go.

"I'm a big girl, Wyatt."

"I know, but you seem to be doing so well lately and—"

I sit back away from the smell of his cologne and away from his strong thighs. "I am, but I hate it when other people know something I don't, especially when it has to do with me."

He's silent for a while, his hands still on the iPad and his gaze aimed out his patio door. Without a word, he hands the iPad to me.

"Thanks."

He stands and disappears into his kitchen. I'm not sure if he's leaving me alone or if he's mad or what.

I press the button to turn on the screen. There's Buzz Wheel's logo at the top of the page. Below is a picture of Jeff at Liquory Split with a black eye, and another picture of his car on cinder blocks without tires and the hood propped open, revealing the empty space where the engine used to be.

Jeff Brickle has finally shown his face in Lake Starlight. Not sure if someone had a tracking device on him, but he was here no longer than an hour before he was sporting the shiner you see in the picture below. Someone's trying to keep the runaway groom from running back out of town based on the condition his car was left in. Can't say he didn't deserve it. The sheriff says they have some suspects, and I think we all know who he'll be questioning first. It's worth mentioning that there are no witnesses to the crime and Jeff surprisingly says he didn't see who jumped him. Interesting all around.

I FLICK THE SCREEN OFF AND SIT ON THE COUCH, MY mind racing over what happened and who might have done it even though it's not hard to put two and two together.

"I should mention." Wyatt walks in with two glasses of liquor. No ice, no chaser, no mix. He sets one in front of me. "A few weeks ago, after I brought you that Chinese food, I left you asleep on the couch. When I left, Rome was in the hallway. He somehow swindled a key from Joel and... well, long story short, he knows about Jeff taking the honeymoon with someone else." He tips his glass back, swallowing it all in one gulp.

My stomach introduces itself to my feet. "What? You told him?"

"I didn't really have a choice. He saw me coming out of your apartment, went inside, and saw you there. He wanted answers."

My chest tightens and I stand, pacing toward the door. "You said you wouldn't tell."

"I had no choice. He saw you." His eyes plead with me.

"You could've told him I changed my mind. It's just so embarrassing. I was a fool, a fucking fool, and everyone knows it. Do you have any idea what that feels like?" I yell, my hands clenched at my sides.

"I can imagine."

I laser focus at him. "Imagine? Live it. Feel everyone's eyes on you, the questions murmured behind your back. Deal with everyone thinking you somehow missed something and wondering how you didn't know the person you were set to marry didn't want to marry you. I overheard someone at the Lard Have Mercy saying that I probably put an ultimatum to Jeff to get engaged in the first place because I'm a spoiled princess who wanted what she wanted when she wanted it." I throw my arms in the air. "Now my brothers do this and think them getting in trouble is going to help me?"

I whip his door open and stomp over to mine. He follows me, but I grab my coat and my keys and slam my door shut, heading toward the stairs and ignoring him.

"That person is an asshole and should keep their mouth shut. Where are you going?"

I grab my phone from my jacket pocket and dial Rome. "I'm going to kick my brothers' asses and get this cleared up."

"I'm not sure that's a good idea. Just let it die. Don't fuel any more gossip."

I put my hand in the air. "Whatever."

I run down the stairs, but I'm not at my car more than two seconds before the door to the building springs open.

"Brooklyn!" Wyatt yells.

I turn to see him jogging toward me, his own jacket on. "What?"

"I'm going with you, but we're walking, because by the time we get back, neither of us will be able to drive."

"You're crazy, it's a mile."

He shrugs, grabbing my hand. "It's a nice night." He drags me to the sidewalk.

We're halfway there when I figure out his plan because I've already calmed down considerably.

"Don't be mad at your brothers. They're defending you in their own way." His shoulder bumps mine.

"I know. They've done stupid shit my entire life. Usually with the best of intentions though."

I don't blame my brothers. I just hate that I'm in Buzz Wheel. I'd be lying if I said I wasn't happy they hit him and stripped his car.

"Speaking as an older brother, we're assholes if we don't protect our sisters."

"Explain something to me then. How come you guys can be so protective of your sisters and moms and every other woman close to you, but treat a woman you have a romantic interest in so poorly?"

We walk under a street lamp and he glances at me. "I don't treat women poorly."

I roll my eyes. "Let's see, you look like you do, yet you're not attached. You take a job a long way from home, didn't want to bring a date to your sister's wedding… I'd say you're running from someone or something. I can sniff out a commitment-phobe. At least now I can."

We make the turn onto Main Street. Lucky's Tavern and Smokin' Guns Tattoo Shop are all lit up.

"All I'm getting from what you just said is that you think I'm attractive."

I laugh. "Spoken like a commitment-phobe."

He grabs my hand, stopping us, and presses my back against the light pole. "You can call it whatever you want—commitment-phobe, manwhore—but the women I'm with know the score. I haven't sworn off the whole marriage-and-kids thing, but I'm smart enough to know if I don't accomplish what I want before settling down, I'll regret it. And just so you know, I'm not running away from anyone but my father."

His eyes fall to my lips before dipping farther to my breasts, and I inhale a deep breath, entranced by the smell of him. He's dangerous, so dangerous. I thought Jeff destroyed me, but I can feel in my bones that Wyatt would annihilate me.

I'm not sure what's transpiring between Wyatt and me, but it scares me. I don't remember ever feeling this way for Jeff—craving his body on mine, his hands running down my curves, his lips on mine. Because right now, I'd give just about anything for one brush of my lips against his.

"This is Main Street, not your bedroom!" a deep voice yells from across the street.

Wyatt steps away, stripping his gaze from mine.

I glance behind me to see Liam. "Mind your business!"

"You are my business!"

"So I heard."

He holds up his hands. "No idea what you're talking about. I've been working and tattooing people for days." He chuckles. "Want one? It's on me."

"Come on." I nod to Wyatt to follow me across the street. "Nah, you know me. I like pristine skin."

Liam wraps me in a hug so tight, he lifts my feet off the concrete. "How's my pseudo-sister?"

"Ready to kick my brother's ass. And yours."

"I told you, I've been here for days. I'm innocent."

I smack his shoulder when he places me down. "Liam, this is—"

"Hey, Wyatt." Liam holds out his hand.

I wave a finger between them. "You two know one another?"

Wyatt nods. "That night, I went to Lucky's with Rome."

"Ah, the plot thickens. I don't know about you, Wyatt Moore." I poke him in the stomach, not as upset anymore that he told my brother about the honeymoon. Rome was probably bringing some chick up to my apartment. One day he'll have to grow up.

"I was just heading down to Lucky's." Liam walks toward the tavern.

"Great we'll join you."

A minute later, we step into the tavern, finding my twin brothers at a table and my sister Juno with her friend Colton in a booth with Savannah.

I'm about to give my brothers hell when the bar grows silent and everyone stares behind me at the sheriff. *Shit.*

"Rome and Denver Bailey, I need a word," he says, weaving through the tables.

NINETEEN

Wyatt

Rome and Denver snicker as the sheriff stands in front of their table with his thumbs hooked into his belt loops. In the month or so that I've lived in Lake Starlight, I see now how it doesn't resemble Stars Hollow, but this cop reminds me of Barney Fife.

"Hey, Sheriff Miller. How is it being a granddaddy? I ran into Miranda the other day and that boy is going to break hearts." Brooklyn steps in with the sweet talk.

She manages to pull a smile from the sheriff. "Thanks, Brooklyn. I was sorry to hear about your nuptials."

"You mean lack of nuptials." She shrugs as though she's moved on with her life. "Better to never marry than to get a divorce."

"True. Can you give us a minute here?" His eyes set on the twins, both of them leaning their chairs back on two legs, arms crossed.

"Sure thing." Brooklyn signals with her head for me to head to the booth with Juno and Savannah and some guy I don't know.

From there, we'll close enough to hear everything—as is everyone in the bar. The sheriff is clearly not going for discreet.

"You guys take my side." Savannah slides out to head over to the twins' table.

Sheriff puts up his hand. "No, Savannah, we do not need you here."

"If there's questioning, then maybe we need to call our lawyer. Is that necessary, Sheriff Miller?"

I'd hate to go toe to toe in business with Savannah Bailey. She looks like she could strip a man of his balls with one cut-eye.

Liam sits down with his friends, but his vision isn't focused on the sheriff, it's on Savannah. Her cleavage to be specific. Are they a thing?

"No lawyer necessary. I just need to know where Rome and Denver were last night."

They look at one another, neither of them changing their stances. Denver turns toward the sheriff. "Together."

The sheriff blows out a breath.

"Where do you think their tough-ass gene came from?" Juno whispers.

"Totally your dad or Dori," the guy next to her answers, and Juno and Brooklyn giggle and nod.

"I'm not amused, Denver," the sheriff says. "Come on. We all understand..." He glances at Brooklyn, whose forehead falls to my shoulder. "But you can't go around committing assault and vandalizing his car."

Rome holds up his hands. "We didn't do anything.

You're speculating. I'm pretty sure we're not his only enemies."

"I'm also pretty sure your sister is the only woman he's left at the altar recently."

The whole bar sighs. Instinctively, my hand ventures under the table and grabs Brooklyn's thigh. She's not mine, but someone has to tell her it's okay and this will pass.

The twins' chairs fall forward to four legs and their elbows rest on the table.

"You want to know where we were?" Rome starts.

"Yes," the sheriff answers.

"Don't answer anything. I'm calling Uncle Brian." Savannah steps toward us to grab her purse, but Brooklyn can't get it before Liam interrupts.

"They were with me."

The sheriff's eyes shift to Liam, leaned back and relaxed like his best friends. "You're not a very good alibi. You're probably the one who took the tires and the engine."

Liam smirks. "There you go, jumping to conclusions again."

The sheriff does not look amused. "That's it. All three of you, you're coming back to the station with me." He crooks his finger.

The three men stand, willing to go, but I'm sure not even torture would get them to talk.

"I'm going too," Savannah says.

"I'll call my lawyer. We're good." Liam touches her arm and she flings it back.

"Yeah, you probably have a great criminal attorney on call, right?"

Liam narrows his eyes at her. "It's a shame. So damn gorgeous and smart, but you can't unwind and see what's right in front of you."

She blows out a breath and shakes her head.

Brooklyn's hand grips my bicep. "Oh Jesus, look at the circus Jeff has caused. I might as well send in selfies for Buzz Wheel to use because I'll be in it forever."

"No, no, it'll blow over," Juno assures her.

"They were with me." The words tumble from my mouth before my brain can wrap around the reality of the consequences of what I'm doing. Being their alibi means giving the sheriff my real name with the hopes he doesn't tell anyone. Or maybe he won't ask for an official statement.

Everyone stops and turns in our direction.

The sheriff looks at me skeptically. "Who are you?"

"I'm the new manager at Glacier Point. Wyatt Moore."

"Where were you with the boys exactly?" he asks.

Rome and Denver's eyebrows scrunch at us.

Shit. Where were we?

Behind the sheriff's back, Rome gives the smallest of nods at Liam.

"We were at Liam's tattoo place. I keep forgetting the name of it, but this town is new to me."

"Smokin' Guns," Liam says, a smile playing on his lips.

I snap my fingers. "I promise, man, I'll remember one day."

"Were you getting a tattoo?" the sheriff asks, eyes narrowed.

"Me? No. But—"

Rome steps forward. "I got one."

The sheriff's attention falls to him. "Let's see it."

"Sir, it's covered up," Liam says.

"Uncover it. You're the professional."

Liam looks around. "This is hardly a sanitary place."

Sheriff Miller loses the last ounce of his patience. "Fine, let's go to your tattoo shop."

Denver raises his hand to the bartender. "We'll be back."

"Oh, and you can come too." The sheriff points at me.

Brooklyn slides out of the booth and slides her arm through mine as though we're a united front.

"Dumbasses, I swear," Savannah mumbles. "Though if they go to jail for this, I wish they'd have really beaten the shit out of him. He got off easy."

"Feel free to throw a mug his way," Juno teases while she climbs out of the booth.

Savannah rolls her eyes.

All of us leave Lucky's and head three doors down to Liam's tattoo shop. There's a big guy cleaning some equipment, and he follows us over to another bench. Rome strips off his shirt and leans down so his back faces us, showing off a large bandage. Liam washes his hands and puts on a pair of gloves, staring at Savannah as he snaps the gloves into place.

She rolls her eyes.

Liam peels back the bandage on Rome's back, and there sits a blackbird with two lines of script.

"It's beautiful," Brooklyn coos next to me.

"As you can see, Sheriff, it's still healing and fairly fresh," Liam says.

The sheriff nods, the tough-ass act morphing into exasperation. "Go ahead and cover it up."

"Wait," Brooklyn says, stepping forward to read the script. She smiles and looks at Juno, who steps up beside her.

Juno swipes a tear from her eye. "Oh, Rome."

"Cover it, Liam," he says.

But Liam can't move fast enough before Savannah comes over, then she looks at Liam. They share a look I can't describe, as though they're having a conversation with their eyes. Liam nods and his gaze veers to Savannah's waist before concentrating back on the bandage.

"For Mom and Dad?" Brooklyn asks after Rome puts his shirt on.

"Obviously."

"'I will carry you with me. 'Til I see you again.' It's beautiful." Brooklyn sits next to Rome on the bench.

"Fine." Sheriff Miller looks at me. "You were with them the entire time?"

"Yeah. We were here."

"Okay. I'll let this go, but I hope this puts an end to everything, do you understand?" Sheriff shoots them all a warning glare, like a father disciplining his child.

"Yes," Denver says, a serious look on his face.

It's the oddest thing. Rome and Denver have lost their tough, screw-society-and-their-rules mentality. The sheriff is looking at them like lost boys more than men who broke the law. Juno has tears slipping down her cheeks. Even the chip on Savannah's shoulder has disappeared. And Brooklyn, she's taking off her shirt and pushing up off her seat.

Whoa. What the hell?

"Come on, Liam. Give me the same thing but with a feminine touch."

"I'm out of here," Sherriff Miller says and bolts out the door.

"Um... Brooklyn." Rome stands over her. "What are you doing?"

"I'm copying you. I'm assuming you don't mind." She turns to Liam. "I don't want the big wings like he has, but maybe a few smaller birds flying."

Liam looks at Savannah, who blushes.

Seriously, are they screwing behind everyone's backs?

"I mean the fact that you just stripped naked in front of everyone," Rome grinds out.

Brooklyn's forehead scrunches. "A bra is just like a swimsuit."

If I were Rome, I'd argue that swimsuit don't have lace and I'd also mention that she looks way too hot to do what she did without expecting a reaction. Shit. I shake that thought away. Rome is her brother. Of course he wouldn't think the same way I would. The same way that's making my dick grow in my pants.

I really need to get laid to get her out of my mind. She's not even close to my type of woman—the kind who doesn't expect breakfast the next morning. Then add on the fact she's mourning a relationship. Usually I wouldn't care, because it works for the kind of sex I prefer, but for some reason, this girl—this woman—has me caring.

"You have Colt and Wyatt here," Rome says as if she's not getting it.

"And me." Liam raises his hand, although I have to think he thinks of her as more of a sister. Then again, with the looks he's been giving Savannah all night, who knows?

"What happened to 'she's my sister too,' asshole?" Denver repeats the words Liam must have said before they enacted their revenge on Jeff.

"I like revenge." He laughs and looks at Brooklyn, applying an antiseptic wipe on the back of her shoulder.

"What are you doing?" Rome asks.

"Last I checked, Brooklyn is older than you dipshits and can make her own decisions. And you know I think ink is good for the soul." He picks up a book and flips the pages before holding it out to Brooklyn. "What do you think of this?"

"I need a beer." Rome storms into the back, Denver following.

"Get me one while you're back there." Liam laughs, knocking Brooklyn with his fist because he's joking.

"Are you sure, Brook?" Savannah asks, her eyes once again finding Liam. "Blackbirds?" Her eyes fall to the picture before she turns a scathing look toward Liam.

He smiles.

"Oh, this is gorgeous. Did you do this?" Brooklyn asks, pointing at the picture.

He nods with a proud smile.

"Let me see!" Juno rushes over. "Oh, I want one."

"Just when you thought you were off shift," the guy next to me says, laughing, then looks at me. "Sorry, we haven't met yet. I'm Colton Stone. Juno's friend."

"Wyatt."

"I heard." He smiles. Seems nice enough. Dark hair, clean-cut, muscular.

"Small town. Right." I nod and lean back on my heels, hands in my pockets.

"Do we get a special?" Juno asks.

"Both of you, stop," Savannah says. "Why are you getting tattoos?"

Brooklyn looks at Savannah. "It's fun. Come on. Join in for once."

Liam places the transfer on Brooklyn's shoulder.

Savannah grabs her purse. "I have work to do."

"You work too hard," Liam calls after her.

"See you all tomorrow." She waves without looking back and the door chimes with her departure.

Brooklyn's eyes find mine after her sister leaves and Liam's needle buzzes. Rome and Denver bring beers for everyone, and we all congregate in waiting area as Brooklyn takes her pain like a champ. Not wincing once.

This woman, she surprises me every damn day.

TWENTY

Wyatt

Once Liam finishes tattooing Juno and Brooklyn, everyone prepares to leave. The boys are half lit since Rome ran down to Liquory Split. Juno and Colton are the soberest of us. Well, other than Liam. Brooklyn's eyes are a little glazed, but I counted her drinks after her tattoo. She hasn't had that much.

"Want a ride?" Colton asks us.

"Su—"

"Nope. We're good," Brooklyn interjects.

"You sure?" he asks because he's probably thinking what I am—you'll never make it back on both feet.

The hell if I want to carry anyone home tonight.

"It's too nice to drive. Come and I'll show you Lake Starlight." She hooks her arm through mine.

We say our goodbyes to the guys and Juno and Colton.

Once we're outside, I say with a chuckle, "I have a bad feeling I'll be carrying you half the way."

"Nope." She grabs a light pole and swings around it as if we're in a musical.

She's happy, and I find myself smiling at seeing her without the worry of a wedding that didn't happen and the success or failure of her business hanging over her head. Since I started helping her with the business, it's evident she has a lot riding on the essential oil business. Not just money but self-worth.

We turn away from downtown to head toward the lake, which we can follow to our apartment complex.

"Does the tattoo hurt?" I ask.

She looks at me over her shoulder. "No, but I sleep on my back, so I'm a little worried how I'll manage that."

Great, now all I can picture is her in bed.

She walks ahead of me, the moonlight glowing down on her as she picks up small pebbles and tosses them into the lake. "Do you think every kid thinks their parents had a perfect relationship?"

I want to answer, but all I can think is, "God no, just look at my parents." My mom is neglected most of the time because my dad is working. I don't think she resents it, just thinks that's the way it is. The last time I saw them kiss was forever ago.

With my silence, she continues. "I was sixteen when my parents died. In a way, I was lucky. Phoenix and Sedona probably don't remember anything about them. You know what kills me the most about this whole Jeff thing?" She sits on the lake's edge, the moonlight giving her an ethereal quality.

"What?" I join her.

"I used to see my parents kiss and hug and hold hands

when no one was looking. I'd go to the kitchen for a snack or my mom would bring something to the grill for my dad. It was in the most unlikely of places and times that I'd find them in an embrace or a kiss. Their love was so strong. I wanted that, but I think I forced it. Yeah, I'm pissed at Jeff, but maybe he did me a favor." She throws a rock into the lake and it plops in, sending small ripples circling out.

"I think a lot of girls grow up wanting that fairy tale."

"That's just it. I did want the husband and the family, but what I wanted most was that kind of love. Walking up to the man I love because I need his arms around me like my next breath. Thinking I can't go a moment longer without his lips on mine." She looks at me, meeting my gaze. "You probably think it sounds stupid."

I pick up a few of my own rocks. "Not at all. I think as much as you've wanted to find love, I've found a way of dodging it."

She glances at me, her head tilted. "Why?"

"We should get going." I stand, toss some pebbles into the water, then hold my hand out for her. She accepts it, and I pull her up.

"I'll take your silence to mean you don't want to tell me?"

"Why does there have to be a reason?"

She looks at me as though my skin is paper-thin and she can see right through me. She knows there's a reason for me feeling that way and I can't deny she's right, so I'll plead the fifth.

"I forgot to thank you," she says and steps back. "For helping my brothers. I know they did it, and the car thing has Liam written all over it."

"I'm not sure if it was me or the tattoo that made the sheriff give them a break."

She huffs. "Sheriff Miller and my dad went to school together. I think he forgets why Rome and Denver are the way they are sometimes. They were fourteen when my parents died, and don't get me wrong, they weren't angels before the accident, but after, they just didn't give one shit about authority. Austin went rounds and rounds with them during high school. Rome ran away from Lake Starlight to work in Europe for a while, and Denver picked a dangerous job. I guess my parents' dying affected all of us in different ways. But you're right. Rome's tattoo reminded the sheriff what they've lost."

Her matter-of-fact way of talking about her parents' death surprises me. They seem to all be able to talk about it fairly easily.

"What made you step up and get one?" I take her hand, leading her around a mud puddle.

"I just saw it on Rome and thought that I wanted a tribute to them too. You're going to think I'm stupid, but I wanted to be someone else for a change—someone who takes chances and lives for the moment. My eyes have been on the fairy tale since I met Jeff, and I'm exhausted by it all. I want a change. Maybe I don't need a man to be happy." She smiles at me.

My feet slow, and I want to taste her lips. To tell her she's going to knock some guy on his ass one day. Hell, she's already done a number on me. I'm not the lucky guy, but he's out there. One day she'll get her happy ever after. "I think that's a great plan."

We reach our apartment complex parking lot, the lights casting aside the moonlight.

"You need to trust a woman not to hurt you too." I say nothing, and she stops us under a light post. "I'm serious. I get that something happened to mess up your belief in love, but you have to let someone in at some point."

"You sound like my mom."

She laughs. "Well, you've done so much for me and you barely know me."

I feel as if I've known her forever. "I'll consider it."

She shakes her head and abandons me by the light pole, walking to the door of the building.

How bad would it be if I kissed her?

Really bad, I remind myself.

She's finding herself and doesn't need to go missing again by investing herself in a guy whose real name she doesn't even know and who has a real life thousands of miles away.

Instead of running to catch her off guard and planting a long and languid kiss on her lips, I settle for admiring her from a distance.

She's a mirage, because there's no way she can be as good as she appears.

TWENTY-ONE

Brooklyn

The day couldn't be better for my first appearance at the farmer's market. It's sunny and warm and people are already milling around, waiting for it to open.

"Thanks for helping me," I say as Juno puts up the tent over our table with the banner Wyatt surprised me with last night.

"I love this." Juno holds out a business card with my logo and company name. He also had labels, business cards, and postcards made up. "How did you come up with Earth's Potions?"

I continue stocking the table, putting together some of my specialty packages. "Wyatt kept calling them my potions and the idea snowballed from there."

We sit on the folding chairs, and I organize the money and the card reader thingy Wyatt suggested would be helpful so I could accept debit and credit cards. I kind of wish he could be here with me, but my brothers wanted to thank him for being their alibi by inviting him to an axe throwing competition. Men.

"Did Colton go with them?" I ask.

"Of course. I swear sometimes I think he's our fifth brother."

"That's why he'd make a great addition to the family." I raise my eyebrows.

She rolls her eyes. "We're friends. Look, you and Wyatt are friends. Men and women are capable of having platonic relationships." Juno crosses her legs and sips her iced coffee. "Though I still say there's something there…"

I frown. "Is it bad that…"

I lay awake at night, thinking about Wyatt. I make excuses to walk by the front desk to see him every day at work. On my day off this week, I kept the volume on my stereo low so I could hear him come home. Am I fixating on him to avoid dealing with the Jeff fallout or are these feelings real?

"Is what bad?" Holly asks from behind us. She's in a cute pair of shorts and a T-shirt with flip-flops.

"Someone's grown used to our Alaskan summer," I say. Holly's only been in Lake Starlight a year and a part of the Bailey clan for roughly the same, but she fits in so well, I don't quite remember us without her.

She smiles. "Yeah, now if I could only get the tan I used to in Florida." She sits on the concrete step between our chairs. "Does this conversation have something to do with Lake Starlight's hot new bachelor, Wyatt Moore?"

Juno laughs, positioning herself to clearly see me.

"How do you know about Wyatt Moore?" I ask.

"Well, I read that he was the alibi for Rome and Denver, and there was a picture of you two sitting down by the lake last week." She shoots me a "sue me, I read Buzz Wheel on the regular" look.

"For someone who doesn't like to be in the gossip blog, you sure enjoy reading it," I tease.

She laughs. "I know. It's horrible, but I am the high school principal. I need to make sure the kids respect me."

"Then stop screwing in Austin's Jeep behind Lucky's," Juno pipes up.

Holly's face reddens. "It was our anniversary! We were reliving the memory of the night we met."

Juno and I laugh.

"I missed the Buzz Wheel thing. I don't want to read anything about Jeff, and I really don't want to read about what a loser everyone thinks I am."

Holly grabs my hand at the same time as Juno says, "You are not a loser, and no one thinks that."

"In fact." Holly looks at Juno. They don't have to communicate verbally to know they're on the same page. "People think Wyatt Moore might be your prince."

"I just want it out there right now that I was the one who called it." Juno raises her hand as if she's the girl in the front row at school. "As soon as you hit him in the head with that book, I knew."

"You're both wrong. He doesn't want a relationship, and even if I did, it's way too soon after Jeff. Not to mention I basically work for him. But..."

"You kind of like him?" Holly asks, already assured of my answer.

"Like who?" Savannah surprises us all from behind. Her hair is thrown up in a ponytail and she has her running clothes on. "I just beat my best pace for a mile." She smiles, and the three of us stare at her as though she's an alien. "I've been off and couldn't figure out why. How about some 'woo hoo Savannah's?"

I'm thinking you couldn't pay me to run, let alone have a set time to run a mile in.

"Woo hoo, Savannah!" we all say in unison.

"You need to get laid," Juno says.

"Sit down. Do you need water?" Holly slides over, and Savannah sits next to her on the curb.

"Nah. That was a warm-up." She bends forward and picks up one of my bottles. "This is *so* cute, Brookie. Wyatt did this?"

"He hooked me up with the designer. She did a great job at branding."

"Love the name," Holly comments.

"Now I just need them to sell."

"They will." Juno smiles at me. "Maybe I should open a booth for my matchmaking business. I mean, there are so many people who still need to find their person." Her eyes settle on Savannah.

Savannah flips her off. Her usual response when a family member razzes her about either her temper or her love life.

"Let's get back on the Wyatt topic," Holly urges.

"We're talking about Wyatt?" Savannah asks, her gaze on me.

"Because Brooklyn wants to tie him to her bedposts, but she's afraid people will think less of her," Juno fills everyone in as if she's a mind reader.

Ever since that night at the lake, something has shifted between us. I could've sworn he wanted to kiss me. And I wanted to kiss him.

"I do not," I lie. I'm not going to admit that I've fallen for someone so soon after being left at the altar. It feels wrong somehow.

"You so do. I saw it all over your face the other night." Juno points at me in accusation.

"She has a point. When he lied to be Rome and Denver's alibi, a million hearts floated out of your eyes," Savannah says.

"I missed out on the fun." Holly pretends to pout, although I'm sure she and Austin were having some fun of their own.

Instinctively I glance at Holly's left hand. No engagement ring yet.

"You didn't really. These two got tattoos." Savannah thumbs in mine and Juno's direction.

"You did?" Holly asks. "Let me see."

I slide over in the chair and push my tank top over so she can see my shoulder. Juno holds up her ankle to show off the same tattoo.

"You guys got the same one?" The sweet smile on Holly's face tells me what she thinks of that.

"Yeah. Rome got this black bird with the saying, 'I will carry you with me. 'Til I see you again.' for our parents."

Holly smiles the one I'm used to when the topic of my parents come up. Like all anyone remembers is they died too young. True, but they left handprints and footprints all over this town and in our hearts. I try to remember that every time I get down about not having them anymore.

"What about you?" Holly shoulder-knocks Savannah, who must be lost somewhere in her head because she falls into Juno's chair and looks at us as though she doesn't know what we're talking about.

"I'm not one for tattoos," Savannah mumbles.

I look at the street where a light sprinkling of customers are making their way through the booths.

"Well, I told my mom I'd pick her up after her breakfast shift and we'd shop together." Holly stands and pats my shoulder. "So I'll see you all in a little bit. You got this and"—she leans down so she's face level with me—"there's no time limit on grieving one relationship before starting another. Don't stress about the timing. Life is way too short. That being said, I think it's great that you're feeling something for someone else. Just take it slow. One day at a time."

I smile and pat her hand on my arm. "You're the best. Thank you."

"Any time."

She says goodbye to Juno and Savannah, and we watch her walk toward Lard Have Mercy.

"And Holly?" Juno calls, making her turn around. "Maybe relive those memories with the Jeep parked outside of the house. You know, just a suggestion."

Holly's face reddens as people glance in her direction. "Here's a little something Savannah taught me." She holds up one hand to block her flipping off Juno with the other hand.

We all laugh, and Holly spins toward the cafe.

"Way to take the sweetness out of her," I say to Savannah.

She laughs. "She'll always be sweet."

True. Holly doesn't have a mean bone in her body.

"I heard what she told you and her advice is solid, Brook. Don't overthink anything. Not that any of us have a ton of experience in love, but just because Jeff was an asshole doesn't mean Wyatt is. Regardless of what anyone says, love doesn't come when the timing is right. If that were the case, Holly would've met Austin years before she did.

I'm not saying you love Wyatt or anything, but if you like him, explore it. That's all."

Juno clears her throat, and I look away from Savannah to find a woman with her young daughter at my table. She shoots me an apologetic look.

"Hi, I'm Brooklyn," I say with a smile. "That one you're holding is our lavender oil to help you sleep."

That's pretty much how the rest of my afternoon goes. Introducing myself to those I don't recognize, explaining all the different oils and the benefits of each. Wyatt had a good point when he told me to stick to four to start off. I decided on Soothe, Energize, Sleep, and Cleanse. I've set them out in a four-pack as well as individually. I doubted his keep-it-simple plan at first, but he was right.

By the time five o'clock comes and everyone around me is putting their booths away, I've sold a good number. A number I'm proud of.

"Wait!" Grandma Dori runs—or goes as fast as she can —down Main Street, waving money.

"Grandma." I sigh with a smile as she approaches.

"What's up, G'ma?" Juno says, putting the merchandise that didn't sell into a box.

"I'm buying everything you have left," Grandma says.

My shoulders falter and I shoot her a look.

"I am, Brookie. I want to support my granddaughter, and all the ladies down at the center want some. I'm going to be their supplier."

"Watch who you say that in front of," Juno says.

"Oh, get your mind off the wacky tobaccy." She waves off my sister.

I sneak a peek at Juno, whose eyes are rolled so far into her head, I'm afraid they won't find their way back.

"Are you still smoking that crap?" Grandma asks.

"Where's Colton? He's usually five steps away from you. I still say he's a bad influence."

"One time, Grandma. You caught me one time."

"You and Colton," Grandma clarifies.

I stay out of the conversation because the longer this goes on, the more likely Grandma will forget what she came here for.

"We were experimenting," Juno says exasperatedly.

"In your tree house. What else did you experiment with?"

"Don't worry, I haven't killed all my brain cells." Juno pats Grandma's hand and continues to pack up the bottles.

"So you say."

"I'm taking this to the car," Juno grumbles and leaves.

"Wait! I said I wanted to buy it all."

So much for her forgetting. Juno stops and looks at me.

"Really, Grandma, I'm gonna sell online too. It's fine."

"What do we have here?" Rome grabs the box from Juno's hands, picks out a bottle, and tosses it to Denver.

He opens the bottle and smells. "Oh, I think I'm already feeling tired." Denver pretends to fall asleep.

"You guys really are a bunch of dumbasses." Juno snags the bottle.

"I'm buying that, Denver, and I don't need your grubby hands all over it."

He kisses Grandma's cheek. "You say the sweetest things."

She disregards his comment, pushing the money into my palm. "Boys, put this in my car. It's around the corner." She tosses the keys, and Rome snatches them mid-air.

"Whatever you want, G'ma D."

"You all stink. Where were you?" she asks, her nose scrunched up.

It's then that I wonder where Wyatt is. I look down the sidewalk and see him walking with Liam and Austin. He's telling them some story and they can't stop laughing. Oh God, what is he telling them? Please nothing about me.

"We were axe throwing. Turns out the city boy has an arm." Denver opens a cookie that he bought from I have no idea where and takes a bite, his eyes on me the entire time.

I look away.

"You took Wyatt with you?" Grandma asks, a smile forming.

"You know us, we include everyone." Denver shrugs.

"It was probably a thank you for saving your ass from the sheriff," Grandma says, patting Denver's cheek. "Good job by the way."

I shake my head.

"If I wouldn't break my hip, I'd have done it myself."

"I know," Denver says to her.

"So how did it go?" Wyatt says, looking down at the table. "You sold a lot." He should know, he helped me label and fill the bottles.

"Rome has an entire box." I nod to my brother in explanation.

Wyatt looks over his shoulder. "I still say it was a total success."

I smile at him, willing my stomach to stop flipping and flopping like a fish on a dock.

"Holly wants everyone over to the house tonight," Austin announces.

"Dinner's tomorrow," Grandma says.

"Yeah, but she wants to have a bonfire tonight, so all your asses will be there." He points around at the group of us.

"Great," I mumble.

"You too, Wyatt. And Juno, Colton went home to shower, so go surprise him and tell him to come too."

Juno makes an annoyed face.

"Fuck, I'd love it if some chick came to tell me something while I was in the shower and she just pushed past the curtain and my back was turned as her hands slid around me and her wet body pressed to mine as her hands continued until they—*ouch!*" Denver holds the back of his head.

"Children," Grandma says, looking around. "Not to mention you can't talk like that in front of me. It's disrespectful."

"I have a feeling you and Grandpa were kinky back in the day." Denver waggles his eyebrows.

She ignores him, pressing her money into my palm again. "Give me the rest of the goods, Brooklyn."

"What's the deal?" Wyatt asks.

"She wants to buy the rest of my products but—"

Wyatt takes her money and hands her the other box. "Brooklyn thanks you." He smiles.

"I knew I liked you." She turns. "Rome. Box. Car. Now." She turns her attention to Austin. "I'll be there. What should I bring?"

Austin laughs. "Just you."

"Good answer."

Austin's phone rings. "Okay. See you all in one hour." He points.

We all grumble, but it's not as though I had other plans tonight.

"You'll come?" I ask Wyatt.

He pats a few drops of the eucalyptus oil on his temples. "Sure."

There goes my stomach again, not listening to my brain's instructions.

TWENTY-TWO

Wyatt

Brooklyn directs me to Austin and Holly's house. It's definitely in a more rural section of town, with a long driveway through a row of woods on either side.

"This is where I grew up. Except for college, I lived here all my life."

We round a bend and the house comes into view. It's a large home with a three-car garage, all dark wood and high beams. Basically what you'd imagine an Alaskan house to look like—almost like a gigantic log cabin.

"With Sedona in New York and Phoenix in Los Angeles, it's just Austin and Holly here now."

I nod, parking my sedan next to Austin's Jeep. I loved riding in that to the axe-throwing excursion they took me on earlier.

"Did you have fun today?" Brooklyn asks, stepping out of my car.

I round the back to grab the beer I bought while Brooklyn was getting ready. "Surprisingly, I did. Definitely out of my comfort zone, but your brothers are hilarious."

"Not everyone is on the same page as you with that." She glances over her shoulder on the way up the stairs to the front door.

Her hair is down and curled into little ringlets that make me want to wind them around my finger and tug her toward me until she falls into my arms. The sundress she's wearing with her jean jacket shows off her long, toned legs. When she answered her apartment door, I wanted to step in and lock the door so we could have our own private party.

That exact thought is what's making me think twice about her coming to the wedding with me. It's bad enough she thinks I'm the new manager and I'll have to tell her I'm the owner's son, but I'm also going to have to tell her that I'm not staying in Lake Starlight. I know that I eventually have to come clean, but the selfish part of me says to enjoy this a little longer. Besides, we're just friends, not lovers.

"It feels so weird to ring the doorbell, but this is Holly's house now." She smiles as we wait for someone to answer.

Austin opens the door and a large dog springs out, jumping at us.

"Myles!" Austin and Brooklyn scream.

The dog jumps on me, and with the two cases of beer I'm holding, I have no hands to stop it.

"Myles, no," Austin says, stepping onto the porch and tugging at his collar.

Obviously not hard enough because the dog seems intent on sniffing my crotch. This is why I've never really been a dog person. This is always so uncomfortable, and I don't ever want to be in Austin's position.

"Myles," Brooklyn says, her eyes transfixed on what's happening.

I'm sure Austin doesn't really want to reach between my legs, so I try to slide my legs to one side then the other.

"I swear I just showered," I say, trying to make a joke of it.

"I know. I'm sorry. He does this," Austin says.

"*Treat, Myles!*" Holly yells from somewhere in the house.

The dog stops, looks at me, then he jets past Austin into the house to find Holly.

"Fucking dog. He's caused me nothing but trouble. Did you hear what he did?" Austin asks us as he holds the door open.

Brooklyn hangs up her jean jacket on the coat rack, revealing her bare shoulders. Is she trying to make me endure this party with a constant hard-on? Leave the jacket on, woman.

"It might get cold tonight outside," I offer.

She glances at me, her eyebrows furrowing. "I'll get it when we go outside. I'm going to help Holly." She leaves me alone with Austin.

"Obviously she's not into my news." Austin takes a case of beer from me. "Myles knocked up some dog who lives a mile away. Turns out the family is moving, so they came knocking on our door one night and Holly said we'll keep the dog."

"Oh my God!" Brooklyn screams from farther in the house.

"Guess she just met Daisy. The dog doesn't leave Holly's side. She's going to have pups. I told Holly we should leave her at the vet." He walks toward the kitchen.

"You'd think I said leave her on the side of the road from the look I got."

I'm listening intently, or as intently as I can without thinking of his sister naked. Fuck, there's nothing to the dress she's wearing.

"So she's made up a whole birthing station in our mudroom. I'm paying for the vet to make house calls. Damn Myles and his inability to control himself."

I feel a kindred spirit with Myles right this minute.

"Here's Daisy." Austin holds his hand out to a small dog.

"You poor thing." Brooklyn bends down and pets the dog. "Your babies are going to be so big."

Myles walks over, nudges Daisy's head, and Brooklyn pets them both.

"I know. I kept asking the vet if she was sure that she could get them out," Holly says.

Austin rolls his eyes at me, holding his arm out for the beer in front of the fridge.

"What did she say?" Brooklyn asks, a worried look in her eye.

"She said it's fine. They're puppies. But I'm still worried about her." Holly chops up the salad.

Daisy waddles into a back room that I assume is the mudroom.

"What do you need help with?" Brooklyn asks.

Austin opens a beer and hands it to me. "Brook?"

"Wine is good."

"I hope white is okay? It's all I drink." Holly cringes.

"White is perfect."

With drinks in hand, the rest of the Baileys slowly trickle in. I'm slightly thankful the youngest twins and Kingston aren't here. I already feel a bit overwhelmed.

I talk to Denver for a bit about what made him want to be a bush pilot, then I talk to Rome about his days in Europe without asking about specific restaurants. The manager of a hotel wouldn't have visited Europe twice a year and been familiar with them. Definitely wouldn't have backpacked through Europe after he graduated high school. Which I did to piss off my dad. At one point, Juno hands me her match-making card and says she'll give me a discount because she already has an eye on the woman she'd set me up with, her gaze flicking over to Brooklyn.

Luckily, people talk about New York but don't pry too much. I have the lie that I attended NYU, rather than Columbia, on the tip of my tongue in case they ask.

All this reminds me that I have to tell Brooklyn before we leave for New York. I have two months left and I want to put it off as long as possible. Not just because I promised my dad, but more because I'm afraid it will change things between Brooklyn and me.

Dinner was burgers, hot dogs, and a salad. Except for the summer I stayed in the Hamptons on weekends and holidays, I haven't really been a part of a typical cook-out. The food was good, the laughs came in droves, and the scenery is breathtaking. Brooklyn's been smiling the whole time. The times when I see her mind wander and she'd look away or pick up her phone or fidget with her nails have become fewer and fewer. I wonder if Jeff is becoming a distant memory.

"*Austin!*" Holly screams off the balcony. "It's time."

"Jesus, is Holly pregnant?" Rome asks.

"No, dipshit, our dog is," Austin says.

"Male dogs can have babies?" Denver looks at Myles, whose ears have perked up as though he knows we're talking about him.

"Do you ever listen? Daisy, the dog Myles knocked up." Savannah follows Austin up the back stairs.

Grandma stands. "Oh, it's time for me to go."

"Why?" Juno asks.

"I've seen enough births in my life. Come on, Brian and Karen." She beckons their uncle, Brian, and Holly's mom, Karen.

"I feel like I should stay here for Holly," Karen says.

"I'll be right back." Brian kisses her cheek and pats her on the ass.

"You should be lucky Holly's not here, Uncle B, smacking her mom's ass like that." Rome grins and sips his beer.

"One day you'll grow up, Ro." Uncle Brian escorts Grandma Dori up the walkway.

"Night, G'Ma."

"Night, Grandma," they all say in unison.

"Oh, Wyatt." I turn to find Dori stopped right before walking up the stairs. "You can pick me up from the center for the family dinner and drive me over tomorrow, right?"

My gaze falls to Brooklyn. Her eyebrows are up at her hairline.

"Sure?"

"I'll see you then." She nods.

I'm not sure what just happened there.

"Oh shit, I wouldn't wanna be in your shoes. Lecture time." Denver looks at Rome and they share a laugh.

"He doesn't do the dumb shit you two do. I'm sure it's fine," Brooklyn says, but she nibbles on her lips, which I've noticed she does when she's feeling unsure about something.

"I don't do dumb shit. I just bought a restaurant," Rome says.

"I own my own plane. Live in my own apartment," Denver adds.

Brooklyn stands. "I'm heading in to watch some puppies being born."

"Me too," Juno says.

Colton looks at me and raises his eyebrows.

"I'm good here. Give Daisy a pet for me." I rest my ankle on my knee and swig back my beer.

"Juno, let me know if you need me to come in," Colton says.

She nods and turns to join Brooklyn as they head up the steps.

I give him a questioning look and he says, "I'm in vet school during the school year."

"Gotcha." I take another sip of my beer.

"I kind of want to bring one home," Brooklyn says to Juno.

"Oh, Brookie, you're always the caregiver."

The two women continue up the stairs. When they step inside, two sets of eyes land on me from across the fire. Colton's head volleys between us.

"So, Wyatt?" Denver says, sitting up in his chair and resting his forearms on his thighs.

"Yeah?"

"What are your intentions with our sister?" Rome asks.

"On second thought, Daisy might need an extra cheerleader." Colton practically runs up the stairs.

Chicken shit. His day will come. I know it will from the way he caters to Juno.

"We're friends. I'm helping her out with the business."

They look at one another then back at me. "We're not naïve."

"Nor are we cockblockers," Rome says.

"But you know what we did to Jeff?" Denver asks, and I nod. "If you hurt her after what she's already been through, we have a body bag prepared."

I sip my beer, calling their bluff. They sit there with identical expressions of seriousness.

"No joke. She's not something to have a little bit of fun with then toss aside. So if you start it, you better damn well plan to finish it with an 'I do,'" Denver finishes.

"Or get her to break up with you," Rome adds, shrugging.

"Be serious. You saw him eye fucking her," Denver says.

Rome stands and finishes his beer. "Yeah, but Brooklyn's a big girl." He tosses the empty into a trash can. "That doesn't mean I won't kick your ass if I see one tear shed because of you."

"Noted. But we're really just friends," I assure them.

"And I have a fucking unicorn cock." Denver shrugs. "Not that my cock isn't magical."

The twins laugh. I can't help but join in until their faces grow serious and snap back in my direction.

They change the subject to my aim at the axe-throwing competition, but my mind is stuck on what I want with Brooklyn are and how I can possibly keep my cock away from her.

TWENTY-THREE

Brooklyn

Having Wyatt come to the Bailey Sunday dinner isn't something I'd planned, but he doesn't have any family here and it was a nice gesture for Grandma to think about him. I rode with him to pick her up so she didn't say anything she shouldn't. Like, "How do you like Brookie, she's cute, right?"

God, can you imagine having your grandma trying to get you some action? How embarrassing and desperate.

Now we're parked back outside of her senior living community. She decided to leave dinner early because of her sniffles, so Wyatt drove us back. Grandma told me to wait in the back seat for him to round the car. We'll be able to see if he's a gentleman or not she insisted.

Wyatt opens both our doors at the same time. "I hope you feel better, Mrs. Bailey."

Gentleman it is then.

She offers her hand, and he helps her to her feet. "I'm sure I will. Ethel was a little under the weather a few days ago. The old bat probably gave me something."

"Nice way to talk about your best friend," I say.

"A common cold could kill me at this age," she says.

Wyatt smiles at me, opening the door to the building for us.

"Good evening, Dori, did you have fun with your family?" the girl behind the desk asks. I watch her concentrate more on Wyatt than my grandma.

"I did. Have you met Wyatt? He's new to Lake Starlight."

"I haven't. Nice to meet you, Wyatt." She licks her lips. Could she be any more obvious?

"Nice to meet you..."

"Nicole." She twirls her hair around her finger.

Seriously?

"Nicole." Wyatt smiles.

If I cared, I'd mention to Wyatt that we're not on the *Love Connection* so move it along to Grandma's apartment. *Whoa. Where did that spurt of jealousy come from?*

"And you know Brooklyn, my granddaughter."

Thank you, Grandma.

"I haven't met you yet. Hi, Nicole." I wave. I don't get quite the welcoming smile Wyatt did.

"Hi."

Luckily Grandma hurries and we reach the hallway to her apartment quickly. I'm still examining the fact I want to scratch out some girl's eyes for looking at Wyatt as though all she needs is a spoon to eat him up with.

We stop outside Grandma's door and I soak Wyatt in.

There's no doubt he's attractive. Not in the Lake Starlight way. His polished edges stick out here. The way his hair is never out of place. His wardrobe of mostly button-down shirts. Skin that feels like he bathes in coconut oil daily.

Regardless of his physical appearance, he's a nice guy, and I can't say the thought hasn't crossed my mind—what if I had met him before Jeff? I've also thought he might be a great rebound to get over Jeff. But being jealous of another girl admiring him? That feeling came out of nowhere. I wasn't even the jealous type with Jeff.

"Brookie, in my purse," Grandma interrupts my inner monologue.

I round the two of them and find her keys then unlock her door. Wyatt holds it open while we both step through, and Grandma walks around, flicking on the lights. She steps into her living room and glances at the picture of her and Grandpa, then turns around to face us.

"Why are you two still here? Go." She shoos us with her hand.

"Jeez, you're welcome," I say.

"Thank you." She walks toward us, still shooing us out the door.

We back-step until we're out of her apartment.

"Have a good night you two." She smiles and closes the door.

Wyatt and I look at one another, confusion on our faces.

"She's an odd one," I mutter.

"So are you!" Grandma says from the other side of the door.

"Good night, Grandma," I chuckle and wave to the peephole. I walk down the hallway toward the front entrance. "She totally set us up."

"I figured, since she bragged about your speed skating when you were six the whole way here, that she was trying to tell me something." Wyatt smiles at me. His perfect teeth gleam under the florescent lights of the lobby.

"Good night, Wyatt and Brooklyn," Nicole says, stripping Wyatt's eyes off me.

"Night," he says.

I turn away and roll my eyes, jealousy intensifying instead of diminishing.

We round his sedan and I wonder what he's going to do in the winter. No way this thing will get him where he needs to go without leaving him stranded a time or two.

He opens the door for me, and I slide in. The car smells of him—his fresh scent mixed with eucalyptus now. I pick up a bottle of my oil that's resting in the console and smile.

"Mine." After getting into the driver's seat, he takes it from me. "Trying to take my goods?" He drops it back into the cup holder and turns the key in the ignition.

"You like it, huh?"

"So much so that I stole another bottle, but I figure it's a bonus for helping you out." He winks.

My stomach swirls with excitement. "I'm glad. My brothers never try it. They think it's girly."

He snaps his seat belt and pulls out of the parking lot. "I'll endorse it for them. I suffered from the worst headaches for months until you gave me my first sample."

He drives down the windy road that leads to Northern Lights Retirement Residence, and I wonder yet again why they chose to make the road so challenging when a lot of the residents still drive. Then again, I've never heard of an accident here.

My mind wanders to Nicole and why jealousy was my

first reaction, which makes me question why Wyatt's never crossed the line between us. All the times he's snapped his hand away when our fingers brush or the way his eyes sometimes venture anywhere but on me...

"Are you gay?" I ask the question that was supposed to be asked only in my head.

He stops at the stop sign and looks at me, eyes wide. "What?"

"I'm sorry. It's none of my business. Ever think something and accidentally blurt it out? Ignore me." Heat burns my cheeks.

He doesn't move, one hand on the steering wheel and one in his lap. "Why would you think I'm gay?"

"Um... I don't. Let's just forget it." I motion for him to get driving so I can escape this car and lock myself in my apartment for the foreseeable future. Or at least until I have to go to work tomorrow.

"That's not going to happen. Do you think I'm gay because I like your oils?"

Why can't someone want to leave the assisted living right now? *Because it's nine o'clock and all the residents are in bed.* We could be sitting here until five in the morning without anyone having to honk at us to move out of the way.

"Not really. I'm just..." How do I even word this to avoid making myself sound like a runway model he shouldn't be able to resist?

"I get that I'm not as outdoorsy as your brothers, and yes, I've gotten manicures and massages, but I have no idea why you'd think I'm gay."

"It's just that you and I... we haven't..." I stare out the window at the dark streets of Lake Starlight.

"You think because I haven't come on to you, I'm gay?"

He's hit the nail on the head, and I want to slink down the seat and disappear under the floor mat.

"No!"

"You do." His cocky voice alight with humor says no matter how much I fight it, that's what he believes.

"But not because I think I'm all that. And yes, you like my oils. But you eat lunch alone at the restaurant every day. I haven't seen you talk to another woman, let alone flirt with one. You spend all your time with me when you're not working. Nicole was obviously interested in you."

"Nicole?" He throws the car into park. It's too dark to see his facial expressions since there's no street light close to us, so I can only use his tone to judge his reaction.

"The girl back there." I thumb toward the retirement residence.

"She's, like, twelve."

"She's clearly in her twenties."

"Early twenties if that."

I throw my hands in the air. "I'm sorry I asked. There's nothing to be offended by."

"I'm not offended. But just so you know"—he leans toward me—"I'm not."

"Okay." I cross my arms.

"Let's go home." He straightens up, moves the car into drive, and presses on the gas.

He seems agitated and I don't understand why. It was a simple question. One with a yes or no answer and he didn't seem like he felt I'd invaded his privacy for asking.

With a huff, I watch as Main Street passes by. Only Lucky's is lit up, since Liam closes Smokin' Guns on Sunday and Monday and all the other businesses are closed.

It's not until we pull into our apartment complex that I

finally find the guts to address the heavy feeling in the air between us. "I'm sorry."

He parks the car and slides the key out of the ignition. We sit in silence for a minute before he responds.

"Don't be."

I open the car door and dig inside my purse for my keys. I want to go to bed and wake up tomorrow and pretend this never happened.

"Hold up." Wyatt jogs to catch up to me and inserts his key into the lock of our building. He stands in front of it, blocking me. "This is stupid. Why are we kind of fighting over the fact you asked me if I was gay?"

"You tell me." I cross my arms.

"It's not that you asked if I was gay. It's just..." He looks out at the dark lake then looks back at me, uncertainty marring his perfect features. He steps forward, his hand sliding up to cradle my cheek.

I inhale a deep breath, staring into his eyes, and lean into his warm touch.

"Have you considered the fact that maybe I'm waiting for you to be over *him*?"

My eyes fall to his lips, and his tongue slides out. My insides feel as though a pinball was just shot out and it's running through my body.

"Are you?" I whisper, leaning in a little closer.

He closes his eyes and the pinball sinks to the pit of my stomach. "We need to talk. There's something you need to know before this goes any further."

A shiver—not the good kind—spreads over my skin. "What?"

His hand slides off my cheek, grazing down my arm until my hand is in his. "Let's go inside. We'll both need a drink for this."

He opens the door of the building and my hand remains in his. As we round each level of the stairs, adrenaline courses faster and faster through my veins. What's happening? What could he possibly have to tell me? Part of me is cursing myself for getting the ball rolling on this conversation in the first place.

It's all moving so fast, but I don't want it to stop. I want to know if Wyatt's lips are as soft as they look. I want to know the feel of his hands as they explore my body. Will he be as gentle with his physical touch as he's been with me in regard to the business? Does he like it hard and fast or soft and languid?

He glances at me over his shoulder when we reach the third floor, and I'm pretty sure I see the same questions in his eyes. Whatever he has to tell me won't change how I feel. I'll want him regardless.

His head falls into the crook of my neck. "I really want to kiss you right now."

A shiver of goose bumps scatter up my spine—the good kind this time. "Then do it," I whisper.

He shakes his head, placing his lips right under my earlobe. "Not until you know everything."

Bang!

Both of our heads shoot up, staring in the direction the sound came from. It's then that I realize my apartment door is open.

"Stay here," Wyatt says and walks over to my door then disappears inside.

He's crazy if he thinks I'm staying here.

"Who are you?" I hear Wyatt ask.

"I should ask you the same thing." I recognize the other voice.

Those shivers now chill my body bone deep. I round the

corner and all the exhilaration coursing through my body dies. "Jeff?"

Wyatt turns around, something akin to disappointment in his eyes.

"Hi, Brooklyn. We need to talk."

TWENTY-FOUR

Wyatt

The guy standing in front of me is Jeff?

I guess the black eye should've clued me in. But he's not someone I would picture Brooklyn with and I struggle to understand how she was engaged to him. He's... for lack of a better word—and I'm not trying to sound like I'm into some high school hierarchy bullshit—dorky. Who buttons the top button of their shirt if they aren't wearing a tie? He appears so clean-shaven, I can't help but wonder if he can even grow facial hair. His hair is big and unkempt and unstyled. This guy's never met a bottle of gel in his life.

I ignore the ping of jealousy in my chest and turn my attention to Brooklyn. The pink flush from minutes earlier in the hallway has paled. Her mouth hangs slightly open, and her arms are limp at her sides like a gorilla's.

"Should I go?" I ask her.

She says nothing.

Jeff steps over the small box at his feet. "I thought you'd be at Sunday family dinner?" He stops walking before passing me. "Not on a date."

That he has the nerve to try to make Brooklyn feel guilty for anything has my head rearing back.

"Get the rest of your stuff, though Joel has the majority of it." Brooklyn drops her purse on the table and busies herself in the kitchen. "Do you want coffee or tea, Wyatt?"

Um... what?

"Why does Joel have my stuff?" Jeff asks.

"Well, I don't know, Jeff, maybe because you left me at the *altar,* and I was pissed off and before I knew what happened, your shit was on the lawn outside. Oops." She smiles sweetly, busying herself with the coffee pot. "Coffee or tea, Wyatt?" she asks as if I'm a child who's purposely ignoring her while playing his video game.

"Coffee is fine." I'd rather have three fingers of whiskey, but I'm not arguing with her.

"I'll just come back another time," Jeff grumbles.

Brooklyn opens the cabinet with the coffee mugs and sets them hard on the counter. Anyone can tell she's trying to control her emotions, but it's coming off as slightly psychotic. "*No!* You get your shit now or never."

I step back to leave the apartment. Clearly this is between them, but then again, I feel protective over Brooklyn.

"Cream or sugar?" she asks, and I'm processing so much, I don't immediately answer. "*Wyatt?*"

"Sugar," I answer, although I take my coffee black. Why did I say sugar?

Jeff raises his eyebrows at me like "see why I dumped the bitch?" My fists clench at my sides, and even though I thought for a split second I should be protecting him from Brooklyn, I'm back to wanting to kick his ass.

"Go about your business, Jeff. Wyatt and I have to talk about something." She shoos him away with her hand just like her grandma did to us a half hour ago at her apartment.

A laugh bubbles up in my throat and I swallow it.

"Well, since most of my stuff is at Joel's, I should be done quickly." Jeff walks back down the hall.

"And you'll be leaving the key! This is not your apartment!" Brooklyn calls after him.

"Let's not forget that I paid for first and last and the deposit," Jeff responds.

He clearly has a death wish.

"Well, let's square everything away then. You owe my family fifty grand for the wedding!" she leans over the counter and yells down the hall.

"Should I go?" I whisper.

"What?" Her head whips in my direction, her eyes narrowed.

These past couple of months, I've never seen this side of her.

"It doesn't matter, I'm moving to San Francisco." Jeff's voice sounds from down the hall.

"To sell that great app," Brooklyn mocks him with a dopey tone.

Jeff stomps back down the hall. "I did sell the app."

Brooklyn's face falls.

Jeff looks at the kitchen table, littered with Brooklyn's supplies for making her oils. "I see you're back to your magic healing powers."

I place my hand in the air, stepping in front of him. "Okay, I was giving you some leeway but—"

"Are you dating him?" Jeff ignores me.

"What business is it of yours?" I ask. I glance out the side of my eye to see Brooklyn slowly shutting down—the fight is leaving her.

You know what? Fuck this. I'm taking charge.

I place my hand on the back of Jeff's neck, squeezing enough to grab his attention. "Let's pack your shit and get you out of here."

Once we're at the closet, I take everything that looks manly and drop it in the box.

"Hey, that's my fishing stuff."

The tackle box breaks open and the contents spill out into the box. "Sorry." I slide over Brooklyn's coats, finding fishing rods. "These yours?"

Brooklyn could be into fishing. I don't know.

"Yeah." He holds out his hand.

I break them over my knee and shove them in the box.

"What the—"

I ignore him, putting down the flaps of the box so I don't need tape. "There's one. Anything else yours?"

"No."

Anyone can see that Jeff's not a confrontational guy. I kind of wish he'd throw a punch so I'd have an excuse to beat the shit out of him.

"Then let's go." I pick up the box and push it into his arms, which he fumbles at first.

We walk down the hall.

Brooklyn's waiting for us, her hands on her hips. "We're going to talk."

The box slips from Jeff's hands because he's either a complete weakling or she's taken him by surprise.

"Is that a good idea?" I say to her over Jeff's head.

Brooklyn's sharp blue eyes pierce mine, making me think I should sink down behind Jeff and be invisible. This side of her? The side where she's not taking any shit? I knew he hit a nerve when he mentioned her oils, but I love that she picked herself up, dusted herself off, and is ready to get the answers she deserves.

"Wyatt, do you mind leaving us alone for a while?"

I want to answer yes, I do mind. But Brooklyn doesn't belong to me.

"I'll be across the hall if you need me." I slide out from behind Jeff and squeeze her forearm in an act I hope portrays that I'm here for her.

Nothing more is said. I leave her apartment, shutting the door while wanting only to be on the other side with her.

Then it dawns on me.

What if Brooklyn wants Jeff back?

I rub my chest. Damn, something from dinner must've given me heartburn.

I guess it doesn't matter if I confess the truth to her. What's transpiring on the other side of that door might stop whatever was starting between Brooklyn and me anyway.

TWENTY-FIVE

Brooklyn

When the door clicks shut with Wyatt's departure, I point at the couch. "Sit."

"I get that you're upset, and I wish I had more answers. Don't worry, I'm leaving and you'll never hear from me again."

He sits on the couch and I sit in the chair adjacent so I can clearly see his face. Jeff isn't one to talk about feelings, but he can't mask what he's thinking either. And I have questions I need answers to before I can move on completely. Although I wasn't expecting it to happen tonight, I'm not letting the opportunity go.

"Why didn't you talk to me?" I ask, crossing my legs and sitting on the edge of the chair.

He slides back and lays his arm along the back of the couch, looking anywhere but at me. "It all just snowballed."

"That's what happens with a big wedding."

He rolls his eyes. "I get it. I pushed the big wedding."

"Yeah, you did, then you left me responsible for telling our guests that it wasn't going to happen."

"I knew you wouldn't have to do it. I mean, your family's like *The Brady Bunch*."

I inhale what I hope is a calming breath because my palm is getting itchy and it wants to smack Jeff across the face. "Did you ever love me?" I ask and brace myself for the answer.

His eyes meet mine and it's there. At least something is. "I still love you, Brook, but I don't want to live in Lake Starlight forever. We want such different things."

"Why didn't you talk to me about that then? Maybe we could've compromised."

He blows out a breath and his head falls back. "Come on. You know as well as I do that you're never leaving here."

"Well, you could've at least broached the subject with me."

"It's more than that. I mean... don't you ever feel like maybe we were just great friends?"

"No, I thought you were my future husband. I was in love with you. I know you wanted to move to San Francisco, but after everything that happened with my parents, it's hard to leave here. Don't you get that?"

"Think hard. Do you think you were *in* love with me? I mean, when's the last time you wanted me? Like, couldn't keep your hands off me?" He sits forward on the couch more.

This is where his decision about stepping out on our wedding came from? I didn't give him enough sex? "That's what happens when you're together a long time."

"It happened after two months. And it's not just the

physical stuff. I don't even know how to explain it. You became so accommodating."

"You ran out of our wedding because I gave you your way too many times?" I throw my hands in the air.

"When I met you in college, I remember thinking, 'This girl takes on life like she wants everything it has to offer.' But once we got back here and started talking about marriage and kids, you let me have my way all the time. Why do you think I pushed you on all the wedding stuff? I was hoping you'd push back."

I head to the kitchen, grabbing a beer that Wyatt brought over the other night. I tip back the beer and guzzle a large amount. "Let me get this straight. You broke up with me because I gave you your way?"

"I didn't want my way. I wanted you to fight me on it. I wanted the Brooklyn I met at that bar who made me go on five dates before I could kiss her. The one who blew me off because she had an exam in three days. The one who always did what *she* loved."

The memories of Jeff and me in college run through my mind like photographs scattered on a table. I *was* different back then, and these last couple of months, I've felt so much like the person I used to be.

"You were okay with working in housekeeping. Which is fine. But when I met you, you had all these plans. You were the girl who wanted to move to San Francisco with me."

I look at the floor. I'm almost ashamed of how I was then. I was more than willing to leave my family because being around them was too painful. The memories of my parents sliced me whenever I walked into our house. But now that more time has passed, I draw comfort from being around the rest of my family.

"You're right, I was different." I lift my eyes and see the lavender I picked yesterday at the family house on the table in front of me. "But you were the one who always made me feel like essential oils were just a hobby and not worth my time."

He chuckles. "Because it's just that—a waste of time. You aren't going to make any money playing with herbs and scents. You have a degree in art history. You should be doing something with that."

"Why?"

"Because you spent a shit-ton of money getting the degree. That's why we should've gone to San Francisco. You could've found a gallery or taught a class. Here there's nothing for you."

I gulp down another sip. "There's my family."

"And there you have it. Listen, I'm not sure what to say. I know I handled it wrong, but in the end, I think the decision was the right one."

"Who's the brunette?"

Our gazes lock. He doesn't deserve to psychoanalyze who I was then or now.

He runs his fingers through his uncombed hair and looks at the corner of the room. "Just someone I met at a bar in Sunset Bay. No one serious."

"You took her on our honeymoon," I get out between clenched teeth.

He nods.

"Is she moving with you?"

He nods again, still not looking at me.

"It's serious enough that you're moving in with her? Did you cheat on me?"

He nods.

"Look at me."

His head slowly rises until his eyes are set on mine.

"Say it."

"I cheated on you," he says in a defeated voice.

"When?"

"A month or so before the wedding. I don't remember."

I set the beer bottle on the coffee table. "You can't remember the day you cheated on me?"

My anger is boiling again and soon it's going to spill over. I'm not sure if I'll be able to control myself.

"Jesus, I don't remember, okay?"

"Because it wasn't important to you." Which means he was never as invested in this relationship as I was. If he was, he'd remember the day he decided to ruin us.

"What?" he asks.

I shake my head. This conversation is pointless. I have all the answers I need—the ones that really matter.

"Leave." I point at the door.

"I thought you wanted to talk?"

"I'm done."

"You're done?"

I close my eyes, gripping the side of the chair. "Yes." I pick up my head, hoping my eyes reflect the feeling of finality inside me. "Have a great life."

"I'm sorry—"

I raise my hand to cut him off. "It's over."

He stands, rounds the couch, and picks up his box. I walk over to the door before him and open it up.

He stops right before leaving. "I hope I didn't ruin your belief in love. You always loved the fairy tale."

"Well, you know the saying."

He tilts his head.

Lord, please forgive me for this.

I kick him in the ass and push him out the door. He

loses his footing and the box flies out of his hands while he lands face-first on the carpeting in the hallway.

"You have to kiss a lot of frogs before you find your prince." I slam the door and inhale a cleansing breath.

I don't feel better about how things ended between us, but I do feel a sense of closure. That's what I've needed to really move on.

TWENTY-SIX

Brooklyn

There's a knock at my door and although I'm sure it's not Jeff, I look through the peephole anyway. Wyatt stands on the other side with a bottle under his arm and two glasses in hand.

I open the door, and he walks in without asking.

"Saw him leave and I figured you might need this." He pours two shots of Jack Daniels and hands one to me. "So is it good riddance or congratulations?"

I scrunch my forehead. "Congratulations?"

He shrugs. "I've seen couples work out after much worse." He clinks my glass and downs his shot.

"Not us. We're done—put a stamp on it and mail it to Siberia." I down the whiskey with a grimace.

"Interesting comparison." He pours another shot for both of us. We clink and down them. "You feel good?"

"Like I could sleep for ten hours."

"That's good?" He picks up our glasses and heads to the couch. I guess he's not leaving any time soon.

No complaints on my part.

"It's good. It means no stress, I got closure."

"Mind me asking what his excuse was?" He pours another drink, but I wave him off. If I get drunk tonight, work will suck tomorrow.

I shrug. "He had a lot of excuses, which to me means he was grabbing at straws because I'm perfect." I bat my eyelashes.

A slow smile forms on his lips. "Clearly."

Now I'm smiling. I want to jump into his arms and thank him for being such a great friend. Would I have recovered from this so quickly if not for Wyatt? I don't know.

"Truthfully, he had a few points though," I say.

"Name one?" He rests his feet on the coffee table, getting comfortable.

"Well, when he met me, I didn't want to come back to Lake Starlight after graduation. The me back then would've moved with him to San Francisco."

"And?" He sips his drink instead of downing it like a shot.

I shrug. "He's right."

"You changed?"

I nod.

"People change." Now he shrugs.

"Yeah, but... there's a reason for my change."

Wyatt doesn't say anything, patiently waiting for me to share more.

"My parents died two years before I went to college. When I got there, it felt like a fresh start, you know? No one knew me as Brooklyn Bailey, the girl who lost her parents. It was so refreshing. I felt like I could reinvent myself. And I kind of did." I look up from knotting my fingers in my lap. Wyatt's listening intently, as always. "I never wanted that feeling to end. Jeff met me right in the middle of that phase of my life. But then right before graduation, I knew I had to come home. I couldn't leave Austin and Savannah to hold the family together on their own. I was the third eldest, so I told Jeff we'd move here temporarily."

"But…"

"Once I got here, Austin was in a good groove after Rome and Denver left for college. Savannah was turning the company around. They didn't need me, and the town had settled, no longer looking at the Bailey kids with pity. I slowly remembered why I loved it here and why I wanted to raise my kids here."

"So staying here is important to you?"

I nod. "I think so, but then I wonder if maybe I just didn't love Jeff enough. Maybe if it was someone else…"

He sips his drink, his gaze leaving mine for the first time in our conversation. "I guess you won't know until you're in that situation again."

Something passes over his face, but when his eyes catch mine, he smiles as though he's masking something.

"Wasn't there something you wanted to tell me?"

"It can wait. Jeff coming tonight is enough for you to deal with." He downs the rest of his drink and places the glass on the table. "I just wanted to check on you. I'll make myself scarce now that I know you're doing so great."

"No." I sit on the couch next to him. I touch his forearm to keep him where he is, and heat travels from my fingertips up my arm. "Tell me."

He sits straighter, and now it's his hands knotting between his legs. He stares at me, and that peaceful feeling that had started to settle in my body and mind twitches because in all the months I've hung out with Wyatt, I've never seen this look on his face. He seems... nervous.

"I like what's developing between us."

"Me too, but with you being my boss, how will that affect our jobs if—"

He nods and raises his hand for me to stop. I stiffen, preparing for disappointment once again.

TWENTY-SEVEN

Wyatt

"That's the something I needed to talk to you about."

"Oh." She straightens her back and inhales as though she's physically preparing herself for bad news.

Well, it is bad news. I should be on the other side of the room to deliver this news. She's got an arm I'm already familiar with. I look around for any books within her grasp and breathe a small sigh of relief when I don't see any.

"Regarding the whole boss thing. I signed a contract that says I can't be in a romantic relationship with any of the employees."

Her face falls, but she recovers quickly. "So one of us would be fired?"

You, you would be fired. "There's more."

"Okay..."

I know she won't see this coming. I mean, my dad checked everything. My name was stripped from the company website. I grew this scruff to disguise myself, although I don't think it does a great job. Then again, did no one here Google my father's name? Our family photos would be easy enough to find. But people here take you at your word. They don't automatically assume people are lying.

I grab her hands. "My name is Wyatt—"

She laughs and shakes her head. "Obviously." When she notices I'm not laughing, her face drops.

"My last name isn't Moore. It's Whitmore."

Her face tilts, a chunk of hair falling in front of her eyes. "Whitmore?"

I nod.

"As in..."

"Whitmore Hotels. My dad is the owner of the company."

Her hands grow cold and limp in mine before she pulls them away from me. "You lied?"

Her question is so quiet, for a second, I wonder if I really heard it. But the way every muscle in her face falls, I know my mind isn't playing tricks on me.

"My dad wanted me to come here and appraise the hotel, figure out what is and isn't working. Have a hand in figuring out what needs to be done to make it a success again. The only person who knows who I really am is Mr. Clayton. And now you."

"And you're going to be the manager of the hotel?"

I hadn't anticipated that question. "Until I get it up and running. Then someone else will come in to take over and I'll go back to New York."

She picks up the bottle of Jack, pours a shot, and downs it. Pours another and downs it.

"You're upset," I say, like the idiotic man I am.

"Me? No. I'm not upset." She downs another shot with a grimace then holds her hand over her stomach. "I mean, you're a millionaire pretending to be a regular Joe. You've weaved yourself through my life, knowing you were going to leave. Why would I be upset?" She pauses for another refill of whiskey but doesn't throw it back. At this point, I'll be carrying her to bed. "How convenient that you moved across the hall from me."

She turns away from me but stays on the couch.

"That was purely a coincidence. Believe me, I wish you didn't work for Whitmore Hotels."

She glances at me. "That's funny, I still think of it as Glacier Point, but tell me, Wyatt *Whitmore*, what are the plans for the resort?" Her eyes are laser focused on me, though I can see the effects of the alcohol bearing down on her. Her sweet smile and gentle manner have been stripped away.

"I... um, well... I'm figuring out what's been working and what needs improving." When I figured I needed to come clean, I didn't prepare myself for this round of questioning. I kind of thought she'd either jump my bones or kick me out. I never thought she'd want to know my specific plans for the hotel.

"And the employees?"

"New guidelines are going into place."

Her eyes narrow. Those beautiful big blue eyes aren't so endearing at the moment. They're kind of scary. "New guidelines? Like the whole write up thing?"

I raise my eyebrows. News travels fast. I can only assume Mr. Clayton is where this game of telephone began. "Yes."

"You can't do that! There are people who have been working there forever. Just because they're going through a hard time doesn't mean you can make it harder by getting them fired. Or I guess in your case, firing them yourself."

I hate this feeling in the pit of my stomach—like I'm disappointing her. "I'm not sure what you want from me. I'm trying to be honest."

"Honest would have been you coming here the first day and saying, 'Oh, I'm not only your boss, I'm the owner.'"

"I'm not the owner. This is my dad's stupid plan. He's always..." I let my words trail off. I'm not going to delve into my issues with my father right now.

She huffs and crosses her arms. "I think I need to be alone."

"Really? We can't figure this out here and now?"

Her arms drop. "What exactly are you looking for with me? A fling while you're here? Some fuck buddy for when you have to come into town to check on the hotel?"

I blink several times, thrown by her remarks. I knew our attraction was growing, and hell yes, I want to sleep with Brooklyn. What heterosexual male wouldn't? But I guess I never thought too much about the fact that I'm leaving because I had the whole "who I really am" thing hanging over my head the whole time. "I don't know. I just enjoy spending time with you."

She pours another shot of Jack for me and grabs the one she never drank. "Let's play a little game of Never Have I Ever."

"I'm not playing some college drinking game."

She downs the shot. "Funny. I figured you'd be up for it since you seem to like playing games."

I blow out a frustrated breath. "I'm putting a lot on the line. If you tell someone or someone finds out who I am, my dad will retract his promise to me."

"Promise, huh? Tell me, what do you get for slumming it in this small town?"

I shake my head. "That's a tad dramatic."

She shrugs one shoulder and crosses her legs, propping her elbow on her knee, holding her chin and waiting for my reply.

"I've been promised one of the chains of hotels."

Her eyes widen. "Wow, you must be so excited." She stands and walks into the kitchen, though a little wobbly, and opens the cupboards, looking for something. "So what do you have to do to earn this chain?"

"I have to work my way through Glacier Point and report back to him with a plan. If I can figure out a way to get the resort back in the black, he'll consider it a success."

"Huh." She opens a bag of Oreos and drops a whole one in her mouth, then she stares at me while she chews.

"I had no choice but to keep my real name a secret, but everything you know about me is real."

"Except for the number of zeros in your bank account and the fact you'll be putting a forwarding address in at the post office soon." Another Oreo goes into her mouth.

"Well, yeah, but I still have months left here. Who knows what could happen between us..."

What am I saying? That I'd take her back to New York with me? I'm not that guy. I don't want to do to her what my father's done to my mother—left her waiting until he was finished with whatever business he had to attend to and expecting her to be there when it suited him.

"Nothing is going to happen now." A third Oreo makes its way into her mouth.

"It's not?" I stand and make my way into the kitchen.

She rolls her eyes. "You're kidding me, right? Did you

think I'd subject myself to heartbreak, knowing you're leaving? Especially after Jeff?"

I rest my hands on her kitchen chair, not sure what to say.

"It might be easy for you to sleep with someone and not care at all, but it's not for me."

A fourth Oreo now. I want to tell her she's got some black crumbs around her mouth, but I'm not putting myself in the ring to get knocked out.

"Fine. We won't sleep together." I raise my hands.

"Fine. We're on the same page." She covers the Oreos and puts them back in the cupboard. "You can leave now," she says more to the cupboard door than to me. Her back is still to me while she stares straight ahead, hand on the knob.

"But you won't, right? Tell anyone, I mean."

If her eyes shot missiles, I'd be in little chunks all over her apartment from the way she looks at me over her shoulder.

"I'm just asking because if my cover is blown—"

"Just go!" she yells, so I make my way to her door and leave.

I want to blame my dad for putting me in a shitty position, but this is on me. I knew I shouldn't have gotten involved with Brooklyn Bailey from the get-go.

TWENTY-EIGHT

Brooklyn

There are few people I can trust with my newfound knowledge, but I need to talk to someone before I self-destruct or join the nunnery. Reagan is out since she works with me, so I go with the next best thing.

I pick up my phone and wait, tapping my fingers.

"Hey," Rome answers.

"Can we meet up to talk?"

"Uh oh. Do I need to kick Wyatt's ass?" He turns down the radio in the background.

"No, but you need to keep a secret."

He laughs. "You know I'm the Bailey vault."

"Um... not so much about Jeff taking our honeymoon with another girl."

"That was extenuating circumstances. Denver would've been pissed if I had all the fun myself."

"And Liam?"

"We're practically triplets." He laughs. "I'm down at the restaurant, trying to rehab part of it. Lucky for you, Denver got called away and Liam is with some chick."

"Do you have any other friends?"

He laughs again. His big, hearty, good-natured laugh that makes me feel a bit better. "No."

"I'll be right over."

I hang up and grab my jacket and my keys. I'm almost out the door before I head back and snatch the Oreos from the cabinet. I'm a stress eater. Leave me alone.

By the time I open the door of Rome's new restaurant just off Main Street, it's pretty late, but since this is Alaska, it's not dark yet.

"Hello?" I call out when I enter, but Rome can't hear me since he's banging away with Linkin Park blaring. I take one more glimpse through the big front windows then wind through to the back of the restaurant.

Rome is shirtless, slashing at a cabinet with a sledgehammer.

I pick up his phone and lower the volume.

"Hey, Brookie." He grabs his white T-shirt and wipes his forehead, walking over to me. "Want a beer?" He opens a refrigerator and pulls out two.

"No. I rode my bike over because I've drunk too much Jack."

He jumps onto a cabinet, popping off the cap of the beer bottle. "I thought Wyatt was supposed to be your bodyguard?"

I pick up a wad of paper and throw it at him.

He laughs when it falls in front of him. "So what's up?"

"You know, Wyatt's helped me a lot."

"Whoa!" He holds up one hand. "If we're talking help in the bedroom, it's a hard no. You gotta go to Savannah or

Juno. Maybe go to Holly. She's up for sleeping with strangers in their car."

Poor Holly will never live that down.

I stick out my tongue at him. "No. It's not bedroom stuff."

He drops his hand. "Then carry on."

"He's not Wyatt Moore, he's Wyatt Whitmore."

It takes Rome a second before he nods. "As in—"

"Yep."

Although it was big news that Mr. Clayton sold a few months ago, since he's still involved in the daily operation of the place, no one feels like much has changed.

He tips back his beer. "You sure you don't want one? I'll drive you home."

I shake my head, hopping up on the counter and stuffing my hands under my thighs.

"Well, he's your boss. He already was though, right?" He shrugs a shoulder.

"Now he's not just the boss, he's the owner." I clarify even though that's not the entire problem.

"He owns Whitmore Hotels?"

"His dad does."

He rolls his eyes. "I was gonna say he's young, but then I'm sure one of us would have taken the reins from Dad at some point if he hadn't died. Probably still would've been Savannah but who knows."

"Okay, so you need to keep that under wraps. He's here to see how the hotel is operating and what needs improvement. I guess his dad figured they'll get the real story if Wyatt doesn't say who he is."

"This is the easiest secret to keep because I don't give a shit." His eyes stay on me. "But I'm thinking that's not the reason you're here."

"It's not."

"You like him?"

I nod.

"And what? You're afraid Reagan will be upset that you're dating the owner?"

"No." I stare off anywhere but at him. "He's not staying in Lake Starlight. He's leaving once he's done with his assignment. Moving back to New York."

"Aah. Gotcha." He hops off the counter, throwing his bottle into the recycling bin. "So this is more about the fact that you have feelings for him and he just told you he's leaving."

"Not that I think we're, like, fated to be together forever, but..."

He quirks his lips to one side as he looks over his shoulder at me. Yeah, I'm not Rome. Or Denver. Or Liam. Hell, even our most responsible Bailey, Austin, had one-night stands. But I've never had one. Truth is I don't want one.

I'd love nothing more than to have the weight of Wyatt's body over mine. To feel his gentle caresses and the scruff of his beard along my skin. But I can't do that while knowing for certain that it's headed nowhere.

"Some of us are just better at the whole leaving thing," Rome says.

"Why though? Why can't I say 'screw it, let's have fun while you're here'?"

He laughs, putting on his safety glasses. He uses a crowbar to pull up molding at the base of the cabinets. "That's not you. If you sleep with him, do it right before he leaves, not months before. You're a girl, which means feelings come with sex. Better not to leave time for those feelings to fester."

"You don't have feelings when you have sex?" I quirk an eyebrow.

He chuckles. "I have a lot of feelings, but none of them involve my heart."

"Why can't I be you?" I say with a sigh.

"Because you're my Brookie." He drops the crowbar and wipes his forehead with his arm. "There's no shame in not wanting to screw someone just for fun. I love that about you. You've saved me a lot of bleeding knuckles. But you have to know what you're getting into."

"What do you mean?"

"You're, like, a few months off Jeff. Have you thought that maybe Wyatt is just your rebound?" He blows out a breath, wearing that look that says, "I probably shouldn't say this because the other Bailey boys might kick my ass."

"But we're friends too."

He shakes his head as though he can't believe he's the one stuck in this position. "Even so, it doesn't mean he can't be the guy who gets you over the first guy and acts as a bridge to the new guy. Not that I want to tell you what to do, but a guy like Wyatt isn't Lake Starlight material. Why not have fun with a guy you won't have to see for years after?"

"Because it makes me a slut."

He rolls his eyes. "When will women realize that having desires and needs does not make you a slut? I hate that fucking word. The key is to get your mind straight." He taps his temple. "So you can keep this straight." He taps his chest.

I consider Rome's words then think about the way my stomach fluttered with butterflies when Wyatt cornered me in the hallway before we realized Jeff was in my apartment. How every time Wyatt walks into a room, a smile splays on my face. How when he leaves at night, I wish he was slipping into my bed instead of one across the hallway.

"I don't know. I think I'm better to keep him in the box."

"What box?"

"The 'Do Not Touch' box."

He shrugs in a good luck gesture. "I hope he stays in there for you then."

I jump off the counter. "And you won't tell anyone who he is, right?"

"Nah, but I'm wondering if he wants to invest in a restaurant."

"Rome!"

He laughs, raising his hands. "I'm kidding." He grabs his phone off the counter and hops down. "Come on, I'm driving you home."

"Thanks, bro."

"Any time." He takes a few steps toward the entrance. "Oh, and I was thinking maybe you could create a scent to make people hungry?"

I chuckle. "I'll see what I can do."

"There's my little potion-maker." He swings his arm around my shoulders, and we leave the restaurant I know will be a success once he has it open.

***

THE NEXT MORNING, I FEEL AS THOUGH I CAN'T BEGIN my day until I talk to Wyatt. Since he's in the manager's office, it'll be easy for me to slide in without being noticed.

I knock.

"Come in."

I step in and shut the door. Wyatt slides his chair away from the computer. He's in a suit today. A professional suit that upon closer inspection, I can tell costs more than my entire wardrobe. The way it lays on his shoulders and nips in at his waist says it's custom tailored.

"I'm glad you're here." He stands and rounds the desk, coming toward me.

If he touches me, I'll never get out what I decided late last night while I lay in bed. I hold up my hands and he stops mid-stride.

"You're still angry?"

I shake my head. "No. I understand why you couldn't tell me, but this thing between us..." His clear blue eyes look at me, and I think somewhere deep down, I know I'll never hold the willpower to stay away from him, but I have to try. "I can't. I'll still go to the wedding with you, but I need this to stay platonic. Okay?"

He nods, sliding over to the front of the desk.

Now that I see him like this, I know I was stupid not to see how much better this version suits him. He's in his clothes, doing what he's supposed to be doing. The bellhop, housekeeping, and front desk versions of Wyatt weren't him. Not really.

"Okay." He shrugs.

"Easy as that?" A small part of me is disappointed he isn't fighting me on my decision which yes, I realize makes me very difficult to please.

He crosses his arms. "I can't say I don't want more from you. I'd love nothing more than to spend my months here with you in my bed, but hurting you would kill me."

Okay, so I'm not disappointed anymore. Just kind of hot and bothered with a warm, mushy feeling in my chest.

"So platonic it is. And you don't have to go to my sister's wedding," he says.

"A deal is a deal. You've helped me so much with the business."

"It's okay. Honestly, I'm fine with it. My mom will get over it."

"Well." My hand latches onto the doorknob behind me in fear that I'll turn my back on the words I just said. "I won't. I'm going."

He smiles. The one that I love the most. As if I made his day. "Okay, then. I'm booking the airline tickets today. If you're okay with it, we'll stay at my condo. If not, I can line up a hotel for you, but I have two bedrooms so…"

"Your condo is fine. Thank you."

"I suppose we can't hug it out, huh?"

I shake my head, my palm hurting from the pressure I'm exerting on the doorknob.

"Glad we're straight."

"Yep. Okay, heading to work now." I open the door.

"One more thing."

I turn back to him.

"Reagan? She's missing again."

I blow out a breath. Ugh. With everything going on, I've yet to check in with her. "I'll call her."

"I did. This is her third time in two weeks."

I shut the door and step forward. "It's her mom. She's sick."

Wyatt rounds the desk to sit back down. "I'm not asking for her excuse. I'm just telling you that you're alone on your shift today. I'll deal with her."

"What do you mean you'll deal with her?" I tilt my head.

His eyes widen. "It's not for you to worry about. This is my job."

"You can't fire her. You don't understand." I sit in the chair in front of him.

"She's missed too much time. I'm sorry, but this is where management has to step in. A hotel can't function with a housekeeper who misses work almost once a week." From his expression, it's clear that if I say anything else, I'll be overstepping. "You need to clock in before you're late."

Both our gazes move to the clock on the wall.

I leave his office. Once the door is shut, I'm thinking the whole platonic thing will be easy if he keeps being such a dick.

TWENTY-NINE

Wyatt

It's been three weeks of trying to keep my hands in my pockets when I'm around Brooklyn. To stop any flirtatious comments. But that doesn't mean my body isn't drawn to her. When we're watching television, we both kind of lean toward one another. Hell, I went against my better judgment and gave Reagan a warning instead of writing her up or firing her. She asked for part-time until her mom is settled, and I agreed only because it would make Brooklyn happy.

Brooklyn looks at me when I hand her the ticket. "First class?"

"Will that give me some mile-high perks?" I ask, guiding her toward the security area by placing my hand on the small of her back.

She glances over her shoulder and I retract my hand.

Why, three weeks after our talk about being platonic, can I still not control my hands or my tongue around this woman?

We get through security, where Brooklyn chats with one of the security guys she knows.

She grabs her bag after he's done wanding her. Was that really necessary? "It was nice seeing you, Duke."

"You too, Brook. Call me when you return and maybe we can meet up at Lucky's."

I scowl at the guy, picking up my own bag and slipping back into my shoes.

"Do you want something to eat or drink?" I ask as we pass a few restaurants and stores.

"Do we have time?"

I glance at my watch. "We have an hour before boarding since you like to adhere to the whole two-hour rule."

"There's a reason for the rules," she sing-songs.

"Yeah, and it's for major airports, not this one."

She narrows her eyes at me. "What are you trying to say?' She pokes me in the stomach.

Maybe she feels like I do now that we're away from all the eyes and ears of Lake Starlight. Like we can actually enjoy each other's company without worrying about what it does or doesn't mean.

"Did you break your finger?" I ask with a grin.

It takes her a minute to figure out my joke, then she shakes her head and walks toward a small restaurant. "Such an ego on you."

She asks if we can be seated by the window to watch the planes take off. I allow her to take charge for us, and a slow stirring begins in my stomach. This trip could change things.

I slide into the seat across from her.

"The burgers look good, but so does the wrap." Her mouth twists while she tries to decide.

I don't know if she's always like this or what. We haven't been to a ton of restaurants together because she's still freaked out about that damn Buzz Wheel thing. For a gossip blog, they can't be that good since they haven't been able to figure out I'm not Wyatt Moore.

She drops her menu on the table.

"What are you getting?" I ask.

"I'm deciding when she comes."

"Interesting." I lay my menu on the edge.

"What are you getting?"

"The bacon cheeseburger. Having to see my father makes me want to stress eat."

She tilts her head. "Tell me about him."

I lean back in my chair, watching a plane speed down the runway. One good thing about being in Lake Starlight is being away from him. "We don't get along."

Her lips scrunch. "I'm sorry."

"It's fine. It's been our relationship my entire life. I would've never gone into the hospitality business, but my sister won't do it and if I don't, it dies with my dad."

Am I going to tell her everything before she meets them? Hell no. There's some of my family past that just needs to stay there.

"But if you don't love it—"

Luckily, the waitress comes over and takes our order, distracting me from having to answer.

"I always wonder what my relationship with my parents would've been like," she says before sipping the water the waitress brought over. "We didn't have the best one when they passed, but I was sixteen. I wasn't like Rome and

Denver, who tested each and every boundary, but I thought I was smarter than them."

I laugh, glad she changed the topic to her. Then again, she's always willing to share her past and talk about memories that might be painful.

"Would my dad have tried to get me into the business? Or calm Rome or Denver down? There's so much that might have changed if they hadn't died."

I clutch her hand. "You'll never know, unfortunately. I'm sorry."

She shakes her head but squeezes my hand. "You need to have a relationship with your dad. Speaking as someone who lost her parents, when they die, you don't want unresolved feelings."

I slide my hand from hers. "You'll understand when you meet him. And when you do, please don't think we share the same thoughts on things."

She sips her water again, her eyes on the runway. We both know she's letting me skate away from telling her about the real problems between my father and me.

"Tell me about your mom or your sister." She sits up straighter in her chair.

"Well, we'll start with my sister. She's marrying my friend from college. They met when she came to see me my senior year. Her biggest ambition is to be on *Real Housewives of New York*."

"Not a bad ambition." She winks.

"Well, she's got the dramatic flair to fit in perfectly." I sip my drink. "We're not close like you and your siblings. We tolerate one another, but that's about it. Bradley, her fiancé, is going to run for Congress." I try to not roll my eyes, but it doesn't work.

She laughs. "You're not in agreement?"

"My worst fear is that he'll publicly cheat on my sister and I'll end up in the newspapers for having to beat the shit out of him. Bradley wasn't exactly faithful to anyone back in college."

"If you only tolerate your sister, why would you care enough to beat up Bradley?"

I shrug. "She's still my sister. I'm not on board with the whole wedding thing, but I promised my mom to keep my mouth shut."

"Which brings us to your mother."

I smile.

"I see the soft spot in your family."

I nod. "My mom is worried I'll die alone, so prepare for a heavy push about us being a couple."

The waitress brings over our food, and Brooklyn unwraps her silverware from a paper napkin. I could've taken her to the airport's first class lounge, but she doesn't seem like she'd enjoy it as much as this.

"Please, you've had to endure Grandma Dori for months."

I'd never say it, but I don't mind. If it wasn't for Grandma Dori, I never would've gotten to know Brooklyn the way I have. "Let's just say if my mom and your grandma got together, we'd be married in a month."

She laughs. I shouldn't enjoy the fact she doesn't seem put out by my comment, but I do. My mind has made some mental slips the last few weeks, thinking that I could enjoy a life with Brooklyn. Picturing coming home from work and watching television with her rather than going to the latest restaurant opening or gallery showing. Walking around town and seeing where we end up rather than taking a town car everywhere. Falling asleep next to her after making love.

We finish eating, and I'm happy that the topic of my

family had been put on the back burner. I'm not sure what Brooklyn will think when she meets them. Not just my immediate family, but my extended as well. There aren't many of us Whitmores because there have been so many falling-outs. My dad ends up alienating most of my family.

A half hour later, I pay the bill and we head to our gate.

"Are you cool with flying?" I ask, sitting next to her at the gate and letting my arm rest on the chair behind her.

"Love it."

I smile. "Good. Me too. I usually sleep."

She scrunches her eyebrows. "Not this time." She digs into her bag and pulls out a pack of cards. "We're playing rummy."

"Too bad we can't play strip poker." I grin.

She pokes me in the stomach. "You better stop with these comments. We're just friends, remember?"

I smile, wishing she was mine to kiss when she's this cute.

THIRTY

Brooklyn

"Brook," Wyatt's voice whispers in my ear. "We're landing."

My eyes flutter open, and I tilt my head. His baby blues could put me in a trance. "I fell asleep?"

He chuckles. "You did."

"How did the movie end?"

I remember us playing rummy, doing the crossword puzzle from the paper he bought, and then the movie.

"It's a romantic comedy. They end up together."

I sit up and pile the blanket over my lap, my ears popping from the descent. "Of course they did, but how?" I stretch my arms, and Wyatt's gaze fixates on my breasts. They perk up from his attention.

"The typical way—the guy had to do the begging."

I hand the blanket to the flight attendant as she passes.

"Well, that's the way it usually goes because the men are always wrong."

His hands move to my ribs and he tickles me. "Want to try that again?"

I wiggle in my seat, and the plane takes a big dip. The woman behind me yelps.

"One day you're going to run toward a woman instead of away from her." The words fall from my lips before I can lock them inside. I hope he doesn't think I'm implying I want him to run after me. To change his life course for me.

"Don't go to Vegas with that bet."

My smile falls and I slink back in my seat. He stops tickling me and faces forward. Just like that, it's back to feeling awkward. Before I knew he was leaving town, our relationship was so easy, and now it's so hard. *Because I thought it was headed somewhere, but he was only heading in one direction—back to New York.*

"Can I ask you a question?" he whispers.

Most people around us are busy putting their stuff away and watching the plane dip below the clouds.

I adjust my seat belt. "Sure, what?"

"Is this hard for you? The platonic thing."

I shrug when in truth, pretending I see him as a friend goes against everything in my nature. Reaching out to touch him but retracting my hand. The flirtatious banter that almost slides out of my mouth before I swallow it back down.

"So I'm alone in this?" he asks.

I take him in. He's dressed differently today. Like he's ready for pictures to be taken the minute we step off the plane. His hair is usually impeccable and his beard trimmed nicely, so it could be his clothes that's making me see him in a different light today. But it makes no difference to me whether he's dressed like this or wearing a T-shirt and running shorts—I want him just the same. A craving heats my blood every time I look at him.

"No. But..."

"Listen, my family isn't going to understand me brokering a deal to bring a date to my sister's wedding. I'm not asking you to kiss me or anything, but some affection will be necessary if I want my mom to believe that you're a real date."

"You can't tell her I'm a friend?" Nerves have my heart rate pitching a fit.

He blows out a breath and looks out the window at the skyscrapers that come into view. Anxiousness crosses his face. "She'll push me toward someone else. She's obsessed with me finding someone. There's this woman... she's the daughter of my dad's friend. They usually push me toward her at these kinds of events."

"Are you asking me to be your fake girlfriend?"

He bites his bottom lip. "Would it be that bad? We go to the wedding, then in a week, I tell my mom we broke up."

"I don't like to lie." Which is the truth. Plus, I'm a shitty liar. Then again, I have a feeling that pretending to be Wyatt's girlfriend might be the easiest lie ever. I'm more concerned about how I'll feel after than during.

"You don't have to say you're my girlfriend, just be my real date."

I don't know if it's the look of desperation in his eyes or the thought of him being directed some other woman's way, but the word is out of my mouth before he has to make any further argument. "Sure."

He smiles at me and grabs my thigh, squeezing. "Thank you, Brooklyn. You're really... something." He retracts his hand.

Yeah, might as well order that stockpile of wine and Oreos because when Wyatt flies out of Lake Starlight and back to New York for good, they'll be all that's left to comfort me.

WYATT'S CONDO IS WHAT I EXPECTED—BLACK AND stainless steel. There isn't a drop of color in the place unless it's coming from an article of clothing or a book.

"This will be your bedroom." He opens a door and I find more of the same. Gray walls, black bed frame, black-and-chrome dresser, and a steel-colored comforter.

"Just curious, you're not actually a vampire, are you?"

He laughs. "I like black." He steps into the room and sets my bag on the chair in the corner of the room, next to a big flat-screen television. "You have your own bathroom, which I already stocked with freshly washed towels."

"You did?"

A sheepish look crosses his face. "Someone did... for me."

I roll my eyes in a playful way. I'm not sure this life would ever be for me.

"Make yourself at home. There's food in the fridge and pantry. I'm going to take a quick shower before the rehearsal."

He's out of the room in a flash, and I hear him cross the tiled floor into a neighboring room. I look around and wonder where the yellow brick road is. This isn't the Wyatt I've come to know. The one who brings me food. The one who says let's walk instead of drive. The one who's happy sitting in my colorful apartment, watching old reruns. I suspect that the Wyatt who lives here goes to dinner at nine at night, wakes up at six to work out, then showers and puts on his suit before having his hired driver pick him up curb-side and take him to the office.

Sitting on the bed, I fiddle with my phone. I wish I could call Reagan or Juno or Savannah so they could talk me through this. I feel as if I fell for a man I didn't even know.

There's too much raw truth in that statement. I've pushed aside my feelings for Wyatt because if I accept how I feel about him, it will make it hurt worse, but the truth is, I'm going to hurt no matter what when he leaves. Maybe seeing him in his element will help, because the man who lives here is not the man for me.

I turn on my shower then go through my suitcase to find something to wear. I open the closet door and find a row of empty hangers. As I hang up my dresses, I wonder if I'll look like Cinderella pre-fairy godmother when I meet all his rich friends and family.

I shake my head. They can think whatever they want. I don't care.

I almost believe it.

THIRTY-ONE

Wyatt

We step out of the car and I pass the keys to the valet. Brooklyn's jaw dropped when we took the elevator to the parking garage where my BMW was waiting. My jaw dropped before that when she stepped out of my guest bedroom wearing a dress that dips low in the back, revealing all her delectable skin. I'd love to slip my hand past that backline and feel goose bumps pop up along her spine. This whole platonic thing sucks.

The hotel doorman opens the door for us and Brooklyn thanks him, stepping into the foyer. We follow directions on the small sign indicating that the rehearsal dinner is being held in the Acorn Room. The hallway is littered with men in suits and women in dresses, but I don't recognize one of them.

Unease presses down on me the closer we get to the Acorn Room and I latch my hand to Brooklyn's. She doesn't appear worried, and I hate the gnawing feeling growing inside me that says she should be. The women are catty, the men flirtatious. I pray Haylee will be the sister I know she is and help Brooklyn through tonight. Then again, that's selfish of me since it's Haylee's big night.

Brooklyn glances at me, her shiny blond hair hanging down in loose waves. "Relax. I promise not to act like a small-town girl."

I still can't help but wonder if she's prepared for the manipulative Upper East Side crowd. I stop us right before we reach the door, pressing her back to the wall. "Promise me one more thing?"

My fingers tuck a strand of hair behind her ear. She's so innocent. Why did I ever agree to let her see this side of my life? It takes everything in me to not whisk her away from here to avoid her being tainted by these people.

"You've been strung tight since we left your condo. Relax." Her hand presses against my chest. She tilts her head with her usual easy-going smile. Lips I'd love to press mine to right this moment in some desperate attempt to steal a little bit of her goodness while I can have it because once I step through those doors, I'll transform into a man she doesn't recognize.

"Whatever happens, don't leave without me. If we get separated, seek me out."

"What? Why?" Her forehead wrinkles.

"Just promise me." I lay my hand on her cheek, and she leans into my palm.

To anyone outside of our bubble, we're a couple in love.

Truth is, I wish... forget it.

Her hand covers mine on her cheek. "Okay. I promise."

My thumb swipes across her soft skin.

"Can we go in now?" She giggles. Too bad I can't take this naïve girl and place her in a bottle.

"Sure."

I entwine our hands. We're about to walk into the Acorn Room, but we don't get a chance before Veronica Adley almost bumps into Brooklyn. Not exactly the person I would've chosen as Brooklyn's first encounter this evening. I would have preferred she hang with some of the nurse sharks before meeting a great white.

"Wyatt?" Veronica's dark eyebrows shoot up as though she's surprised to find me at my sister's rehearsal party. She grips my shoulders and does the whole air-kisses thing. "I'm not so sure about this beard." Her finger and thumb grip my chin, twisting my head in either direction.

"I like it," I say.

She drops her hand. *Thank God.* "You know me, I always like everything baby soft."

Her implication is clear, and Brooklyn's red cheeks say she's not as naïve as I thought.

"Oh." Veronica notices my gaze dipping to my side. "You must be the date." She puts her hand out between them, and Brooklyn releases my hand to shake Veronica's. It appears civilized, but I know better.

"Brooklyn Bailey."

"How cute," Veronica says, looking over Brooklyn's dress. "I could eat you up."

With her fangs. An image of Veronica wiping the blood dripping from her chin is clear in my head.

"Thanks. I love your dress too. You look beautiful." Brooklyn's compliment is genuine.

"Thanks." Veronica turns to me. "What about you, Wyatt? What do you think of the dress?" She runs her hands down her waist and over her hips.

"It's nice."

"Nice?" She rolls her eyes, focusing on me as though Brooklyn isn't even standing here with me. "Come on. Give me one of the good ones like you used to."

See what I mean about malicious? The compliment she gave Brooklyn was done so she can make it clear there was a time when I thought Veronica was the most stunning girl I'd ever meet. Then again, I was sixteen and easily led around by my dick. Seeing Brooklyn and Veronica side by side, I realize that, at twenty-nine, I hadn't seen the world yet even if I had been all over the globe, I hadn't been to Lake Starlight. I hadn't met Brooklyn Bailey.

"My mom's probably looking for us." I sidestep Veronica, which she allows.

Veronica's eyes cast a judgmental gaze over Brooklyn one last time. "Have fun. Oh, and just a tip. The finger bowl isn't soup." She touches Brooklyn's arm and smiles.

"Ignore her," I whisper in Brooklyn's ear, leaving Veronica at the door.

"Well, she's a treat."

"So sweet she'll rot your teeth. Let's find my mom."

I search the crowded room. Everyone has drinks in their hands and has yet to sit for dinner. We missed the rehearsal earlier because of when our plane arrived but it's fine. If you've been in one wedding you've been in them all.

I spot my mom on the other side of the room, talking to Haylee, which is great. I'm hoping Haylee will help block Mom from gushing over Brooklyn as though she's Bruce Springsteen, my mom's favorite.

"Come on." I squeeze Brooklyn's hand, leading her toward my mother. We stop along the way to say some brief hellos.

When we reach them, my mom and Haylee glance over.

Something must be going on because Haylee forces a smile. Look at that—she's already perfected the role of a congressman's wife.

"Big brother," she coos, squeezing me tightly around the neck.

Brooklyn drops my hand, allowing me to wrap both arms around my sister. Her mass of dark hair almost suffocates me.

"Save me," Haylee whispers. She steps back and looks at Brooklyn, then at me again.

In the meantime, my mom hugs me lightly with a kiss on the cheek. Her interest isn't on me, and we both know it.

"This is Brooklyn." I place my hand on the small of her back as though I'm presenting her like a prize. "Brooklyn, this is my mother, Eva, and my sister, Haylee."

My mom smiles. Brooklyn puts her hand out between them, but my mom steps forward and squeezes Brooklyn in a hug so tight, she might snap her in two. Haylee and I share a look behind Mom's back.

"Well, why don't you just welcome her to the family, Mom?" Haylee says.

Our shared look turns deadly. Haylee laughs, rolling her eyes at me.

"It's so good to meet you. I haven't heard nearly enough. Come on, I'll get you a drink and you can tell me everything."

"Mom, I'll take her to get the drink."

But my mom already has her arm slid through Brooklyn's and is pulling her toward the bar.

"I guess I'll say my hello another time?" Haylee asks.

My mom ignores us, and I watch as my mom carries on about who knows what, leading Brooklyn away from me and closer to the shark-infested waters.

"Stop it. Mom will take good care of her." Haylee grips my upper arm. "She's cute. What is she doing with you?"

I shove my hands in my pants pockets. "Since she just found out who I really am three weeks ago, I'm pretty sure this is a farewell tour."

Haylee tilts her head as though she's confused. I'm not surprised. She's been so deep into wedding planning, I'm shocked she even knew I was in Alaska.

"Dad had me go work at the new resort incognito. Brooklyn works for the hotel." I grab a glass of champagne from one of the passing waitstaff. I'll take anything to calm my nerves right now.

"She works at the hotel?"

"Housekeeping." I swallow back the entire glass before setting it on a nearby table.

"You brought a maid as your date?"

"Don't be a judgey bitch. It's not becoming of a politician's wife."

"I'm not. I'm just surprised." She touches my forehead. "Did Mom and Dad send you away for some brain rewiring?"

I shake my head. "I've always been more down to earth than all these people." I throw my head to the side, casting judgment on everyone here.

She laughs. "Just because your good friend was the student aid kid at Trinity doesn't mean you're down to earth."

"Anyway, keep it on the down low. Veronica's already showing her true colors."

"Green was never her color."

I pick up two champagne glasses, hand one to Haylee, and clink our glasses. "Congratulations, sister. You snagged yourself a congressman."

"If I didn't love him, I'd leave him just because of that."

We both know she wouldn't. Then again, maybe I'm cynical.

We sip our drinks. My gaze searches the crowd near the bar. My mom has now sat Brooklyn down and she's laughing at something.

"So you want to tell me what the deal is with you two?" my sister asks.

We both stare at my mom and Brooklyn.

"We're friends, but don't burst Mom's bubble, okay?"

"Huh." Haylee places her half-drunk glass on the table nearby.

"What?"

"Oh, nothing. Good to know you're still blind as a bat. I guess even the fresh air in Alaska can't clear that head of yours." She pats my back and walks to her bridesmaids three tables in, checking over her shoulder to make sure I understood.

Well, if Haylee thinks there's something more between us, then my mom will too. It's a win.

I start to approach the table my mom and Brooklyn sit at, but Bradley intercepts.

"Wyatt, thanks for coming, man." He pulls me into a hug, practically picking my feet up off the floor.

I like to think I'm a big guy, but Bradley played rugby, and let me tell you, he looks like what you imagine a rugby player would. Tall, broad, and muscles bulging everywhere.

"Congratulations, you get my sister for the rest of your life. I don't envy you in the slightest."

He laughs before downing the rest of his champagne. "Let's get a real drink."

I peer around his body to find Brooklyn and Mom still engrossed in conversation. "Sure."

"So who's the girl?" Bradly asks, as I knew he would.

"A friend."

"From Alaska?"

We reach the bar, where each of us order our drinks.

"Yeah."

"I was going to say one thing isn't like the other."

"Jesus, what is with everyone here? So what if she's from a small town?"

Bradley stirs his drink and stares at me. He takes out his stirrer, licks it clean, and places it next to his drink on the napkin. "I meant she's way too fucking good-looking for you."

Maybe I need to loosen up. Maybe my family won't think less of her because she doesn't have the money or status the majority of people in this room do.

I sip my scotch, hoping it allows me to calm the fuck down. "Well, I could say the same thing to you. Here's to marrying up." I raise my drink.

He clinks mine. "Isn't that the truth."

We sip our drinks. The burn from the alcohol feels like relief down my throat.

"Now if only I can get her away from Mom."

We turn toward the table, seeing my dad right beside my mom.

"Fuck," I murmur.

"Nothing good will come of that." Bradley cringes and pats me on the back. "Talk to you later."

I knew I shouldn't have let myself get comfortable. That's exactly when the enemy will decide to attack.

THIRTY-TWO

Brooklyn

Wyatt's mom is adorable and everything I expected after overhearing her hounding Wyatt to find a date. She's asked me all the questions a mother would of the new woman dating her son.

"And your father, honey? What does he do?"

Here comes the tricky part. This is a happy affair, and my answer always brings people down. "He passed. Ten years ago."

She places her hand over her heart then over my hand. "I'm so sorry."

"Thanks."

"And your mother?"

I just have to say they passed together. Why didn't I do that? "She passed at the same time. Snowmobile accident."

Her eyes widen, and I ignore her tears welling. If I

address them, she'll let them fall and she's the mother of the bride.

I look around. Where is Wyatt when I need saving?

"I'm sorry. Life is so unfair. We've had our own unfair obstacles, but nothing as devastating as losing your parents at such a young age." Her hand is back over her heart now.

"Like I said, it was ten years ago."

"How old were you at the time?"

"Sixteen." I sip my glass of wine. I let Mrs. Whitmore order it for me since I didn't want to order the wrong thing. People keep staring at me and I don't understand why.

"Who raised you?" Eva asks.

I swallow, trying to remain polite. "My brother."

"Heartbreaking." She looks off in one direction then the other, composes herself, and sips her own wine. "How did you meet Wyatt?"

Finally, a topic I can handle. "Work. I work at Glacier Point Resort."

"You do?"

Shit. I probably shouldn't have said that.

She looks around again and leans in. "Let's keep that between us. If Wyatt's dad found out he's sleeping with an employee, it would be bad all around."

I blanche, wanting to shrivel up and disappear.

"Oh no. I didn't mean that it's beneath him. It's the employee-and-boss thing. As you know, Wyatt's there for a reason and it isn't to fornicate with the employees." She smiles. "But you're absolutely breathtaking." She grips my hand and I have no idea if I should feel complimented or insulted.

I smile and sip my wine, hoping he rescues me soon.

"And who is this?" A man I don't need to be introduced to—because his son looks so much like him—kisses Eva's cheek and sits next to her. He extends his hand in my direction. "Abe Whitmore."

"Brooklyn Bailey." I shake his hand.

"Bailey?" He clicks his tongue along the roof of his mouth. "Have we met?"

"No, I don't believe so."

"You look familiar... Bailey..." He snaps his fingers and points at me. "You're here with Wyatt?"

"Yes, Abe, this is Wyatt's date." Eva smiles almost as if she's reassuring me this will be over in a second and to just grin and bear him for a moment.

"Bailey Timber?"

"Yes." I nod.

"When I scouted out Glacier Point, Mr. Clayton raved about your family like you're the Kennedys. You must do well in that town."

"My sister, Savannah, runs the family business now."

"Her parents passed," Eva whispers.

Not one ounce of sympathy mars his face. I'm happy I don't have to reassure someone else that I'm okay, but what does it say about him?

"Of course Wyatt goes off to Lake Starlight and finds himself one of you guys and not some normal girl."

His mom laughs but checks to make sure I am too. I'm not. I don't understand the joke, nor do I think because my last name is Bailey that I'm better than anyone else who lives in Lake Starlight. But I'm not impolite and I'm doing something nice for Wyatt.

"I see you've met Brooklyn?" Speak of the devil. He comes up behind me, resting one hand on the back of my chair.

"We have. She's lovely." Eva smiles at me.

"Yes. She is." Wyatt dips down and presses his lips to

my cheek. A million-watt surge courses through my veins, but I try to tamper down my surprise and my arousal. "I'm going to take her out to the balcony."

His hand grazes down my arm until my hand is firmly in his. Then he lifts it and I stand from the chair.

"Have fun, you two," his mom says. "It was wonderful talking with you."

"You as well," I say.

"Wyatt, come by the house tomorrow morning. We need to chat," Abe says.

"It's Haylee's wedding day. No business tomorrow. Actually, no business this entire weekend," Eva says.

"That's ridiculous. I'll be making deals during the reception." Abe laughs, but no one joins in. He doesn't seem to notice as he picks up his drink. "Come, Eva, the Feldmans are here."

"Mom. Dad." Wyatt nods and leads us out of the room and onto a balcony that overlooks Manhattan.

I gasp. "Wow…"

He guides me to the railing. The lights of the skyscrapers are almost blinding.

"Something, isn't it?"

"It's beautiful." I saw everything on the way to the hotel, but up high like we are now, and at night? It's spectacular.

"I'm glad you're here, but I apologize if anyone said anything offside when I wasn't around. It's easy to forget how vicious the people here can be."

This remark isn't his first of this variety. He's been paranoid since we left his condo that people would treat me poorly. Veronica wasn't great, but it's obvious she's jealous. I don't know the details of their past, and I don't care to.

I circle around so my back is pressed to the railing. Wyatt doesn't step away, leaving us close. Too close for platonic friends, but I don't push him away. I don't want to and I'm tired of fighting against myself. "Why do you keep saying things like that? Did you run away to Lake Starlight for a reason?"

His gaze shoots to the skyline behind me, but the light on the balcony above allows me to see what's in his eyes. Wyatt isn't transparent, he keeps his expressions in check, but usually a stirring of something is evident in his blue hues. "I never thought much of it until I went to Lake Starlight. I was content in the dog-eat-dog world this city breeds. But..." He looks at me and tucks a strand of my hair behind my ear. I fail to mention he's ruining all the hard work I put into making it look naturally wavy. Having his touch on me feels right. "You make me wish I was someone else."

"Why?"

He steps closer, and his hand splays along my cheek as it did when we first arrived. His touch is intimate. If I don't want this to go any further, I need to say so now. But I can't deny I want Wyatt, and Rome's words ring through my head.

"You're so angelic. So pure. So perfect. But I'm far from it."

His words make me feel as if I could float away right off this balcony.

"You talk about yourself like you're an assassin or something. You're not, right?"

He laughs, his head tilting back. The moon shining on his neck... God, I want him. I shouldn't, but I do.

"No, I'm not that, but I was raised to get what I want, damn the consequences."

I lean closer to him, wanting him to see himself the way I do. "That's not the man I know."

"You know the Lake Starlight Wyatt Moore, not the New York Wyatt Whitmore."

I cover his hand on the railing with mine and step into the small space separating us. Damn the consequences. "Be the man *you* want to be."

"You make it sound so easy." His eyes search mine.

"I'm not sure I understand what's so hard about it."

The pain on his face tells me I still don't understand. Why can't he be the same Wyatt in Lake Starlight and New York?

"Come on. We should get back inside." He grabs my hand, but I don't let him lead me. He looks over his shoulder, and when he sees my expression, he turns back around. "What's the matter?"

"This." I wave a finger between us. "I want you to share with me whatever is the matter. Is it family? Your dad? I see how he might be hard on you, but you only get one family. Unfortunately, I know how precious family is. Time with them isn't guaranteed."

"See what I mean? You're way too good a person to be here."

"Maybe you just don't know the true me yet?"

He chuckles, reaching for my arm. "Let's go inside before I kiss you under the moonlight." He stares into my eyes.

The breath leaves my lungs in a giant whoosh. "Maybe you should."

He quirks an eyebrow at me. Apparently seeing that I'm serious, he steps forward, forcing me back until my back is pressed to the railing. "You want me to kiss you?"

I lick my lips in anticipation, drawing his gaze.

The Wyatt I know is genuine. Yeah, he lied to me about his name, but he was right that night in my apartment. His name doesn't change the man I've grown to know these past months. Still, do I want to chance another heartbreak by crossing that line?

"Yes. I want you to kiss me." I hold his gaze so he can see that I mean it.

"Really? What happened to being friends?" His arms cage me in, and he steps forward, leaving no space between us.

The heat from his body calls to me, and I can't help the way I press into him. "I can't do it anymore. I need to feel you."

"Feel me?"

I throw my hands in the air. "You know what I'm talking about."

He says nothing, but his smirk says all I need to know.

"You do too, right? I'm not in this alone?"

He chuckles. "You sound like me three weeks ago. If I kiss you, you know the score? No dating, no serious relationship?"

"I do."

"I'm serious. I'm not a man who will change. If you allow me to kiss you, I need to know you understand and accept it. I don't want to hurt you."

"Thanks for the warning." I smile, but I can't tell whether or not he's convinced.

"Okay then." He nods.

"Okay," I say in a breathy voice.

"Close your eyes."

"This isn't my first kiss."

"Just close them."

"Fine." I close my eyes and lick my lips.

"God, you're beautiful," he says, his voice growing even closer.

The wind shifts and runs under the hem of my dress, but it's a relief to the growing heat between my thighs.

"Ready?" he asks, and his voice is so near, my heart races with anticipation.

"Um-hmm."

I brace myself. This is it. I'm finally going to kiss this man, and when I do, I'm not going to think about tomorrow or what happens when he leaves Lake Starlight. I'm not going to worry about our destiny. I'm just going to enjoy kissing and touching and hopefully having sex with him. The future be damned.

"Our first kiss will not be with one hundred people bearing witness," he whispers into my ear and goose bumps scatter along my neck.

I open my eyes and he's right in front of me.

"Because once my lips land on yours, I'm certain I'll turn into a caveman until you're naked and writhing beneath me."

I blow out a breath and try to calm my pounding heart.

"Now let's get tonight over with so I can get you back to my condo and get you out of that dress."

"Boy, New York Wyatt is kind of dirty."

He laughs. "Told you I was different here."

"I kinda like it." I giggle, allowing him to take my hand and guide me to the doors leading inside.

"Then you're in for a great night. Make sure you finish your meal. You'll need the energy."

I'm so busy laughing when he opens the door, I fail to realize that every set of eyes is on us.

The man with the microphone at the front of the room says, "You'd think you were the celebratory couple."

"Sorry." Wyatt raises his hand, looking a little sheepish.

"Typical Wyatt Whitmore!" some guy in the crowd yells.

Wyatt ignores him and rushes us to our table, where his dad is beet red. I don't know the man at all, but I know that can't be good.

THIRTY-THREE

Wyatt

The fact that my dad's eyes are laser focused on me should have my attention focused on silently apologizing for the spectacle I made by coming in late. I guess it shows that I haven't changed as much as I'd like to think I have. But instead of my dad, it's Brooklyn occupying my mind.

She's a permanent fixture in my thoughts at this point, but it's usually because I'm trying to figure out some way she can fit into my life after I leave Lake Starlight. Right now, I'm trying to decide what I want to do to her first when we get back to my condo. Or whether I should even allow us to cross that line. I'm not naïve—she's going to get hurt because Brooklyn doesn't let someone come into her life like that without growing attached.

Is that what she realized? That no matter if we slept together or not, she'll be affected when we part, so she might as well take what she wants? If so, then why shouldn't I do the same? Because as much as I try, I see no way she'll fit in my life. At least not in any way that won't tarnish everything good about her.

"Hey, you," she whispers, her hand sliding to my knee under the table.

I smile at her. I can't seem to not smile when I look at her. "Hey."

"You okay?"

I nod, sliding my hand under the table and squeezing hers. She's too damn good for me. It was easier to pretend that wasn't the case back in Lake Starlight. But here, with reminders of the person I used to be, the person I'm trying so hard not to be anymore, it's so much more obvious.

"Brooklyn, tell me about yourself," my dad says while cutting up his salad.

"I'm not sure what to say." She's stiff, and that sweet smile is now filled with anxiety as she moves her hand from mine and grabs her wine glass.

"You mentioned your sister runs your family business. Do you work alongside her?"

My dad is so busy eating, he doesn't see the way her eyes shoot to me then my mom and back to me. Why are my mom and Brooklyn acting cagey?

"Who cares what she does, Abe? I want to hear about Lake Starlight." My mom looks at Bradley's parents and grandparents. "The pictures Wyatt posts on Instagram would steal your breath. It looks so beautiful there."

Bradley's parents politely smile and look at me.

"How do you expect me to know her if I don't know what she does?" my dad interrupts my mom's attempt at changing the subject.

I'm definitely missing something here. My mom hasn't

been this on edge since the day I got my rejection letter to Harvard Business School and my dad wouldn't stop asking why I hadn't heard back from the school yet.

"Because that doesn't say who she is." My mom smiles sweetly and touches my dad's arm as though they actually love one another.

My dad slides a tomato off his fork into his mouth and looks at Brooklyn, waiting for her to answer.

I place my arm around the back of her chair, tired of whatever is going on here. "She works at Glacier Point."

My mom's gaze dips to the table, and a small groan comes from Brooklyn's throat.

"You do?" My dad places his silverware on either side of his plate and wipes his mouth with his napkin. "In which department?"

Brooklyn sits up straighter and leans forward. "House-keeping," she says in a low voice as though she doesn't want anyone else to hear it.

My dad's narrowed gaze lands on me. I'm familiar with his look of disappointment. It's the same one I get with any life decisions I make. But what I don't like about this one is that he's displeased with Brooklyn.

"You're a maid?" he clarifies.

She swallows her wine. "Yes, but um..." She looks at me for a moment. "Wyatt has been helping me start another business."

"What kind of business?" My dad directs the question to me instead of Brooklyn, but I won't respond for her.

"Essential oils," she says.

My dad's eyebrows rise. He's not exactly the type of guy to dab lavender onto his wrists to help him sleep.

"Oh, I just tried a sample when I was shopping the other day." My mom looks at the ceiling. "I think it was vanilla almond, but I don't remember what it was good for."

"Yes, when we flew to Paris last month, the flight attendant passed around little vials of lavender oil." Bradley's mom nudges his dad, who looks about as impressed as my dad. "Remember when I thought they were handing out cocaine?" She laughs.

My mom, of course, joins in.

"There're a lot of benefits to vanilla oil," Brooklyn says.

"Really? Like what?" my dad asks, sounding skeptical. I'm surprised he hasn't pulled me away from the table yet.

"Well, it relaxes you. If you put it in a diffuser and fill in a room, it helps calm your mind. It also works to nourish hair and skin."

"I think that's what the lady told me." My mom is more excited than the topic warrants, but I know she's desperate to let Brooklyn shine. "I think she mentioned that in the winter it helps with dry skin?"

Brooklyn nods. "Yes."

"You're telling me she spends a small fortune every year on all this health and beauty crap, but all she needs is a little vial of your oil?" My dad laughs with Bradley's dad.

I grind my teeth. "Brooklyn gave me some eucalyptus for my headaches, and it's helped." I smile at Brooklyn, hoping to give her the encouragement that what she's doing matters.

"Oh, that's wonderful," my mom says, turning to Bradley's mom. "Wyatt has suffered from headaches since he hit puberty. Sometimes the migraines were so bad, he'd lock himself in a dark room."

Bradley glances at me with mock concern.

No need to mention I haven't had to take meds nearly as much since I moved to Lake Starlight since I haven't suffered from as many headaches. Although I feel one coming on now.

The waitstaff clears away the salads.

"Wyatt has been so wonderful in helping me get everything set up," Brooklyn says.

"That's very altruistic of him, since he's there to do a job for me." My dad doesn't look at me now, which means his anger is brewing.

"Oh, he's done great things with Glacier Point as well. Although he may be a little stricter with the employees than they're used to." She smirks at me, and my heart swells that she's trying to boost me up to my father.

"Not strict enough. We're not in the black yet."

"Now, Abe, we shouldn't talk business at the table." My mom's hand lands on my dad's forearm, but he ignores it.

I tilt my head. "How would you know?"

"Did you think I wouldn't be keeping an eye on what was going on?"

My insides go cold. Of course. I should've known he'd never trust me enough to manage a hotel on my own. Brooklyn grows quiet, and I try to calm myself before I grab my dad by his shirt and knock him out.

Everything I've been through with my dad comes barreling through my mind like a freight train. All the disappointed looks, the comments meant to undercut any self-confidence I had, and the jabs that I'd never find success. How he can't count on me or trust me to do the right thing. What he really means is I'm not him. That somewhere along the way, I strayed from his vision for me. I might be riding on the train track right next to him, but we're on different paths.

"Speech time," the DJ says over the microphone, and the lights dim.

"I'll be right back," I whisper to Brooklyn and stand.

"Do you want—"

"No. I'll be right back," I assure her, even though there's a good chance the hotel might have a hole to patch in the drywall later tonight.

I shake a few more hands of family and friends on my way out the door, but I don't release a breath until I'm finally in the hallway and heading to the bathroom.

"Wyatt!"

I turn to find Veronica walking toward me.

"Not now." I put my hand in the air and continue heading to the bathroom.

I push open the door and stare at myself in the mirror. What the hell am I doing with my life? Why do I still let him control me and demean me? Why do I let him get to me?

The answer is the same as always. He holds my future because I was too weak to start on my own path out of graduate school. I fucked up as a rich punk in my earlier years. Now my only chance of living the life I dream is to abide by my dad's rules and put up with his shit.

"This is familiar," Veronica coos. "Of course, usually your hands would be up my dress already." She laughs, leaning against the bathroom wall.

What the hell is she doing in here?

"I'm not in the mood for your antics." I wash my hands as if I wasn't moments away from having a breakdown.

"Antics? You never complained before."

"I'm here with someone." I dry my hands, but she pushes off the wall and stalks toward me.

"Goldilocks? You know she can't give you what you want. She doesn't seem like a back-scratcher or a fuck-me-in-the-men's-room type of girl." Her finger runs down my chest.

I grab her hands and place them to her sides. "Maybe that's what I like about her."

"I'm curious. Does she know your past? That you're not some saint?"

I shake my head. "Get off it. What I have with Brooklyn is none of your business. And you act like I have some deep, dark secret. So what if I fucked around?"

She laughs, unleashing her hands from my grip. "Please. You've fucked practically every girl on the Upper East Side and half of Tribeca. We both know this relationship of yours will last about five minutes. We're meant to be together. Me and you. Destined since childhood."

"You seem to think we're in some demented teen movie. You know what we were together, and who I was with you isn't who I am with her."

"I never heard complaints," she purrs.

She has a point. Veronica was a girl to call at the end of the night if I hadn't met someone else. She was on the same page though.

I head to the door, but she cuts me off. "Come on, Wy. Remember all the fun times?"

I grip her hand and sidestep her. "Those days are over."

"Don't worry. I'll welcome you back after she finds out you're no prince."

I open the door and step out, rage burning inside me.

"Wyatt!"

I turn toward my dad's voice, thankful it's not Brooklyn because Veronica picks that moment to walk out of the men's bathroom.

My dad's vision flickers to her. "Veronica."

"Good evening, Mr. Whitmore. You make such a handsome father of the bride." She bows her head, smirking at me.

"You always say the kindest things. If you'll excuse us, I need a word with my son."

"Of course, Mr. Whitmore." She saunters down the hallway, glancing back at me over her shoulder.

I roll my eyes and turn my attention to my father.

"You sneak away to have a fling with Veronica in the men's room?" My dad's judgmental tone says that even if I dispute it, he'll think I'm lying. Not like it would be his first time catching me doing something I shouldn't.

"No. I'm not you."

He tilts his head, appraising me, probably trying to figure out what I know. He has no idea what I know. "Listen, I get that you want to hit me where it hurts and bringing a maid to your sister's wedding is a great way to get back at me for whatever reason it is that you hate me for this month, but you're playing around with that poor girl's emotions."

I stuff my hands in my pockets. "Why do you care?"

He nods toward the balcony. I follow like the obedient son I'm usually not.

"I don't. But I can't have the Whitmore name tarnished when we're just building a reputation in Alaska. Her family is a big deal around that area. You using her to get back at me is only going to make those people hate us more than they already do."

"Maybe I like her."

He laughs into the night sky. "Wyatt, you're the most selfish person I know."

"Are you including yourself in that assessment?"

"Yes, and that's the sad part."

"You don't know me."

I'm remaining calm, but my dad's flared nostrils say he could explode at any moment. "I know you use people to get what you want. That you're stringing this girl along, promising her some future of having millions and never wanting for anything."

"I think you're confusing me with you."

"Let's get something clear. You are to break it off with this girl tonight. Send her on a plane home, and maybe we'll discuss the hotels Sunday after your sister leaves on her honeymoon."

"Sorry." I pat him on the shoulder because I know he hates it. "Not going to happen. I like her, Dad. Deal with it." I turn to leave.

"You like her enough to throw our deal off the table?" He turns around.

Right before I reach the doors, I turn back to face him. "You and I both know you might need me a little bit too, and you're not going to throw that away just because I'm dating a maid."

Then my jaw drops to the floor because from the other side of the balcony steps my mom with Brooklyn. Their faces make it clear that they overheard me.

Fuck my dad, did he set me up?

THIRTY-FOUR

Brooklyn

"Excuse me," I say, trying nicely to shrug off Wyatt's mom's hand.

I step forward but realize Wyatt's there, so I circle back around to the doors Eva and I came through.

"Brooklyn." Wyatt's voice is closer than it was moments ago.

"Oh dear," Eva says right before I open the door and step back into the rehearsal dinner.

Haylee and Bradley are with a group of friends at the table closest to me. I smile, tip my head down, and try to manage a quiet exit.

"Brooklyn!" Wyatt's voice booms through the room.

Obviously, he'd rather make a spectacle of himself.

"Wyatt chasing a girl. That's a new one," some guy says from the circle of friends with Haylee and Bradley.

"Fuck off, Ian."

Pushing back tears, I swallow the saliva coating my throat.

"Excuse you," Veronica says as I accidentally shoulder-knock her while trying to escape the room. "Now that she's gone—"

"Go to hell, Veronica," Wyatt says right before his shoes click along the marble hallway.

Hearing him gain on me, I speed up my footsteps to the elevator, hoping he doesn't catch me. I pass the stairway, thinking that might be a better option.

Realizing I have no way to escape, I turn around, and Wyatt stops, his torso shooting forward from the sudden movement. He grabs my arms to steady himself.

"Stop following me. Enjoy your night. I'm leaving."

"Not without me you're not." He reaches past me and presses the button to the elevator.

"Leave me alone," I bite out.

A few guests from another event room trickle out and head toward the elevators. I smile politely at them.

"You don't understand. I don't think of you like that."

"Then why would you say it?"

We both talk while staring straight ahead at the elevator doors. I watch the numbers, waiting for my escape to arrive.

"It's my dad, he brings out the worst in me." He runs his hand down his beard.

The two older ladies who are now standing behind us discuss the food from the event they attended. Apparently the beef was subpar and the lettuce in the salad was wilted.

"Don't go blaming everything on your dad. You've been different since we got here."

"I know," he says quietly.

"Then let me leave. Let me go," I plead.

The doors open and I step in before everyone else can

get off. Impolite and childish, but Wyatt isn't going to say, "Sure, go back to my condo and I'll give you time to think." He doesn't work like that. At least from what I've seen.

"Excuse me," he says to the people trying to get in behind us. "I don't mean to be rude, but I have to talk to my date, and we need some privacy."

"Wyatt!" I say.

"Lovers' quarrel." The one lady looks at the other. "Of course. But just so you know, if you stop the elevator for a little kissy kissy, you can't hold it too long before they call the fire department. I learned that the hard way." She laughs, and her friend knocks elbows with her.

"Noted. Thanks." He steps in and presses the door close button.

I lean into the corner and cross my arms, looking anywhere but at him.

"We have about thirty seconds to get one thing straight." He steps in front of me. "What I said was an asshole remark and I didn't mean it the way it came out."

"Then why did you say it?" Tears prick the corners of my eyes.

"I told you, my dad is a bastard who likes to pull people's strings. Tonight, I played the part of puppet."

"It shouldn't matter anyway because it's not like we're anything but friends."

"Brooklyn..." He runs his hand down his beard.

"What?" I narrow my gaze.

"You know as well as I do that's not true." He steps closer. With his hands resting on my cheeks, his lips meet mine.

Rather than fighting him off, I find my hands loosening and dropping to my sides while stars fill my vision.

Our first kiss isn't anything like I imagined it would be.

When I thought of us actually kissing, I thought he'd be gentle and soft and tentative. I thought hesitant lips would linger over mine, unsure if he should cross the line because I'm the girl who was left at the altar and I need to be dealt with while wearing velvet gloves. But Wyatt's kiss is explosive and dominant and controlling. I don't have a ton of experience, but this kiss is by far the best I've ever had. His low groan and the way his hands grip just a tiny bit firmer as I welcome his tongue into my mouth has heat pooling between my thighs.

My hands move to his forearms, and all the corded muscle that lies under his suit jacket flexes. I'm transported to another world. A world where this man is mine.

The bell rings, indicating we're on the main floor, but Wyatt doesn't dislodge his body from mine as the doors open. He closes the kiss as though it pains him to do it. "Come home with me?"

"Well, my stuff is there, so..." I raise my eyebrows, and he chuckles.

"Way to ruin the mood." He takes my hand and escorts me from the elevator. "Sorry for the delay," he tells the people who witnessed us making out. Before I grasp what happened, he hands the valet his ticket and wraps his arms around my waist, pulling me into him. "I'm sorry I hurt you."

I stare into his eyes. He has some questions to answer and maybe I'm foolish for putting them on the back burner to spend tonight with him. But I want one night where I finally take something for myself. "Thank you for your apology."

"I can show you how sorry I am back at my place." He winks.

I laugh, falling into his chest and sliding my hands

around his waist. I inhale his cologne and bask in the feeling of my cheek against his chest. In a city far away from home, with a man I wish could be my forever, I know I need to commit this to memory because it's destined to be temporary.

THIRTY-FIVE

Brooklyn

When we enter Wyatt's condo, he tosses his keys on the table by the door.

"Drink?" he asks, already heading into the kitchen, shrugging out of his suit jacket on the way. He disposes it on the back of a chair and grabs a wine glass and a tumbler.

I sit on the couch, unsure how this whole thing works. I haven't been with a man other than Jeff in over five years. I doubt Wyatt is expecting me to change into my pajamas and get under the covers before we have sex. Jeff loved the bed and had whined about his back when I tried to initiate something on the kitchen table once.

I wish I could call one of my sisters. Or my brothers. I should've asked Rome for pointers the other night.

Yeah, right. Like Rome would have been forthcoming.

Get out of your head, Brooklyn.

Wyatt comes over. He's already unbuttoned and rolled up his shirt sleeves. "Wine?"

He hands me the glass and I take it. The liquid sloshes a bit because I can't control my anxiety about what's about to happen. I sip it before it ends up spilled all over my dress. "Thanks."

"Do you want to stay in here or go outside?" he asks. "It's not too cold out."

Is he expecting me to have sex outside? I mean, I'm game when I'm snuggled up in a tent or a sleeping bag, but on his balcony with witnesses in every direction? Is that the kind of woman he wants? Because I'm not her. I bet Veronica is though.

That thought has me wrinkling my forehead.

"Hey." His hand falls to my face and his thumb rubs my cheek. "There's no pressure."

No pressure to have outside spectator sex?

He offers his hand and I accept it, rising to my feet. His free arm slides behind my back and he seems so casual, so at ease.

"You look like you're about to throw up." He buries his head in the crook of my neck. "You're the one in control, okay?"

I nod, though the movement is a little stiff.

He entwines our hands and leads me outside, where the noise of Manhattan on a Friday night accosts our ears. These windows must be made of something pretty awesome to block out all this noise.

He sits on the lounger, placing his drink on the table. "I'd love for you to join me here." He pats between his legs. "But I'll understand if you don't want to."

"Sure." I place my wine glass next to his tumbler and slide onto the lounger, my back to his chest.

His fingers brush the strands of my hair to one side so his chin can rest on my shoulder.

"It's a beautiful city," I say. It's not as beautiful as the view from Glacier Point, but it's nice.

"It's louder than I remember." He chuckles into my ear and places his lips on my shoulder right where it meets my neck.

Shivers scatter up my spine in waves and I find myself leaning toward him. I make some non-committal noise, completely distracted by the feel of him pressed against my back. When I adjust a bit, my hands land on his legs.

"You smell amazing." His arms wrap around my middle. The fabric of my dress is thin, and my skin is scorching under his touch.

"So do you." I tilt my head, and he captures my lips with his own.

This is a different kiss. It's slower and more languid and his fingers graze down the side of my face. I could swear I'm in a dream. That my eyes will pop open and I'll be alone in my dark bedroom, living out a private fantasy.

"I need to tell you something. Before we go any further, there's something I want you to know." He casts one more small kiss on my lips as though he's worried it will be our last.

"Tell me later." I circle around and kneel between his legs, taking his head in my hands. "Forgive me ahead of time if I'm awkward with all this."

I place my lips to his, but he shakes his head and tears his face away from mine.

"What do you mean?" he asks, a line forming between his eyebrows.

"This. I haven't done it."

He looks panicked for a moment. "You haven't—"

I wave him off. "I'm not a virgin." He visibly relaxes. "I've just never initiated... you know."

"I don't want you to be anxious. If you don't want to—"

"No, I do, that's the whole point. But the anxiety of waiting for it to happen is killing me."

He laughs. "Do you want to strip me bare and go at it right here?"

I sit back and stare down between us. "I'd rather go inside. I'm not big on the exhibition thing."

"Oh, Brooklyn, you are—"

I stand from the lounger, feeling stupid. "Naïve?"

"No, not naïve."

I go inside and head toward my bedroom, but Wyatt grabs my wrist and twists me around. I fall into his hold.

"Stop running away from me. I was going to say, you're perfect." His lips land on mine and he grabs under my thighs, hoisting me into his arms.

My hands hold his head to mine. I never want him to stop kissing me. Our mouths are frantic, as though one of us could disappear at any moment.

"Don't ever think badly of yourself, because to me, you're perfect. So fucking perfect I'm another man around you. A better man."

His fingers find the top of my zipper, and he lowers it inch by inch as he casts open-mouthed kisses along my chin and down my neck.

"Stand for a second," he mumbles, lowering me to the floor.

His gaze falls down my body and back up, his hands sliding under the straps of my dress until they fall past my shoulders. He guides them down my arms, watching my body intently as the material slips past my breasts and over my navel. His breath hitches as it passes my hips and cascades to the floor.

Without a bra, I'm practically bare in front of him. I step out of the dress and toward him, my fingers fumbling with the buttons of his shirt. He continues to watch my movements, his hands molding to my sides and sliding up and down my skin until he hooks his fingers on either side of my panties. He's only teasing me though, because he leaves them on.

His chest is smooth and his stomach flat, and once I have his shirt completely undone, he shrugs it off, leaving it to join my dress on the floor.

After sliding out a dining room chair, he sits and pats his legs.

"What about your slacks?"

"If I take these off, this will be over much quicker than I'd prefer." He pats his legs again and I waste no time in straddling him. He twirls my hair into a ponytail and grips the strands at the back of my head, tilting my head where he wants it and licking up my throat. "Do one thing for me tonight?"

A moan is my response.

"Just be here, present with me. Don't worry about what I might be thinking because I'm only thinking about being inside you and praying that I last longer than my fifteen-year-old self."

I giggle, and he latches on to one of my nipples, sucking it, and my giggle morphs into a moan. My head falls back and my lower half grinds against the growing erection in his slacks.

He doesn't make it hard to enjoy the way he worships my body. His kisses are little morsels of admiration for my naked self. His groans are a confidence booster that assures me I'm what he wants.

Just when we're in a rhythm, he stands and my back hits the cool glass of his dining room table. My legs hang over the side, but his fingers slide my panties down my legs, and he pushes my legs up onto his shoulders.

Thank God for I kept up with the waxing, even if I opted out of Brazilians.

"A landing strip," his husky voice says.

"I might live in Alaska, but I'm not a cavewoman."

He chuckles, sitting in the chair and sliding my ass down the glass toward him. "I thought you'd be neatly trimmed."

"You thought of me?"

"From the moment you hit me in the head with the book." He smiles at me.

A giggle escapes my throat until his tongue swipes up my center, at which point it dies off into a moan. All I can think is how marvelous that feels and I hope he never grows tired of it. He laps at me until I'm a needy mess, begging for more. When he plunges a finger inside me, I gasp. When he adds another one, I moan. When he adds a third, I lift my hips and grind into his hot, waiting mouth. The more I buck, the more satisfied noises come from Wyatt, and I'm racing toward the point of no return. His fingers grip my hips and I know there'll be marks there afterward. That thought slingshots me up one more level on the arousal meter.

"Oh God!" I scream, my hands searching for something to grip before my orgasm rips through me. One hand finds the edge of the table, but I'm too far away from the other, so I press it to the glass behind me, my entire body practically rising from the need coiling inside me.

His tongue strokes my clit again and again. My thighs tense, the lower half of my body completely off the glass until I climax, falling over the crest, his name slipping past my lips. He extends my bliss by not relenting throughout my orgasm, and I grip the glass table so hard I fear I'll break it. Eventually he slows his movements, settling me back down on the glass, allowing me to come back to him after the best orgasm of my life.

When I lift my head, he's sitting back in his chair, watching me with lust-filled eyes. He rubs himself through his slacks. "You're beautiful when you come."

I feel my cheeks flush and I slide to the end of the table, my quivering legs finding the floor, but I quickly fall to my knees, my hands on his belt. "Let me watch you come now."

He allows me to open his pants and pull him out. My hand wraps around his impressive dick, stroking it.

"When I'm inside you." He guides me up under my arms and digs a condom out of his pocket. His gaze stays on me as he takes off his pants, boxer briefs, and rips the condom open, sliding it down his rigid length.

I wouldn't think I could come again so soon, but watching him spurs another round of desire inside me.

"I'd love you to ride me, if you're up for it."

"Not outside though?" I ask.

He chuckles and tucks a strand of my hair behind my ear. "Not outside." He sits on the dining room chair, waiting for me.

I don't make him wait long.

THIRTY-SIX

Wyatt

I think I blacked out when Brooklyn came a few minutes ago, but watching her step toward me, trusting that I'll get her through our first time together, fills me with the confidence of a man who deserves her.

She straddles me, and I position my dick at her opening. One day she'll guide me. Baby steps. She sinks down on me with a moan.

Fuck, she feels incredible.

I grab her hips, and she anchors herself with her arms behind my neck. She's slow at first, allowing me to cup her pert breasts and suck on her nipples. She likes that. I can tell by the way her eyes roll back into her head.

We find a groove and a rhythm. I know I'm getting no sleep tonight because this won't be enough for me. My appetite for Brooklyn might never wane.

"You feel so good," she says, her hands now on the

back of the chair. She's rising and falling up and down my length, deliberately building our orgasms. God love her.

"I don't even have words to describe this," I say, leaning back to watch the pleasure unfold on her face. Eventually, I grip her ass cheeks and quicken the pace, unable to keep myself from claiming her any longer.

"Wyatt." Her hand hits the back of the chair.

I keep the pace, the sweat between our bodies making the sliding against one another that much sexier. "Don't stop, baby."

My lips cast kisses anywhere I see skin. My orgasm barrels through me without warning, and all the pious thoughts in the world won't stop me from exploding. I thrust as deep as I can get, and she gasps. Her thighs tighten, and the same noise that tumbled out of her mouth when she came before falls out now, pushing me over the final hurdle until I still inside and stretch up to claim her mouth with my tongue.

After I come, I fall back into the chair and she comes with me, her hair a sweaty mess. My condo smells of sex and it brings a smile to my face, however early caveman that might be.

"You're amazing," I whisper, and goose bumps cascade across her skin.

Yeah, I need to figure out a way to keep her because I'm not ready to let go. It's a startling realization, but I'm not one to lie to myself.

"Shower?" I ask.

"And food?" Her breath is still fighting to return to normal.

"I'll order and we'll shower while we wait."

"Perfect."

I pick her up and her feet fall to the floor. I already miss the feel of her pressed against me.

I GRAB ANOTHER PIECE OF PIZZA FROM THE BOX between us. Brooklyn's wet hair is entwined in some sort of twist on top of her head, and she's dressed in a comfy pair of pajamas I've seen her wear back in Lake Starlight. I think it's safe to say she wasn't planning on doing what we did.

"So you never moved away for college, huh?" she mumbles over a piece of pizza.

"I went to Columbia, much to my dad's displeasure."

"Why?"

"I didn't get accepted at Harvard." I pick at my pizza. The reference to my father brings a knot to my stomach. It's time I come clean with her about a lot of stuff.

"Well, Columbia is a great school."

"It's not Harvard, especially in my dad's eyes."

"It's better than Idaho State." She picks a piece of mushroom off her pizza and pops it into her mouth.

"Why'd you go there?" I sip my beer.

She looks off into the distance. "I have no idea." A small giggle floats out of her. "I mean, a lot of my friends went there, so I did too. I was so hell-bent on getting out of Lake Starlight, I don't think I cared where I went."

"I kind of felt that way about New York when I went to Lake Starlight. I just wanted away from here." She glances at me with a look that implies I should keep going. "What?"

She shrugs. "I'm just wondering. I get that your dad is controlling, but why did you want to run away?"

I drop my pizza onto the plate and figure the beer will do me better if we're going to have this conversation. She's let me in her head more than once. Doesn't she deserve to visit mine? My stomach clenches, and I prepare myself to disappoint her.

"You don't have to—"

"When I was nine, my mom was diagnosed with cancer."

"Oh, I'm sorry." She reaches across the couch and touches my leg.

"Thanks, but she's been good since. I mean, she beat it."

"That's wonderful." She squeezes my knee.

I wish that was the end of my issues. But what my mom's challenge taught her didn't have the same effect on me. My mom looked at her life with a fresh lens, a restart, but all I saw was how love was a lie, not something you could rely on.

"It is. It was a hard road. Part of that time in my life is a blur, but other parts are vivid, like a movie playing inside my head." I sip my beer, buying myself some time to run over those memories, however painful.

The times when the nurse wouldn't let me in to see my mom. When my jokes would bring a pained smile to my mom's face, but not a laugh. When Haylee's dress-up fashion shows didn't make Mom's eyes light up. The times I'd rush upstairs after school, only to be shuffled out of the room by the nurse because my mom needed her rest. The cries I'd hear late at night that her music couldn't mask. The footsteps of my dad coming home late rather than right after work. My parents' fights where she'd beg him to be there for her.

Brooklyn gives me the space I need until I'm ready to lay everything out there.

"My parents' marriage was never great, from what I can remember. My dad never hit my mom or anything, but he'd make condescending remarks once in a while, and he was absent a lot. They didn't show affection in front of Haylee or me. I never thought much of it until my mom got sick. She was always sad, and my dad seemed to be even more scarce during her treatments than he had beforehand." I look out the window, wishing for not the first time that I could only focus on the fact that my mom survived, not everything else.

"You don't have to tell me anything you don't want to." She slides closer, her hand coming to my cheek.

I look at her long and hard. If anyone deserves to know my biggest struggle, it's this girl. The woman who's slowly making me think I might be wrong about the whole love thing. "I want to, it's just... I've never told anyone this before."

"Take your time." She pulls my hand into her lap and covers it with both of hers.

I sip my beer again. I should have poured myself a scotch instead. "My dad was rarely home before she got sick, but after she was diagnosed, he never even made it home for dinner. He'd come home late at night or say he had to travel somewhere. The longer that went on, the more depressed my mom seemed to become. Haylee and I tried everything and anything to make her happy, but we weren't enough."

I stare into her blue eyes to gain the strength I need.

"One night it was late, and my mom had just fallen asleep. I went downstairs to my dad's office. I wanted him to buy me a new joke book because none of mine were working anymore. I was quiet because my dad had this thing about us running or making any noise in the house. I was trying to behave so he'd take me or let the nanny take me to get the book the next day."

I take a deep breath, steeling myself for the next part.

"The giggling should have clued me in, but my dad had associates over all the time. It seemed like everyone in his world worked late. The door to his office was cracked open a bit, which I remember being surprised about because my dad was always paranoid about people overhearing him when it came to business. When I peered in, I saw my dad at his bar, pouring a drink, and I cracked the door open further, thinking it was okay if I went in. Then a woman came up behind him."

A cold chill runs down my spine remembering how her arms wrapped around his waist. The way her cheek laid on his back and her eyes fell closed. "My dad put down the drink, turned around, and kissed her."

"Oh, Wyatt." Brooklyn raises to her knees and hugs me.

I pull her into my lap, wanting her close. "I watched them kiss and my dad pull her closer. I'd never seen him do that with my mom, and I didn't understand why he was doing it with some woman I didn't even know."

"Did you go in?"

I shake my head. "My dad would've killed me. I thought if I went in, I had no chance of getting the book."

"I'm sorry. No kid should have to see that."

I nod, rubbing my hand up and down her thigh. "It kind of screwed me up for a long time. I don't even know if my mom knows. I've never had the nerve to ask. I hid it from her because I didn't want to hurt her, and I hate myself for it."

"Why does your mom stay with him?" she asks without judgment.

I shrug. "I think she loves him. Even if she does know, I'm not sure it would matter, but it's been eating at me for twenty years. Maybe that's why I let her convince me to bring a date to the wedding." I smile and lean my forehead on hers. "I'm happy I did though."

"Me too." Her arms go around my neck.

I inhale a deep breath, wishing that was all I had to tell her, but that's only what spurred me to live my life the way I did. "Anyway, my mom beat her cancer and I never found my dad with anyone else, even as I got older and followed him or looked for signs at meetings or social events. But I was an angry person—at my dad for treating my mom the way he did and at myself for not having her back."

"Wyatt, you were nine—"

"Let me get this out."

She nods and presses her lips together.

"I did stuff I'm not proud of." I run my thumb over her soft cheek. "I've slept with a lot of women, and I never wanted a relationship with any of them. Not that I led them on, but I treated them poorly, putting their feelings aside too many times. Sex was a distraction I used to keep from thinking of the reality of my family situation, and I didn't give much thought to who I might be hurting. Veronica and I had a strictly sexual relationship for years. She helped me cope with the anger of my dad by—"

She puts her finger to my lips to stop me. "You don't owe me any explanation about your past."

"But I was a shitty person."

She smiles and her head falls to my shoulder. "You're not now."

"How can you be so sure?" I whisper.

She kisses me right under my chin. "Because ever since I met you, you've done the right thing. Not to mention the fact that you've helped me get through the second worst thing to ever happen in my life." She pulls back and moves her leg so she's straddling me, then places her hands on my cheeks. "The fact you feel there's a need to tell me you're pretty much a manwhore with no feelings says you're not who you think you are."

"You know the Lake Starlight Wyatt, not the New York one."

She shrugs with a smirk. "There are things to like about both of them."

Forgetting the pizza, drinks, and the deep talk, I stand, picking her up with me. "Are you sure you're not some angel sent down to save me?"

She hugs me and nibbles on my earlobe as we walk toward my bedroom. "Don't go putting labels on me I can't fulfill."

"Are you suggesting you have a naughty side?"

Her body vibrates against mine with her chuckle. "A good girl never tells."

I drop her on the bed. "I promise, your secret is safe with me."

I crawl on top of her, my lips meeting hers. I want nothing but to stay in this bubble with her for the rest of my life.

THIRTY-SEVEN

Brooklyn

We walk into the building the ceremony is being held in, Wyatt's hand on the small of my back. Wyatt's been good at distracting me from the fact that I'll be attending my first wedding since being left at the altar. But between the two of us, I'm not sure which one needs more support. Wyatt's feelings toward his father aren't going to disappear, and after last night, I'm not sure where they stand. Poor Haylee. I can't imagine how having her brother and father fighting on the day of her wedding affects her.

"Wyatt!" A guy who I'd peg at eighteen or nineteen is handing out programs, and he does the whole shake-and-hug thing with Wyatt. "I saw you for a fleeting moment last night, chasing"—the guy's eyes fall to me—"you." He puts out his hand. "Ian."

"Brooklyn." I smile.

The guy has a clean-cut jock-look, with a charismatic

smile that probably assures he's not home alone on a Saturday night.

"This is Bradley's brother," Wyatt says to me.

"Also his usher. You'd think the whole blood bond would mean I'd be a groomsman." Ian rolls his eyes in a dramatic fashion.

"I'm just a guest, so you're one step above me." Wyatt pats him on the back.

"All of his government friends got the prime jobs. I will say though, they throw a helluva bachelor party." His eyes widen. "You missed out."

Wyatt looks at me for a second. "No, I didn't."

A floating sensation rises in my stomach, so I place my hand to cover it. One day at a time, I remind myself.

"Come on, I'll take you to the bride's side." Ian squares his shoulders toward the aisle and holds his arm out to me.

"Thank you." I eye Wyatt as I slide my arm through Ian's.

"My pleasure. It's an excuse to disappear for a second."

I ignore Ian mostly because when we step into the room, I'm awe-stricken. Cherry blossom trees are planted on either side of us, the branches positioned to make an archway. Both sides of the aisle are filled with hydrangeas in white, pale pink, and even a periwinkle one every now and then. It's breathtaking, and as Ian shifts our direction away from the aisle, my body protests, wanting to walk under the cherry blossom trees.

"This way," Ian says.

I trip on the edge of the aisle runner, but Wyatt comes up along the other side and catches me. I know my cheeks must be pink. "I'm sorry."

Once I'm on grounded feet, Wyatt steps back to follow us and Ian laughs.

"It's just so stunning."

"Yeah, it's cool. My cousin got married last year and she had some cherry blossoms, but it wasn't this elaborate. Then again, it wasn't a Whitmore getting married either."

"I'm sure her wedding was just as beautiful," I say absentmindedly, still taking it all in.

We round the back row of chairs and I slow my steps, wishing I could sit back here.

"Well, the bartender didn't card, so that was good." Ian slows down midway up the rows and I think he's going to deposit me there, but I'm wrong. "Let's slow down. I'm not into this usher thing. You're fine, but the old women, they're touchy." He glances behind him and leans in. "Wyatt's great-aunt once removed grabbed my ass."

I can't hold in my laughter. "I don't know what's funnier. The fact she did that or the fact you know the relation so well."

He shrugs. "People tell you who they are because they want to be seated as close as possible. Mrs. Whitmore gave all the ushers strict instructions about where each person was to sit though."

"Are you flirting with my date?" Wyatt asks from behind us.

"Sure am, and she's going to give me the first dance." Ian winks at Wyatt.

"As long as I get the last, I'm good with that," he mumbles.

I motion toward a free row. "I'll just sit here."

"Sorry, Mrs. Whitmore can be a tyrant, so you're up front." He eyes the front. No one is sitting in the first two rows.

"In the second row?" The shock must register on my face.

He laughs. "Sorry, you're first row, fourth seat in, right next to Wyatt in seat three."

I inhale a deep breath as nerves make me jittery.

Wyatt's hand finds mine and he pulls me over to his side. "Brooklyn, this is my aunt Edith."

The redhead wearing a hat with a large flower hanging off the rim smiles at me but doesn't offer her hand. "She's a pretty one, Wy." Her eyes skate over me, concentrating on my hips. "She'll hold a baby just fine."

Ian busts out laughing.

"Thanks, Ian, we're good," Wyatt says.

"Okay, I already told Brooklyn the details, but you're in the first row, buddy." He pats Wyatt on the back and heads back to the entrance.

"Thanks, Ian," I say.

"When you get bored of him, call me. I'm into older and more experienced women."

I shake my head with a smile because I'm not that much older than him, but it's refreshing to have someone make me laugh right now.

"I have to get Brooklyn situated and walk Mom down the aisle," Wyatt says to his aunt. "I'll see you after the ceremony."

He leans down and kisses her cheek. Aunt Edith's eyes remain on me the entire time, and it's so unnerving that I look away.

"Nice to meet you," I say.

"You too, darling." Again, she eyes my hips.

My hands move to cover up her view, but Wyatt's hand finds mine. His footsteps increase speed until we're at the front row.

I sit in the fourth chair as instructed. "She's interesting."

"Move one over, baby," he says.

His term of affection throws me for a second. I glance at him and he smiles, waiting for me to move. Does he even realize he said it?

"Ian said I'm seat four and you're in three."

"Good thing I'm the rebel in this family. Scoot."

I slide one over. "But your mom—"

"My mom will be ecstatic that you're still here with me. Okay, I have to go walk my mom down. You okay?" He sits in the fourth chair.

"Yep. I'm good."

He nods, but he doesn't look convinced. "I'll be back before Ian can steal you away from me." He kisses my cheek right by my ear. "By the way, I'm the only one you're dancing with tonight."

I giggle.

"Did you think I'd share? I'm way too selfish for that." He kisses me one more time then stands, heading out of the row of chairs.

My stomach flips. I need to bring my beating heart back to a two. Right now, it's at a ten from the way Wyatt's made me feel both last night and today, but he's been vocal about his reasons for not wanting commitment and he hasn't said that I've changed his mind. I need to keep my head on straight.

Needing something to do while I sit here, I message Rome, since he's the only family member who knows exactly who Wyatt is. My siblings know I've left town to go to a wedding in New York with Wyatt, but they don't know that it's a wedding of this magnitude.

Me: *I'm at the wedding. How is everything in Lake Starlight?*

The three dots appear immediately.

Rome: *Your favorite brother just used his big muscles and smart brain to install his new fridge.*
Rome: *How are things there? Without all the girly details.*
Me: *Good. It's beautiful. Lots of cherry blossoms.*
Rome: *Cool. How's Wyatt? Again. No pervy details.*
Me: *He's good. We're...*
Rome: *Nope.*
Me: *Getting along.*

I want to ask Rome what I should do, but admitting my feelings for Wyatt is akin to admitting I can't compartmentalize what's happening between us.

Rome: *So why are you texting me?*
Me: *Wyatt has to walk his mom down the aisle, so I'm by myself in the first row and I don't know anyone.*
Rome: *You're a friendly girl. Make some new friends.*
Me: *This is not our crowd.*
Rome: *??*
Me: *Uber rich. Like Gossip Girl rich.*

Rome, Denver, and I were obsessed with *Gossip Girl* growing up. It's one thing we kept up even after Mom and Dad passed.

Rome: *Find me a Serena van der Woodsen.*

Veronica comes to mind, although Serena was much nicer than Veronica.

Me: *Do you think you'd want to settle down then?*

My thumb hovers over the delete button. I can't ask Rome that. But someone bumps my back while getting into their seat behind me, and instead of hitting delete, I press Send. *Shit.*

I look over my shoulder to find a man holding a woman's purse. That was obviously the culprit that hit me.

"Sorry, sweetie. She carries bricks in here." His smile reveals a set of perfectly straight and white fake teeth.

"No problem."

I glance at my phone and see three messages from Rome.

Rome: *Why would you ask…*
Rome: *Brooklyn, I was strict with my instructions.*
Rome: *Rebound. Rebound. Rebound. ONLY for a rebound.*

I frown because his thoughts on the subject most likely match Wyatt's.

The music starts.

Me: *It's starting. Gotta go.*
Rome: *Just remember Brookie, we've got the Buzz Wheel, so we're pretty important too.*
Rome: *Gif with the caption 'Gossip brings people together'*

I shake my head and stuff my phone into my clutch before tucking the purse at my side.

Shifting so I can see the doors, I catch Veronica five rows back, next to Aunt Edith. The old woman is pinching

Veronica's skin and saying something Veronica doesn't seem responsive to. At least I'm not the only one being sized up for motherhood.

The doors open, and Bradley's mom walks in with her arm around Ian's. His floppy hair is such a dramatic contrast to every other male in the room. Wyatt might be the only one with a beard. Other than a few well-groomed mustaches, there isn't a lot of facial hair in this bunch.

Ian smiles and walks up the aisle with more swagger than needed for an event like this. That's likely why he ended up on usher duty. Stopping by the end of the front pew, his mother sits next to Bradley's dad, who shoots a warning glare at Ian.

Once the three of them are seated, the music changes. Wyatt and his mom wait in the archway. Through the crowd of people, our eyes find each other, and he winks, spurring the same stomach flipping and flopping as though there's a circus performing in there.

He steps out, and as Eva wipes tears with a tissue using her free hand, he says something in her ear that brings a smile to her face. A small laugh bubbles up out of her. They're amazing together, and knowing what I do after last night, I see their bond more clearly. It must have been traumatic for a little boy to witness his father cheating on the woman he holds up on a pedestal. Especially when she was fighting for her life.

My own tears well up as I remember how I'd planned around moments like this for my wedding because there was no mother or father of the bride. I blink back the tears and remember that I'm okay without Jeff in my life. It was for the best that we didn't marry. When I open my eyes, I catch someone staring at me in my peripheral vision. I turn my head to find Veronica's dead eyes on me.

Ignoring her, I watch as Wyatt kisses his mom on the cheek and waits for her to sit before taking his seat next to me. Eva squeezes my hands and looks at me with pure excitement on her face. Wyatt places his arm on the top of my chair and slides as close as he can get.

Bradley and his groomsmen come out and stand at the altar. He's sweating but smiling. I'm guessing my groom would have thrown up or passed out entirely.

We all watch a small ring bearer and flower girl walk down the aisle.

"Kids of Bradley's friends," Wyatt whispers in my ear.

The bridesmaids come down.

"All her sorority sisters except the matron of honor. She is, or was, our nanny's daughter." I look over my shoulder, and he chuckles. "We don't only associate with rich people."

I lean back into his strong chest. "I didn't say that."

His one hand crosses over and lightly grasps my hand. "You're making this more tolerable. Thank you for coming."

I return his squeeze and look back. He kisses me briefly. Lucky everyone's eyes are on the doors to see if the bride has shown her face.

The music changes, and I find the bridesmaids made their way down the aisle as Wyatt and I stole a moment for ourselves. We rise, and Eva takes my hand. Wyatt witnesses the action and smiles at me. As all three of us turn toward the doors, I catch Veronica's eyes on me once again.

Haylee and Bruce stand in the doorway, her eyes only on Bradley. I glance at the groom and find the biggest smile I've ever witnessed on a groom's face as she steps onto the carpeted path. It's then that I realize I'm thankful my wedding was canceled. I want a guy who looks at me that same way when I'm walking down the aisle.

From the corner of my eye, I peek at Wyatt, finding his attention on me. When I turn to look into his eyes, he bends down.

"You okay?" he asks.

"Perfect. Everything is perfect."

THIRTY-EIGHT

Wyatt

No one in the room feels the shift, but I do. Something is brewing between Brooklyn and me. I can't explain it, but in this room full of people, I only see her. The way she smiles and talks with everyone after I introduce her. She's ventured to topics far away from the weather and occupations. She's growing comfortable in a world I never felt at ease in.

We've had dinner, watched my dad dance with Haylee, Bradley with his mom, and then Haylee and Bradley.

"Let's go," I whisper in her ear, distracting her from a conversation with some guy who works with or went to graduate school with Bradley. He's been chatting with her for the past fifteen minutes as I watched from across the room.

"This is my..." She looks at me.

"Her boyfriend. Wyatt Whitmore." I put my hand out for the guy. "Sorry to interrupt."

Brooklyn sips her champagne with a small smile. Does that mean she likes that I referred to myself as her boyfriend? It was a bold move. I hate that I did it out of jealousy, but the word felt good coming from my mouth—at least when it's Brooklyn I'm talking about.

"Jake Reynolds." He shakes my hand firmly. "It's okay. I should find my buddies anyway. We have a prank planned for Bradley."

I smile.

"It was nice talking with you, Brooklyn, and if you're ever in Brooklyn, look me up." He winks.

What a tool.

"Nice meeting you, Wyatt." He waves, downing his drink, and disposes of the glass on a nearby table before heading through the crowd.

"That's cute the whole 'Brooklyn when you're in Brooklyn' thing." I welcome myself to her champagne.

Her arms wrap around my waist, her chin resting on my chest. "Is that jealousy? And the boyfriend bit? Really?"

"What can I say? If you're not mine, you're nobody's." I down the champagne and place it on the table next to Jake's empty tumbler.

She giggles but doesn't let me go. "I'm not sure I'll ever understand you."

She has no idea how true that statement is.

The music shifts from a fast beat to a slow song.

"Dance with me?" I ask.

Her eyes turn dreamy. "Love to."

I escort her to the dance floor, finding a space between some other couples because I don't want to be a spectacle. If my mom sees us, she'll be requesting to talk to the banquet manager to nail down a date. I can hear her now. "They book up fast."

"Jake's comment got me thinking. Why did your parents name you Brooklyn?"

She wraps one arm over my shoulder, and I hold her other one between us.

"I never told you?" Her eyebrows raise.

I shake my head.

"I'm going to name all my siblings and you tell me what they have in common."

"Okay..."

"Austin, Savannah, Rome, Denver, Juno, Kingston, Phoenix, Sedona..." Her eyes widen. She's clearly waiting for me to catch on.

"City names?"

She nods. "My mom was a travel writer, so as disgusting as I used to find it, we were each named after where we were conceived."

I tilt my head. "But Rome and Denver?"

Her shoulders wiggle. "They had a layover in Denver on their way to Rome."

"Ah." My head falls back, and I spin her around quickly.

"So when Jake said if you ever get to Brooklyn... you've never?"

She shakes her head. "This is my first time east."

What an idiot I am. I never even thought that this might be her first time here and all we've done is wedding stuff. "Well, we're not leaving New York before you see the city you're named after."

She smiles and puts her face on my chest. "I'm happy right here though."

We sway, and she allows me to lead. As "Dance with

Me" by Morgan Evans plays, the lyrics can't help but mean something to me. The feeling inside me that says I'd be a fool to lose her is so strong, but we live on opposite sides of the world. Maybe I'm enough for her to move out of Lake Starlight—I shake off that absurd thought. Everyone who knows Brooklyn knows she's meant to live the rest of her life there.

"Tomorrow, before we fly out," I assure her, but she never looks at me, content with where she is.

Right now, I envy her ability to live in the moment.

WE WAIT FOR THE BOUQUET AND THE GARTER TOSS, which neither Brooklyn nor I caught, thank God. My mom would have shuffled the preacher over and told him to marry us then.

Brooklyn is at the table and I'm at the bar, getting another drink, when my phone buzzes in my pocket. I set down the drinks and pull it from my inside pocket. *Rome?*

"Hey, Rome."

My dad comes alongside me. "We still need to talk."

I plug my other ear with my finger so I can hear Rome over the music.

"Wyatt, thank God. Brooklyn isn't answering her phone."

"Sorry. We're at the wedding." I walk away from my dad. He probably doesn't even realize, since he's having a different conversation while waiting for the bartender to make his drink.

"It's probably better that I got you anyway. I've got some bad news."

My entire body stiffens. "What happened?"

"Denver was on a flight with some guy who wanted to do a survival excursion. The plane went down. No one can find the plane or Denver. I was going to wait until we had more information before we told Brooklyn, but I got outvoted. What do you think is best? I tell her or you?"

The phone hangs in my hand. He should be telling me what's best. He's known her his entire life; I've known her for four months.

I bring the phone back to my ear. "Um."

"Yeah, I agree. She'll take it better from you."

"Okay?"

"Thanks. Tell her not to hurry home. We've got it handled and we'll let her know as soon as we hear anything."

My eyes search her out. Haylee's next to her, the two smiling and talking as though they're lifelong friends. How did I ever question if she'd fit into my world? She fits in better than me. And now I have to strip that smile off her face. Strip us of this time away, discovering what we could be together.

"You know as well as I do she's on the next flight. I'll message you when I have our flight information."

"It was worth a try. I know you and Brooklyn are... well... I didn't want to interrupt the two of you, but like I said, I got overruled."

"It's okay, Rome. Thanks though. I'll be in touch, and I'm sorry about Denver. I know they'll find him."

"Definitely. He'll probably stroll up to the house in a day or two with some MacGyver story about how he saved himself." His tone doesn't match his words, but I can't imagine what this must be like for him. Denver isn't just his brother, he's his twin.

"For sure. Give everyone my best."

"Thanks, Wyatt."

"No problem."

I hit End and tuck the phone into my pocket. I watch how happy Brooklyn seems. If it was up to me, we would have left after the obligatory rituals, but Brooklyn insisted we stay until the end. She said that it's our job to help with presents and whatever Haylee needs at the end of the evening.

"Wyatt," my dad says from next to me. "Come by my home office after brunch tomorrow and we'll talk."

I turn my focus to him. "I can't. Brooklyn and I have to return to Lake Starlight tonight."

"Tonight?" He sips his drink.

"Her brother is a bush pilot and he's missing. I have to tell her, then I'm calling the airport to see what flight we can get on."

He exhales a displeasured sigh. "Why don't you send her on the private plane, then it can come back tomorrow and get you after our talk?"

I pull my phone back out because I'm going to find us airline tickets now. "Because she's going to be broken and needs someone there for her."

He nods toward a corner that will offer us more privacy. I follow.

"Don't you think this is going too far? I get that you like her, but you're not exactly cut out to be a support system."

My jaw clenches. "Thanks for the vote of confidence."

"I went over the numbers, and she's given you blinders. There are about three employees who are redundant and should be fired."

"How can you talk about business right now? I just told you her brother is missing. Are you that heartless?"

He shakes his head. "You always think the worst of me."

I lean in close, so no one hears—not for his benefit but for my mother's. "You want to talk about me not being a support system? Your wife was battling cancer and you were fucking some whore right under her nose."

He stares at me, and for once, I get the reaction I want. Utter shock. I could almost smile except that it comes at the expense of my mom, so I just feel dirty.

"So excuse me, but I'm going to be the strong one and get Brooklyn home to her family."

"You don't even know what you're talking about," he says to my back.

I turn around. "I saw you. As I was trying to make her smile and laugh every day, you were..." I shake my head, not wanting to think about it anymore. "You're an asshole who likes to keep others down, but I have your fucking number."

His eyes narrow. "You need to watch the way you talk to me."

"Do I? Why? Because maybe one day if I do enough backflips and fall to my knees in front of you enough, you'll grant me part of the company? Stop holding the carrot in front of me."

"I wouldn't have to if you could be responsible once in a while." He downs his drink and holds the glass at his side. "You're a fuckup, plain and simple."

I look him dead in the eyes. "Fuck you."

My mother rushes over, holding her dress so she doesn't trip. "What is going on over here?"

I turn to find a few tables around us trying to act as if they're eating their cake and didn't hear anything we discussed. I hope they didn't hear the part about my dad's infidelity. That would break my mom.

"Oh, just the usual. I'm a fuckup and Dad's perfect. Right?" I shrug and kiss my mom on the cheek. Her eyes pin my dad with a death glare. "Brooklyn and I have to go. She has a family emergency."

She turns in my direction, frowning. "You're leaving tonight?"

"Yes, I'll call you."

She nods. "I hope everything's okay." She looks at her watch. "You'll never get a plane. Use the company jet."

I laugh. "That offer's only good if Brooklyn heads back alone."

My mom stares at my dad.

He pulls his phone out of his pocket. "You have an hour before takeoff," he says, walking away.

"I wish the two of you could be civil for one night."

"I'm sorry, Mom." I hug her.

She pats my back. "I know. Brooklyn's the important one now. Go to her."

"Thanks."

I weave through the tables to where she and Haylee sit.

When my sister brings her head up to look at me, her smile falls. "What?"

"I just need to talk to Brooklyn."

Brooklyn looks at me. "You look way too serious for a wedding." She puts a forkful of cake into her mouth. Her eyes roll back, and she moans. "This is orgasmic."

Haylee laughs, but she knows me well enough to know something is wrong.

"Mom can fill you in. Can you give us a minute?"

Haylee stands. "Of course." Her eyes fall over the reception, and she must spot my mom because she grips my hand right before heading in the direction I just came from.

I sit in the chair she vacated. Brooklyn's too busy enjoying the cake to notice the look of dread on my face at what I have to tell her.

THIRTY-NINE

Brooklyn

"Seriously, try some." I hold the fork in front of Wyatt's mouth, but he doesn't open. "Fine. More for me." I slide the sugary goodness into my mouth, and my taste buds say thank you in a resounding chorus.

"Can we go into the hallway for a second?"

I glare at him. "Tell me here." I use my fork to point at my cake.

"No."

I narrow my eyes. "What is it?"

"Come on." He takes my hand and I allow him, but when he grabs my clutch from the table then tugs me through the room, the hair on my neck stands on end.

"I get that I'm hot and you can't wait to strip me bare, but I told you we're staying until the end." My attempt at making a joke falls flat. He continues walking until I stop in my tracks, literally digging my heels into the carpet. "What is going on?"

He turns back around, looks around me then back the other way, moves us to the side, and takes my hands in his one since he's holding my pink clutch. "Rome called. Denver's plane went down."

My throat dries and my stomach drops like an elevator whose wires were snipped.

"They don't know anything yet except that he's missing."

I stare at Wyatt. Here I was going on and on about cake and he was trying to tell me I might be burying another family member?

"Come on. We're taking the Whitmore jet back to Lake Starlight. We have an hour to get to the airport."

I follow Wyatt to the elevators, down to the ground floor, and into a taxi in a surreal daze. I'm not sure I process anything as we pack our bags, he locks his condo, and we head to the airport in another taxi. Wyatt shuffles me onto a private plane, and minutes later, we're in the air.

"What if...?" I stare through the window into the darkness. They're the first words I've spoken since he told me.

Chris, our pilot, comes on over the speaker. "Mr. Whitmore, we have about a ten-hour flight. We have no attendant because of the short notice, but I had the plane stocked with snacks and drinks."

"Thanks, Chris," Wyatt says, unbuckling his seat belt and mine before taking us over to the sofa along the other side of the plane. He pats his lap and grabs a blanket from a compartment and puts it over my body. "Why don't you sleep?"

"I'm not tired."

"You'll need your energy when we get there."

I lean my head on his shoulder, and his hand finds my thigh. "If something happens to him..."

"You can't think about that now. You've told me how resourceful he is. He'll find a way to survive until they find him."

I nod, and Wyatt's gentle hand on my leg eventually becomes mesmerizing. All the late nights of the past few days catch up to me, my eyes drifting closed.

"Brook." Wyatt nudges me, and my eyes pop open.

"I fell asleep?" I ask, the drool on the side of my face a clear indication that I did.

"We're about to land." He tucks a strand of hair behind my ear.

I have no idea what we are, how Wyatt and I are classified or whether I should ask, but right now, that's not a priority. Getting to my family is the priority. "Once we land, I want to go to Holly and Austin's."

"Well, it's late now, or early depending how you look at it."

"They'll be up."

I get off the couch and go over to my seat and strap myself in before digging my phone out of my purse. If I'd been with it before we left, I would've called, but Wyatt was getting me from one place to the next so fast, I couldn't wrap my mind around the fact my brother was missing.

After he buckles himself in, Wyatt holds my hand. The plane lands smoothly, and I look around the private plane, wishing I could've enjoyed this more. We're up and out of our seats before it comes to a stop.

I dial Savannah, knowing she'll be in the loop.

"Brooklyn," she answers. "We're at Austin's. Are you back?"

"Just landed, so we have an hour drive or so. We'll be there as soon as we can."

"Okay, no word yet. They've called off the search until the sun's up."

I nod, knowing they would have. Tears prick my eyes for the first time, but I swallow them back. Not now. There's nothing to cry about. Denver will come out of this like he always does. "Do you know what happened?"

"Not really. They say something happened with the plane's engine. You know Denver, his ego can get the best of him sometimes. Maybe he tried to push it too far."

"It's that ego that will get him out of this," Kingston yells in the background.

"I'll be there as soon as I can."

"Okay," she says, and I hang up.

"Mr. Whitmore, we've arrived." The pilot comes out from the front, leaving the copilot to do whatever he does. "Your father informed me that you're returning to New York first thing in the morning. Due to guidelines—"

"My father was mistaken. I won't be going back with you."

I look at Wyatt and he rolls his eyes.

"Okay then. I must have gotten it wrong."

"Thank you, Chris. I appreciate this so much." Wyatt shakes his hand.

"I can't thank you enough. Here." I open my purse for a small bottle of lavender and chamomile. I put the vial into his palm and hug him tightly. "I'll send you something more, but hopefully this helps you sleep tonight."

"Thanks," he says and smiles.

"She makes potions," Wyatt says, his hand on the small of my back.

The stairs drop down, and we exit into the fresh Alaskan air. A car is waiting for us.

"What about your car?" I ask, walking toward the dark sedan.

"That was a rental. I told them I'd grab a new one when I returned. They aren't open, so this is it."

The driver puts our luggage into the trunk, and we slide into the back seat.

"A girl could get used to this life." I lean on Wyatt and kiss his cheek. "Thank you for all this."

"You're welcome." He kisses me on the lips. "Let's get you where you belong."

We pull away from the airport and make our way across the dark highways of Alaska toward Lake Starlight, and I wonder where I really do belong. I liked New York. Enough to live there? I don't know. But I'm starting to think it'll be hard for anywhere to feel like home if Wyatt's not there with me.

FORTY

Wyatt

Brooklyn's out of the car before it has a chance to fully stop, running up the stairway and through the front door. I guess the whole knocking thing only applies when we're invited over.

I get the bags, tip the driver, and walk up the stairs, following Brooklyn in since she left the door open. There's mumbling in the other room, and I place our bags by the front door.

Myles saunters around the corner, gets a gleam in his eye when he sees me, then runs toward me.

Shit. I clamp my legs together, but he gets me from behind, his snout pushing up my ass.

"Seriously? You have Daisy, go nail her."

"Well, she's still getting over having his babies." Holly comes around the corner. "Treat, Myles."

Just like days ago, he stops, his ears perk up, then he

runs toward her and snatches the treat from her hands before leaving the room.

"Maybe I should leave them at the door for you." Holly smiles, though it's a tired one.

"That might be helpful." I haven't gotten a chance to talk to Holly much. What I know of her, I learned from Brooklyn or another Bailey family member.

She sits on the living room couch. "I'm trying to give them space. You want to sit with me?"

"Sure." On the way here, I thought maybe I should go to my apartment because I'm not family, but that seemed insensitive and I don't want to leave Brooklyn alone. I sit and stretch, cracking my neck.

"How was your sister's wedding?" she asks.

"Good. We left before it was over, which I'm not complaining about."

She makes herself comfortable in the corner of the couch. "How do you like Lake Starlight?"

I shrug. "I like it."

"More than New York?"

I tilt my head at her. "Am I on trial?"

She laughs. "Sorry. No, I just was curious. You don't have to answer any of my questions. Austin and I... well, I wondered if you saw yourself here long term, you know, because of Brooklyn." She shakes her head. "Oh my God, help me, I'm turning into a nosy bitch. Don't answer any questions."

I laugh. "It's okay. I'm not sure where we stand, to be honest. I like it here, but I'm not sure I'll be living here for the long haul."

She nods but doesn't respond. I kind of wish she'd say exactly what she's thinking.

"Yeah, I can't say much," she finally says. "Austin was the one who had to make the tough decision to stay put."

"Decision?"

"What he wanted out of life. He had a great opportunity that would've taken him down to California. Had to decide if his original dream was worth risking for a different one."

I lean back on the couch, exhaustion creeping up on me. "I don't have a dream."

She blanches. "Everyone should have a dream."

"What's yours?" I lean my head back on their comfortable sofa.

"Mine?"

I nod.

"I always wanted to be somewhere where I was loved unconditionally. Somewhere I wanted to be day in and day out, where I felt like I belonged."

"And that was in Lake Starlight?"

She giggles and stretches her arms out to her sides. "It's funny. I wasn't a fan of Buzz Wheel and all the gossip, but this town takes in outsiders with a blanket over their shoulders and a heartwarming smile. It just fit. I can't explain it. Austin, he's the bonus." She glances at a picture of the two of them on the mantel. "More than a bonus."

Her smile is wide and glowing. I glance at her left ring finger and find it empty.

Barking commences somewhere in the house and she gets up. "Have you seen the puppies yet?" she asks, already heading toward the mudroom.

"No." I'll welcome any distraction from talking about where I see myself long term. Way too much self-discovery after traveling for eight hours.

We enter the mudroom, and the puppies are all nursing on Daisy. Myles is outside the gate, looking on.

"He misses her," Holly says, petting Myles.

One puppy comes to the blocked off area and Myles whines, trying to lick it through the gate.

"Why can't he be in there with them? It's his family." I feel sorry for Myles. Maybe if he could get some from Daisy, he'd leave me alone.

"The vet said to keep them separated for a few weeks. We'll have to start finding homes for these little guys soon." Holly pets a puppy's head. He pushes into her touch, wanting more.

"I know one person who will take one."

Holly smiles. "Yeah, but Brooklyn's apartment puts the kibosh on that."

I nod. She's right. No way Brooklyn can have a dog. Joel would have a conniption.

We sit for a moment, watching Daisy nurse her babies as Myles tries to interact with one of his puppies.

"I'm sorry about meddling. I shouldn't have asked."

"It's okay. Maybe I need to figure out some shit before both of us end up hurt."

Holly sits, crossing her legs, and Myles climbs into her lap. "You want to know what I think?"

"Not sure, do I?"

"I think it might be a little too late for that."

I huff because I have no defense. Holly's a damn smart woman.

ALL THE BAILEYS ARE IN THE FAMILY ROOM. AUSTIN'S sprawled out on the floor, his head on a pillow, his eyes closed. Juno is snuggled into Colton on the loveseat, her legs over the arm. Savannah is at the table, scribbling something down with Rome, and Liam's next to her, staring at a map. They're arguing about pathways through the brush when Kingston comes over with a bag of chips, pointing a greasy finger at a spot and calling them dipshits.

Brooklyn is on the phone. I sit next to her, overhearing her end of the conversation.

"Sedona, I couldn't just grab you. You need to be there for school. I'm sorry." She looks at the phone. "She hung up on me."

I wrap my arm around her shoulders and pull her into me.

"She wants to know why we didn't grab her and pick her up to bring her home, but she has school..."

"I can set up a ticket. Does Phoenix want to come home too?"

Brooklyn looks at me as tears roll down her cheeks. "How did I forget about her?"

"We were busy and in shock."

She nods, but she's not appeased by that answer. She walks outside, and I snatch her phone from where she left it.

Dawn breaks. I'm the only one who stayed awake most of the night.

Austin stretches on the floor when the first stream of light comes into the room. He kisses Holly's forehead and slides out from under her arm. "You up? Coffee?"

"Yeah." I dislodge from Brooklyn's body and follow him to the kitchen. "Any way I can borrow your Jeep?"

"Why?" He grabs the coffee from the freezer and starts making a pot.

"I need to make a run and my car was a rental that I returned."

"Sure. I'm sure we're here until we get word." He grabs his keys and tosses them to me.

"*Hello!*" a booming voice says before a door slams.

"Shit." Austin runs out of the room, but whatever he tried, it doesn't work.

Grandma Dori effectively wakes everyone. "I have a bone to pick with each of you. How could you not tell me my grandson is missing?"

"Because you need your rest and we know eight p.m. is bedtime at the senior home." Rome puts his arm around her and kisses the top of her head. "But now that you're here, we need your expert mapping skills."

Rome pulls out the map they were studying last night. The left side of his hair is sticking straight up, and his pants are almost falling off.

"What? WAZE isn't going to get you to him." She snatches the map from his grasp. She finds me in the crowd and points right at me. "And you. You're a Whitmore?"

Everyone's eyes shift to me. Brooklyn's looking around as if she doesn't know how to react.

"Old news." Rome straightens the map. "So they say he was here last time they had contact so I'm thinking—"

"You're a Whitmore?" Austin asks me.

"You knew?" Savannah asks Rome.

Then all their interest moves to Brooklyn.

"I am. My name is Wyatt Whitmore. My dad had me come to the hotel incognito to figure out how well it was run."

"That reminds me of this show—" Juno begins, but Austin cuts her off with his hand.

"You knew?" he asks Brooklyn.

She bites her lip and nods.

"And you're okay with it?" Savannah asks. They have this double-team thing down to an art.

Brooklyn looks at me. "I am."

"Okay then," Austin says.

"Doesn't that mean you're rich as fuck?" Kington asks.

I shrug.

"Stop it." Brooklyn comes over to me, taking my hand.

Everyone watches with raised eyebrows.

"Yes, he's Wyatt Whitmore, but he's still the Wyatt you all know."

"Except he's rich as fuck." Kingston grabs the bag of chips he had last night and munches on them again.

Rome's phone rings on the counter in front of him and everyone stops.

He looks at it.

"Answer it," Savannah says with urgency.

He slides his thumb over the screen, but it feels as if it happens in slow motion. "Hello? This is his brother, Rome... Uh huh... Okay... Yeah..."

We all wait with bated breath.

"Thank you. Bye." He hangs up and looks at us.

"Well?" Savannah looks as if she's about to crawl out of her skin if he doesn't say something soon.

"They found him. He's on his way to the hospital. One broken leg and they want to check everything else out."

Once all the cheering and hugging dies down, Austin looks at Rome with a serious expression. "What about the guy who was with him?"

"Griffin Thorne, Austin. The music producer."

Kingston shakes his head as though Austin is the out-of-the-times father. He's clearly told Austin a few times who the passenger was.

"He's fine. Completely okay," Rome says.

"Where are they flying him to?" Juno asks.

"They said they'll bring him to Anchorage."

"Let's go then." Austin looks at me. "We'll take Holly's car. Who else can drive?"

Everyone files out chatting, including Grandma Dori.

"Hey." I stop Brooklyn. "I've got something to do. Mind if I catch up with you?"

She shakes her head. "No. Okay."

"Thanks." I watch to make sure everyone is leaving before I kiss her. We don't need any more questions about where we stand, especially when neither of us have the answers. "I'll only be a few hours."

Her eyes dim, but she doesn't say anything. Hopefully once she finds out what I'm up to, she'll be happy again.

FORTY-ONE

Brooklyn

On the way to the hospital in the back of Colton's truck, I pull up the Buzz Wheel to see what the hell it's saying. It's been a while since I got my fix.

The first entry has a picture of Denver and Rome. It's one taken from the *Lake Starlight Tourist* with the two of them from behind, the sunset and mountains in the background.

We all know this picture. The angelic Bailey twin boys. Yes, they're a little rambunctious, and yes, they bring chaos everywhere they go. But they also bring fun and friendship and they've never let anyone struggle with holding something when they're around. We got the bad news last night that

Denver's plane went down and he's missing, along with the hotshot music producer, Griffin Thorne, who was his passenger. Word is that the Baileys are huddled together at the family home, awaiting word.

Please join me in praying for both of their safe returns.

I'll update as I get word.

The second story is juicier, and if it hadn't been for Denver's unfortunate accident, I'm not sure when Buzz Wheel would've found out. The Wyatt Moore who's been in Lake Starlight for the past few months, working as the new manager of Glacier Point Resort, isn't who he says he is. He's actually Wyatt Whitmore, heir of Whitmore Hotels. And to top it all off, I heard Brooklyn Bailey accompanied him to a wedding for his sister in New York City this weekend. Due to Denver's accident, the two flew home on his private jet. Looks like Brooklyn Bailey took a step up from Jeff Brickle. Way to go, girl!

I LOOK AT THE PICTURE OF A JET THEN CLICK THE screen off and look out the window.

Juno turns around from the front seat. "When did you find out?"

"He told me a few weeks ago."

"And?"

"And what?" I cross my arms.

"Something is obviously going on with the two of you. I mean, he kissed you and you snuggled up to him. Come on. Give me the deets. Did you do the deed?" Her overzealous face reminds me of Myles when he sees Wyatt.

My gaze shifts to Colton.

"Colton, plug your ears," Juno says.

"Sure, and drive with no hands on the wheel? That sounds safe." He looks at me through the rearview mirror. "I'd rather not know any details anyway."

"See, Juno." I circle my finger, instructing her to turn around.

She sits back, and Colton turns the radio up. A second later, my phone dings.

"Really, Juno?" Colton asks, looking at her.

I pull out my phone, and sure enough, her name pops up on my screen.

Juno: *Did you guys do it?*

Me: *I don't know. Has Colton got to second base yet? Oh wait, he hasn't even gotten to first yet. Never mind.*

Juno: *Middle finger emoji*

Me: *Now, now, Savannah.*

Juno: *I'm just trying to make sure you know what you're getting yourself into.*

Me: *What does that mean?*

She huffs from the front seat.

Juno: *You know you're a little... nice.*

Me: *Something tells me that nice isn't really what you mean.*

Juno: *I don't want to see you hurt.*

Me: *Well you weren't concerned when you were ready to use your matchmaking skills to claim that Wyatt was perfect for me.*

Juno: *That's when he was Wyatt Moore.*

Me: *What exactly changed your thinking? The fact that he lied or the fact that he comes from money.*

Juno: *Come on. Think about this for a second.*

Me: *Bye.*

My phone dings a few more times, but I'm not going to listen to her negativity at this point. I finally feel happier than I have in months and she's ruining it.

"I'm silencing you," I say after she continues to send me text messages.

"How mature."

"What you're doing isn't fair. You're my sister. You're supposed to be supportive."

Her head whips around. "His real name changes everything."

Colton doesn't attempt to turn the volume down this time. He's probably hoping he drowns her out.

I cross my arms again and stare out the window. "How so?"

"He's like..." She looks at Colton. "Help please?"

He shakes his head and raises a hand that says he is not getting involved in this.

"Another level. I have no idea how to explain it, but his dad owns one of the biggest hotel chains in the world. He grew up in New York City."

"And?"

"It's different from Lake Starlight."

"Oh, Juno, are you afraid he's going to corrupt me and push me to go further than I want? News flash, I'm not a virgin."

She rolls her eyes and turns around, pouting like she always does.

"He's still the same guy," Colton says, turning down the music. "I like him, and I've never seen him do anything but dote on Brooklyn." He smiles at me through the rearview mirror.

I give him an appreciative smile. "Dote? I like your vocabulary."

His smile widens and he winks. Why doesn't Juno date him? He's adorable *and* gorgeous.

"Well, sometimes that's an act. Like a too-good-to-be-true act," Juno shoots back.

Colton stops and parks downtown, following the rest of our family in Holly's SUV. "Good thing we're making a pit stop. Thanks for the wonderful conversation, ladies." Colton turns off the ignition and exits the truck.

Juno turns toward me. "I don't mean to be nosy, but I can't see you get hurt again."

"Relax, Wyatt's a rebound." The word cuts me in half because he's not in the slightest, but I want her off my back.

"Rebound is not a word that should be in your vocabulary."

"You treat me like I'm twelve and I'm older than you!" I exit the car, slamming the door.

Colton grimaces. "Whoa, let's not take your aggravation with Juno out on my baby."

"What's the drama, llamas?" Liam asks.

I glance at Juno. "Apparently I'm a naïve girl who thinks every man is her saving grace."

Rome raises his hand. "I don't think that."

Holly wraps her arms around my shoulders. "I doubt that's what she meant. Everyone is stressed and worried right now. It was a long night. Let's go get some flowers, cards, and stuff to keep him busy."

"I'm getting nudie mags." Rome starts toward the store next to the florist.

"*Hustler*'s the best one." Liam laughs, joining Rome.

"You know as well as I do he'll just pull up porn on his phone." Kingston's off to join the bachelor brigade.

"What about you? How do you weigh in on jerk-off material?" Holly asks Austin as he walks with her toward the florist shop.

He looks at her. "All I need is you."

All us women ooh and aah over Austin's swoon-worthy comment as we approach the flower shop.

"Hold on." Grandma Dori presses her hand to my forehead. "You feel okay? You're flushed."

Did she not hear about the conversation a second ago with Juno?

"I'm fine, Grandma. I didn't realize people in our family were so judgmental, that's all." I square my eyes on Juno.

She throws up her hands.

"What's going on?" Grandma Dori asks Juno.

"Nothing."

We enter the flower shop, Colton deciding at the last minute to join the boys in the other store.

"How can I help—"

Grandma Dori stops the polite lady by raising her hand. "We need a big arrangement. No roses. Something manly. And some balloons too. The card should say, 'Get well. We love you.' Now I need a word with my granddaughters before they start talking about things that should be kept behind closed doors. Thank you."

The lady laughs, tucking her hair behind her ears. "I'll get started."

"Wonderful."

Then Grandma nails us with her get-over-here-now look, so we scurry over to her. "We are family. We do not fight with one another. We love one another. We've had a huge loss in this family before and I thought for sure you'd see how much you need to value the time you have with one another. Denver could have died and you two are arguing about what?"

Neither one of us says anything.

"Put whatever issues you have aside for today. Got it?"

We both nod like the scolded children we are.

"Good." She steps away.

Juno and I go our separate ways in the store, each of us picking out flowers for the big arrangement for Denver.

Forty-five minutes later, Grandma Dori is instructing the poor woman where to put the flowers as if she's the professional florist. I push open the doors, enjoying the warm sun on my face while we still have it.

I take a seat on the bench between the two stores, and shortly after, Rome comes out and sits next to me. They probably all texted one another and sent him.

I give him my bored look. "Did you get all the dirty magazines?"

"I left the guys in charge." He nudges me. "You're sour grapes. Talk to me."

"Everyone in this family thinks I'm an idiot."

"You know what I think?" He leans forward, putting his forearms on his knees and looking at me.

"No."

He laughs. "I think you've developed feelings for Wyatt, and it's cool, Brookie. That's you. Hell, it's half the chicks I know. That's why there isn't a word like player or playboy for a woman. Juno just doesn't want to see you upset. She's your sister, and she loves you. That's all. She doesn't think you're naïve."

"But she thinks she has to warn me?"

He sits back, a hesitant smile playing on his lips. "I get it. I do. This family steps over the line all the time, but that's us. We love each other too damn much." He chuckles.

"I'm still not sure about this carnation." Grandma Dori plucks it out of the bunch as Austin carries the gigantic flower arrangement out of the shop.

"Jesus, he didn't die, G'Ma D," Rome says.

She shoos him to quiet him which he surprisingly does, giving me a look to tell me to think about what he said.

Juno walks to the truck, ignoring me.

How mature.

"And to the hospital we go." Rome points in the direction we're headed then nudges me with his elbow and winks.

I follow Colton to his truck.

"Remember, be nice," Colton says as I reach out to shut the truck door. "Actually, I'll shut it for you."

Right after he gently shuts my door, Juno slams hers. Colton throws his arms in the air as he makes his way around the vehicle. I giggle, and so does Juno.

She peeks around the headrest. "I'm sorry. It's just—"

"It's fine. Let's let it go."

"Okay." She nods.

Colton gets in the truck. "Both of you are riding with someone else on the way home."

We ride in silence until we pull into the hospital parking lot. Colton exits to join the family at the entrance, and I grab the balloons from next to me. Juno and I leave the truck, and she places her hand on my arm to stop me.

"I know I said I was done, but I'm worried and I can't bite my tongue until you hear me out."

I wait a second.

"He's more experienced than you. He's lived a life of privilege, and in my experience, men like that don't think of others before themselves."

"Let it go." I walk away from her, the balloons blowing in the wind while I try to rein them in.

"What's the matter now?" Grandma Dori asks.

"I'm just mad." I stomp ahead, hearing all their footsteps behind me.

"Why is she mad? I fixed this," Grandma says.

"Juno's fault," Kingston chimes in.

"Juno, let whatever the problem is go. She's been through enough. Especially now with this Wyatt fellow being a Whitmore."

I whip around at the doors of the hospital, holding up my hands to stop everyone from entering. The balloons hit me in the face, and I blow my hair out of the way and wrestle with them until I can see everyone. "Can everyone leave my love life alone? I'm good! I'm great actually!" I square my eyes on Juno. "And yes, Juno, I had sex with him, and it was amazing, and I plan on doing it again. Is he using me? I have no clue, but I don't care. For once in my life, I'm laying it all out there without knowing how it will turn out." I reposition the balloons to my other hand. "For once, can this family just stay out of my business?"

Juno steps up. "Brookie—"

"No, don't Brookie me. You of all people should not be

treating me like some young naïve girl. I know exactly what I'm getting myself into with Wyatt, okay? And I'm okay with risking my heart this time around. At least this time I know it's a risk."

I whip back around to find the elevators, but a set of blue eyes and a heavy smirk greet me.

I hand the balloons to Wyatt and walk away to find a hole to crawl into.

FORTY-TWO

Wyatt

"Here." I pass the balloons to Sedona and follow Brooklyn.

"Phoenix? Sedona?" Austin asks from behind me.

I don't get to experience the homecoming of the youngest Baileys. It didn't take a lot for me to get them here—a few red-eye plane tickets—but I wanted to surprise Brooklyn.

"Brooklyn!" I yell as she exits the hospital into a court-yard. She doesn't stop, and I jog to catch up. "Please, stop."

She doesn't until she hits the end of the courtyard and can't go any farther. Unless she wants to scale a wrought-iron fence, she's cornered.

"Brook," I say, coming up alongside her. I slide her veil of blond hair out of the way so I can see her beautiful face.

"I'm sorry you had to hear that."

I step closer. "I'm glad I did." She looks at me, and I wipe one of her tears away with my thumb. "Don't cry."

"I'm such an idiot. Just go." She turns away from me again.

"No."

"Please, Wyatt. I'm embarrassed enough as it is. I don't need to hear any more warnings about staying away from you. Especially from you. That you're not who I think you are. That we have no future. Juno is right. I know I'm on my way to heartache but..." She glances at me for a fleeting moment.

I'm stunned into silence. I've never had anyone pour their heart out to me—for me.

"I can't stay away from you. So." She wipes her eyes. "You have to be the one who walks away here, because I can't do it."

"Look at me," I say softly.

She shakes her head.

"Please, Brooklyn. Look at me."

She sneaks a glance my way, and whatever she sees on my face has her turning all the way in my direction.

"I'm not going anywhere."

Her eyes widen, and she sucks in a quick breath.

"Did you even hear me when I said I'm glad I overheard you? I had no idea if you thought of us as a rebound or what. And yeah, I'm scared to entertain the idea of an actual relationship with someone, but you're the only one I can see trying it for. Do you think I'd do what I've done for you to anyone else? I mean, I left my sister's wedding and took a favor from my dad to use the company plane. I hate owing him anything. I just flew your twin sisters here because you were so upset last night."

A hesitant smile forms on her lips.

"Christ, I didn't even fire Reagan because of you." I step closer, tucking her hair behind her ears again. "You've done something to me, and I'm man enough to admit that I like it. Maybe it's time we talk about what's really going on with us."

She nods, and I escort her to one of the tables. We sit and I take her hands.

"I'm not sure what kind of boyfriend I'll be, but I want to try."

A hesitant smile pulls at her lips. "Okay."

"Can I get graded on a curve?"

Her smile lifts higher. "I don't want you to treat me with kid gloves. I'm a grown woman, and if we do this, I don't want you thinking you have to be perfect or think that you can't break up with me. Tell me if you can't be with me anymore. I know it will hurt, but please don't run away."

I meet her gaze so that she can see the truth in mine. "I promise."

Her eyes sparkle when she smiles this time.

"Can I kiss my girlfriend now?" I shake my head and chuckle. "Damn, that sounded so middle school. Sorry."

"Wyatt." She moves to sit on my lap, wrapping her arms around my neck.

"Yeah?"

"Kiss me."

Easiest request today. My lips meet hers, and I pour all my determination to make this work into our kiss. Too bad we're in public. I close the kiss and pull her into me, needing to feel her pressed against me. I have no idea where we'll end up, but I do know that I'm willing to see where this goes. I care too much about this woman to willingly give her up at this point. We'll deal with the future later.

"Woohoo!" someone screams.

We both look to find the sliding doors opening and closing while some of the Baileys watch us.

"Are you sure you're willing to take me with them in the package?"

I stand and lower her to her feet. "I'd take on a pack of hungry mountain lions if it meant I got you."

She places her hand on my cheek, staring at me as if I'm her one and only. I wait for her to tell me how stupid of a line that is. I'm not used to all this romantic stuff, but she wraps her arms around me and throws herself into my chest again. "Me too."

"Let's go see your brother," I say to her.

"Thanks for bringing my sisters here." She nuzzles her head into the crook of my arm, and I kiss her forehead.

We walk through the courtyard to the sliding doors.

"Shouldn't you all be with Denver?" Brooklyn asks when we reach her family.

"They won't let us up yet. He's getting a room," Rome says.

"Speaking of rooms, if the two of you want to get a room, we'll give Denver your love," Kingston adds.

Juno smiles and hugs Brooklyn, whispering something I can't hear into her ear.

Austin approaches me and puts out his hand. "It means a lot to us that you brought the twins back. Thank you."

"You're welcome."

We all find seats in the waiting area. Grandma Dori's talking to the lady at the desk, probably with the hopes it gets us to Denver's room faster.

Liam clicks on the television to help pass the time.

"He's fucking famous!" Kingston yells.

Liam turns up the television. It's an interview with Griffin Thorpe, Denver's passenger on the plane. He's a big enough deal that he's being interviewed about the accident, and Denver's picture is in the corner of the screen.

"That's who he saved? Griffin Thorpe?" Phoenix runs over to the television and stares at it in awe. "Do none of you know who he is?"

We all shake our heads.

"He could change my career," she says—more to herself than all of us, I think.

"Way to think about Denver, Phoenix," Savannah says, looking up briefly from her phone.

I swing Brooklyn's legs over my lap. We can't seem to let one another go. Talk about a major cockblocker—admit your feelings for a girl then being stuck with her family for hours afterward. All I want to do is make love to her.

Shit, do I even know how to make love?

I panic until I remember when I woke her up in the middle of the night the day of the wedding. I think we may have made love then. Shit, did I know I loved her... no, do I love her? No way. I like her a lot—enough to want to see where this goes—but love is another thing entirely.

FORTY-THREE

Brooklyn

"Thanks for the ride home." I put the key in my door.

Wyatt comes behind me, wrapping his arms around my waist. "Come on. Even I know once you're a couple, you rarely spend a night apart." His lips dip to my neck, casting small kisses along the bare skin.

The question of what will happen when he leaves for New York is on the tip of my tongue. We'll be spending nights apart then. But I can't do that to us. I have to live in this moment, enjoy our time together as though nothing will change.

"Are you asking if you can spend the night?" I turn in his arms, and his lips continue their exploration down my neck as he secures his hands to my hips. "I bet that's not normal behavior for you?"

He looks at me through his thick, dark eyelashes. "You're a special case." His large palm winds around my neck, my hair threading between his fingers. "For lack of a better word, you're the exception."

I turn the knob behind me, and the door falls open. "Okay, smooth talker."

As we fall into the apartment, he works to strip me of my clothing. His hands clutch the hem of my T-shirt to pull it up my body. I raise my arms because I'm more than in agreement.

"Now you've got the right idea." He reaches behind my back and unclasps my bra while his lips land on mine, his tongue slipping into my mouth.

My fingers fiddle with the button of his jeans and the zipper. I push them down and he dislodges his arms from me to shred them from his body, hopping on one foot with his lips attached to mine. We walk backward toward the bedroom, a scatter of clothes left in our wake. By the time we're in my bedroom, he's in his boxer briefs and I'm in my panties.

"Tell me you have condoms," he says in a sexy growl.

My hand stops massaging his length through the cotton. "Shit."

"Yeah, I'll be back." He gives me a chaste kiss and he's out of the bedroom. I hear him dig into the pocket of his jeans. "Naked on the bed when I get back."

My front door opens and closes.

I slip my panties down my legs, wishing I'd shaved this morning. Luckily, I did before the wedding, so the stubble is minimal.

He returns in record time, shoving his boxer briefs off as he tosses a box of condoms on the bed and climbs up to join me. Once he's over me, his hands run over my body slower than ever before. His kisses slow and his touch becomes softer. His tongue searches and explores while his hands move as though he's memorizing my every dip and curve. Somewhere in the frantic act of stripping one another, he's taken a moment to regroup.

"Wyatt," I murmur, my eyes falling shut as he slides on top of me, nudging my legs open with his thighs.

"What do you need?" he asks, kissing every square inch of my body from my neck, venturing down to between my breasts. My nipples are rigid points begging for his attention.

My hands wind through his dark hair. "You. I just need you." My head falls back to the bed.

"I like the sound of that," he mumbles against my heated skin.

His lips never linger anywhere for long, keeping me on my toes and pushing my desperation to a level I didn't know was possible.

I know now that I'll never free myself from Wyatt Whitmore. Even if he leaves me, a piece of me will always be with him. And that piece is my heart.

I ROLL OVER ON MY PILLOW, AND SOMEONE PLACES their lips on mine. I peek an eye open to see Wyatt tying his tie in front of me. The smell of coffee arouses my senses.

"What time is it?" I ask, slowly getting up and resting my back against the headboard.

"It's seven thirty. I have to get to the hotel. We should've talked about this, but since the news came out about who I am..."

"How are you up? What did you get, an hour of sleep?" I wipe my eyes, not ready to talk about Glacier Point or how the employees will feel about being lied to.

"I'm still on the adrenaline rush of taking you so many times." He leans forward to kiss my lips.

I rear back, my hand shielding my mouth. "Morning breath."

He moves my hand and kisses me anyway. Minus tongue, thank God. "Like I was saying. Do you want to go in together or separately? I'll leave it up to you, but Mr. Clayton is leaving today and I'm going to be announced as my real self."

I shake my head, still trying to clear the cobwebs. "When did all this happen? How long have you been up?"

He grabs his suit jacket from the edge of the bed. "You forget. New York is four hours ahead of us."

I nod, dragging the coffee cup off the nightstand. I blow on it. "A girl could get used to this treatment."

He laughs, straightens his shirt inside his jacket.

"You're leaving now?"

"I'll wait for you if you want to go in together."

I sip the coffee, hoping for an immediate hit of caffeine. After Wyatt took his time with the slow circular motion of his hips and promising words in my ear, we ended up in the bath, in the family room, and finally the kitchen when we got hungry. It was an amazing night. I'm not at all in the mood to go clean rooms right now.

"Since you need a ride." I throw the covers off me and slide my legs over the edge of the bed.

"I'll turn on the shower for you. Hurry. Your shift starts at soon, and you don't want to have to report to the boss's office, do you?"

I stick out my tongue. "Maybe I do." I sneak one more sip of coffee and head into the bathroom.

Wyatt follows me. "I think lunches might get a little more interesting from now on." He waggles his eyebrows, and I raise to my tiptoes and kiss him. He grabs my ass and deepens the kiss. "Talk about agony. I have to watch you in a maid's uniform all day?"

"Good thing it's from the nineteen-eighties." I lower my feet and inhale his sandalwood scent.

"Maybe that's my first line of business. Get new house-keeping uniforms ordered. I'll order a special one for you." He laughs.

I step into the shower so we can get going if we're going to be on time. I don't want people to think I'm suddenly getting benefits for dating the boss. But I peek my head out of the shower. "How about I wear the maid costume and you wear the bellhop?"

"I'm seeing your naughty side now." He kisses me then walks out of the bathroom. "I'll put your coffee in a to-go cup."

"You're treating me like a princess," I call after him and smile.

I quickly wash my body and my hair. Twenty minutes later, my hair is slightly damp and ready to be pulled back at work. I walk out of the bedroom in my street clothes, grabbing my coat and shuffling into my shoes. Wyatt is in his suit, my coffee waiting for me in a to-go cup and a granola bar next to it.

"I feel like the slacker of our duo." I accept the coffee and grab my purse and keys.

"You do have to be my chauffeur, so it's an 'I'll scratch your back, you scratch mine' kind of thing." He opens the door.

We walk down the three sets of stairs and out the building. Being in a couple again feels nice. Although I talk a big game about plunging with two feet into this, I still wonder about what's on the horizon for us.

I unlock my car then hurry to his side and open the passenger side door for him.

"Let's not get too carried away." He takes the door and holds out his hand for the keys.

"Come on. It'll be fun."

"Not day one it's not." He snatches the keys and waits for me to climb in. When I stand, wondering if I should give in, he glances at his watch. "You have fifteen minutes to be clocked in before you're written up."

I roll my eyes and slide into the passenger seat of my car. Once he's in and has his seat belt fastened, I soak in this feeling of being with Wyatt. Nothing's changed between us except I get to kiss him, touch him, and have sex with him. All the really good stuff.

We pull onto the road that leads out of our apartment complex, and he rests his hand on my knee.

Yeah, a girl could get used to this.

FORTY-FOUR

Brooklyn

"I wish you all the best. We knew this day was coming when I sold the hotel, but it's hard nonetheless. I never meant to deceive any of you, but as you know, Wyatt would've never gotten the full lay of the land at Glacier Point if you knew he was the owner."

All the staff were called into the private dining area of the restaurant during the time it's closed after the lunch rush and before dinner. Mr. Clayton is saying goodbye and Wyatt is saying hello as the official manager representing the new owner.

Reagan nudges me with her elbow.

"What?" I whisper.

"We need to talk."

"I only found out right before you. I'm sorry I didn't tell you."

"So without any further delay, I present you, Wyatt Whitmore."

Wyatt stands and shakes Mr. Clayton's hand. God, he looks so hot when he's professional and in charge.

"I'm not mad," Reagan leans in and whispers. "But isn't it against the rules to fraternize with the help?" She raises her eyebrows. Who knew Reagan would be the one who read the new employee handbook? When I raise an eyebrow, she shrugs. "I have a lot of time when I'm bedside with Mom."

"I'm not sure what the plan is. I mean, I met his dad this weekend so..." I bite the inside of my cheek.

"I swear, he was good-looking in his bellhop uniform, in that suit, it's a whole other level of hotness." Reagan admires him.

Devon comes in and sits three chairs over from us.

I nudge her. "There's a hot guy just a few chairs down."

"Thank you, Mr. Clayton. Whitmore Hotels feels fortunate to be the trusted hands to carry your hotel through the next fifty years."

Mr. Clayton smiles, and Mrs. Clayton grabs his hand. Love was enough for them to leave their business and move away from the town they've spent their whole lives in.

"I went out with Devon and guess what?" Reagan says.

"What?" I smile.

"We ended up at the nursing home. Mom told one of the nurses she had a shank under her bed and planned on using it on her the next time she turned on a light."

I laugh. Wyatt's eyes shoot to me.

Shit. "I'm in trouble."

"Yeah right. Maybe he'll spank you in his office later." Reagan doesn't look at me.

I wonder if she really feels like I'll benefit in some way from dating Wyatt. Orgasms aside.

"I guess she's been watching these prison reality television shows." She carries on as though her words a second ago didn't put a nick in my armor. "Thankfully, she thought Devon was the warden and calmed down. How embarrassing." She puts one hand to her face.

When I look over, I spot Devon's eyes on her. "I don't think it changed the way he feels for you."

She smiles at him. "Since I jumped him in the car when he drove me home, I'm sure he wants a second date."

"What?"

"Brooklyn and Reagan," Wyatt says and our eyes snap forward. "Mind waiting to have this conversation until after I'm done speaking?"

"Sorry," we murmur.

"Getting the boss upset," Reagan mumbles. "Careful, he might punish you by strapping you to his headboard."

I look at her, my mouth hanging open.

"Like I was saying, Whitmore Hotels couldn't be happier to take over Glacier Point, and I hope that we remain a solid unit striving toward the same goal of making this hotel the premier destination in Alaska. It would only benefit you and Lake Starlight as a whole. I'll be here for the foreseeable future, so please feel free to come to me with any questions or concerns you might have. We'll make any changes slowly, implementing them on a trial basis before making them permanent." His eyes find me. "One last thing before I let you all leave. I'm a transparent kind of guy and I'm aware of the Buzz Wheel blog that's popular in this community. I know they outed me and a fellow Glacier Point employee as being involved. I do believe my private life is just that—private. I hope that ends any and all discussion about that topic."

Is he delusional? Why would he even bring it up?

The room is silent, and I can't help but notice that everyone is avoiding looking at me.

Wyatt claps his hands together and smiles. "That's all. Like I said, I work with an open-door policy."

"Unless Brooklyn's in there." Someone behind me snickers.

My cheeks heat, and I glance back to see that it's Neil.

We all stand to head back to work. Devon stops Reagan, so I figure I'll get started on the suites I left behind for this meeting.

I'm waiting by the service elevators, realizing quickly how different the dynamic will be now that I'm openly dating Wyatt and Wyatt is the known son of the owner. The silver doors slide open and I step inside, happy to find the car empty. Most of the employees will probably linger until they're forced back to work. But Wyatt enters, and the doors shut behind him.

"How did I do?" he asks, cornering me. "I'm not sure I'll ever be in an elevator without thinking of you now."

"You're telling me I was the first woman you kissed in an elevator?"

He laughs, his lips descending on my neck. "One and only."

"We're at work. We can't do this." I wiggle free and step out of his hold.

"What am I missing?" He crosses his arms and leans against the opposite side of the elevator.

"That I'm the girl."

"My girl."

I shoot him a sour smile. "Cute line."

He smirks at me. "Okay, what's the matter? Are you mad about me bringing up our relationship?"

I shrug. "Not that as much as the fact that people are already talking about us."

"So?"

"They think I'm getting special treatment. It's been one day." The doors open and I barrel out. He follows, but I place my hand on his chest. "Just give me some time."

"No, I want to talk about this. I've missed you all day."

My hand falls. I desperately want to sneak into a vacant room to be with him, but I stay strong. "I'm not sure..."

"Just give them time. They'll see it's not the case."

He steps closer, and I don't stop him because I don't want to fight him. My body wants him. My heart wants him. My head wants him.

His arms wrap around me, and we back up to the wall. "I know this is hard—and I'm actually waiting for my dad to talk to me about it since it's against the rules—but believe me, I won't cater to your needs anywhere but off the clock."

"You're such a sweet-talker."

He looks in both directions of the hall and back at me. "Can I get that kiss now?"

"You better make it quick."

He leans down. "As much as I hate to do anything quick with you."

His lips press to mine as the elevator dings. I push him off me.

Reagan walks out of the elevator and eyes the two of us, putting her hand on the side of her face. "I saw nothing."

I plead with Wyatt with my eyes. Does he understand now? Sure, it's easy for him, he's the boss.

"Go," he says, pressing the button for the elevator. "Tonight, we're going out."

"Deal." I kiss his cheek then jog down the hall to catch up to Reagan.

Behind me, the elevator door dings. I resist the urge to look back for one more glance.

"Reagan." I clutch her elbow, and she slows her steps.

"You don't have to leave your boyfriend for me."

"Can you please not do that?"

She quirks her eyebrow at me and rounds the corner into the housekeeping corridors. "What are you talking about?"

"The razzing about Wyatt and me dating and me getting special treatment." We each restock our carts with piles of towels.

"What fun is it for me if you're dating the boss and I can't joke about it?" She moves to the toiletries and snatches a few bottles of lavender oil from my cart. "I've got the suites on the top floor. We're going to pimp your business."

Maybe I'm overreacting and being too sensitive. "You don't think less of me?"

She laughs. "Less of you for sleeping with a hottie like Wyatt? Talk to me, girl."

I stop stocking as it all hits me. I feel as if I've been in the eye of the hurricane. It's calm and serene and I'm loving my time with Wyatt, but outside us, a storm is whipping around. We can't live in the middle forever.

"You want to know my thoughts?" she asks, placing her hand on my shoulder. "I think, as always, Brooklyn Bailey is worrying about what other people think and not what she thinks."

"No. I mean—"

"I'm your best friend. It's my given right to make fun of you for dating the boss. I'm supposed to make innuendos about closed doors and quickies in the stairwell. But I'm *not* judging you. I'm proud of you for finally taking something you want. If the other assholes here are saying anything, tell me and I'll kick their asses." Her arm falls over my shoulders, and she pulls me into her side. "Just have fun and enjoy whatever this is between the two of you."

"Thanks." I smile, feeling better.

"Now what are you going to do?"

My eyebrows scrunch.

"Okay, repeat after me."

"Reagan…"

She puts her hand up, and when I don't, she moves my hand for me. "I promise to have fun exploring my new relationship with Wyatt."

She waits.

I giggle before saying, "I promise to have fun exploring my new relationship with Wyatt."

"And I will not listen to others' opinions."

"I will not listen to others' opinions."

"I will not care if we're reported in Buzz Wheel."

I hem and haw for a second, and she shoots me her best evil eye. "I will not care if we're reported in Buzz Wheel."

"I will sneak into vacant rooms and have sex with my boyfriend."

"Reagan!"

She laughs. "It was worth a try. Take full advantage of all the beds in this place." She kisses my temple and goes back to her cart. "But not in the rooms I'm cleaning."

We both laugh. As always, Reagan has a way about her that makes me feel better about myself.

FORTY-FIVE

Wyatt

Three weeks have passed and my relationship with Brooklyn has only grown hotter as the temperatures plummet. Most of my time is spent in her apartment, except for the rare night I surprise her with dinner at my place. Other than a few slips at the hotel, we've maintained distance at work. She's still a little sensitive about what others might think.

Denver's leg is healing, and he's become even more of a local celebrity after being interviewed on television because the guy he saved was some hotshot in Los Angeles.

I place the box in front of her apartment door and knock. I'm hoping she doesn't slam the door in my face. We haven't known each other for years, but I'm pretty sure I knocked this out of the park. Wanting to see her reaction, I lean on the opposite wall and wait.

She opens the door wearing her apron. I knew I smelled

coconut. I'd struggled to come up with an excuse to leave her on a day off, but I'm happy to see she spent it making new oils.

Her eyes meet mine, an amused look on her face. "Why are you over there?"

I point at the floor. Her gaze shifts down then flies back up to me. Is this what it would be like having a kid on Christmas morning?

"Oh my gosh!" She squats and pets the small puppy head sticking out of the box. "For me?"

I nod.

"But Joel?" Her question doesn't stop her from picking up the puppy and lowering herself to the floor, where she sits with her legs crossed.

"It's fine. I cleared it with him first."

Convincing him was nearly impossible since he has a strict no pets policy. I gave him a deposit and promised I'd be responsible for any damages.

She kisses the black, white, and brown puppy, his ears—which are too big for his size—twitching. "Best gift I've ever gotten."

She stands, the puppy hooked under one arm, and walks across the hallway to me. Her lips fall to mine and my hand slides to the back of her neck, deepening our kiss. She moans.

The puppy yelps and squirms under her arm.

"Just so we're clear, if the dog cockblocks me, there will be a problem."

She giggles and kisses me one more time before nuzzling the dog. "We have to go shopping. And you need a name."

I follow her into her apartment, picking up the box Holly arranged for me. This is the first puppy to leave Daisy and Myles, but I think it made Holly feel better that the little guy was going to Brooklyn.

She holds the puppy in the air and peers underneath. "Boy!"

"I hope that's okay. I mean that it's not a girl. Holly said he'd be perfect for you."

She comes over to me with the dog in her arms and kisses my cheek. "Good thing I like boys."

I look around. "You mean *boy*, right?"

She shakes her head and hands me the dog. "Let me finish this batch and we'll go down to Bark Avenue." After she's back behind her kitchen counter, she looks at me. "Um, Wyatt?"

"Yeah?"

"Hug the little guy."

I look to see I'm holding him with two arms extended in front of me. "I've never had a pet before."

She giggles. "Well, you do now. Let's talk names." She wipes her hands and takes the puppy from my arms. She motions for me to sit down in a chair and waits before she deposits him right back in my lap. "There you go."

She picks up my hand and lays it over the little guy's head, petting from the head and down the back, over and over again until I mimic the motion. Heading back to the kitchen, she glances over her shoulder to make sure I haven't stopped. The little fur ball drops down into my lap, stuffing his head into the small space between my arm and my side.

"What names do you like?" I ask.

"Mocha?"

I shake my head. "Girly."

"Macho?" She laughs.

"What about Jack or Rocky?"

"Ace?" She washes her hands again and takes off her

apron before coming over and kneeling in front of me. "What do you want to be named, little man?"

"You should be the one to decide. He's yours now."

He sits on my lap while Brooklyn pets him. "I want us to name him."

The word *us* causes a prick in my chest. I could be gone in a few months. I've delayed giving my dad my final report because once I do, I'm expected back in New York. We haven't discussed what we'll do. Jeff wasn't enough for her to go to San Francisco. How the hell would I be enough for her to go to New York?

"Let's go to the store, maybe something will come to us," I say.

She takes the dog, and I stand to grab my coat. Thoughts of our future keep plaguing me at night. I want to bring up the topic, but I don't want to stress her out.

"Oh!" she exclaims, startling the little guy. "I forgot to tell you. Guess what?" She picks up an envelope and waves it in front of me. "With online sales, guess what I was able to pay for?"

I pluck it from her hands and see Joel's name written on it. Doing the math in my head, I figure out tomorrow is the first of the month. "Rent?"

Her smile would rain sunshine down on hell. "I can't believe it. I never thought it would be possible." She sets the puppy in the box and wraps her arms around my waist, looking at me. Her hand grazes down the back of my head. "Thank you. I never could've gotten this far without you."

"You did it. I helped you with the business tools, but they're your products. That's what will keep people coming back." I kiss her lightly, my heart swelling with love for this girl.

"You're like a little miracle sent my way." She squeezes

me tightly and I hold her close, never wanting this moment to end.

"I could say the same thing," I say, my voice rough with emotion.

She pulls away, smiles, and hugs me again. I hope we can make it through the storm that's about to rain down on us because I think I'm falling.

"Come on. Let's go shop for this little guy," she says.

She steps back, but I steal another kiss before she gets too far away.

We drive into the small downtown area where Bark Avenue is, just off Main Street. By the time we're out of the store, the pup doesn't have a name, but he has a crate, a leash, a blue collar, food bowls, food, treats, and another three hundred dollars of doggie items. I paid for it all because I can't give her a gift and then have her drop so much on the essentials. I just never knew the essentials were so expensive.

"Let's take him for a walk," Brooklyn says, squatting by the car and securing the leash around his neck.

"Sure." I stuff everything else into my trunk and attach some kind of poop bag container to the end of the leash.

"I never knew dogs needed so much stuff." Brooklyn gets up off the concrete and walks two steps as the puppy stays put. She goes back, pets him, then motions for him to follow her.

I slide up on the hood of my car. "This should be fun to watch."

She looks blankly at me. "Thanks for the help," she deadpans.

"I meant I get to look down your shirt every time you bend over." I watch again as her shirt dips. "I do love that red bra."

"Just so you know, if you can see it, so can everyone else. Do you want me to continue bending over?" Her eyebrows rise.

I hop off the car. "Point taken."

"That's what I thought." She stands, and I nudge the dog when she steps forward.

If anything, he digs his paws into the concrete sidewalk and refuses to budge.

"Do we have the only dog who doesn't want to take a walk?" she asks, and all I can fixate on is the *we* in her sentence.

"You guys took one of the pups?"

I glance over to find Colton walking toward us with a soda in his hand.

"Wyatt surprised me with it." Brooklyn hugs him hello. "How come he won't walk on a leash?"

Colton laughs and holds his hand out for the leash, picks up the puppy, and puts both in Brooklyn's arms. "You need to train him to follow you first."

"But I want to go for a walk."

He sips his drink. "And you can, carrying him."

Brooklyn's lips turn down.

"I thought we were meeting at the gym?" Juno walks over. "What's going on? Whose is that?" She points at the dog.

Colton fills her in. "Wyatt took one of the puppies for Brooklyn."

"Oh, nice. Are you going to be one of those dog owners who carry their dog around?" She inspects the dog in Brooklyn's arms.

Juno hasn't looked at me once since she walked up. That's how things have been since we returned from New York and Juno found out who I am. You'd think I'd scorned her at some point. She was the cheerleader in my corner until my real name came out. Now she's the only one not in the "Wyatt and Brooklyn forever" club.

"No, but according to the doctor"—Brooklyn eyes Colton—"we're not to walk him on the leash until he's trained."

"Not a doctor."

Juno puts her hand on his shoulder. "You will be in a few years." Then she eyes Brooklyn. "I was going to say you're not going to treat him like a baby."

"We should get going." Colton pets the puppy. "Cute guy."

"Bye, guys." Juno waves, still not giving me a fleeting look.

"What's up with your sister? She seems..."

Brooklyn waves me off. "It's her problem."

She walks, so I follow, stuffing the leash inside my pocket. "What?"

"She thinks you could be using me." She shrugs.

"I'm not."

"I know."

I love that Brooklyn's so willing to defend me, but I hate that her sister thinks the worst of me. "I'll talk to her."

"Don't bother. She'll get over it."

We walk in silence, and when Brooklyn's arms get tired, I take the puppy. As we pass by the shops, other Lake Starlight residents smile and say hello to both of us.

"Things are getting serious, I see. You adopted a dog together?" Jack, Austin's best friend, says as we pass his hardware store.

"Hey, guys. What a cutie!" Holly's mom, Karen, stops us outside Lard Have Mercy as she puts up a flyer for bingo night at the VFW hall. "Holly wanted me to take one, but I told her I can't right now, so I'm happy you both took one." She pets his head and smiles before heading back inside.

As we walk around the town, it dawns on me how many of these people I know and who know me now. I don't even think the barista at my coffee shop in New York would recognize me. Hell, the security person at the Whitmore Hotels building made me show two forms of ID when I left my badge at my condo and I pass that guy every day. I gave him tickets to Hamilton for Christmas. Do you know how hard those things are to get?

We sit on the bench by the lake and set the furry guy between us.

"He's really calm. Like scary calm," Brooklyn says.

"He's probably just trying to absorb everything."

"What do you think of Gizmo, like from that old movie *Gremlins*?"

"I've never seen the movie."

Her mouth hangs open. "No way. My dad made us watch it every Christmas. After Christmas morning though. My mom said it was too scary to watch before a man in a red suit sneaked into your house and left presents. But it was a tradition for those of us old enough to watch it." She sighs. "Kingston and the twins never got to experience it with our parents. The rule was you had to be eleven. Austin kept the tradition alive for them, but it wasn't the same. Anyway, I begged my parents for a Gizmo." She picks up the puppy and changes her voice into baby talk. "And you look just like Gizmo."

"Done then."

"No arguments?"

How can I argue? He's hers.

She kisses me and lays her head on my shoulder. "Thank you."

We stare at the lake with the mountains in the background, and I'm amazed by how beautiful this place is and how much I'm enjoying my time here. As the chill is setting in and I'm about to suggest that we head back to the car, my phone buzzes in my pocket. Brooklyn sits up and I dig out my phone.

"My dad," I mumble before sliding my thumb across. "Hey, Dad."

"Your mother and I are leaving New York in the morning. We want a suite, and you better have everything I need by then. I know you've been dragging your feet, but that's drawing to a close now. And I told you to strip the word 'hey' from your vocabulary."

I look at Brooklyn, not about to make her upset by fighting with my father. "Fine. I'll make the arrangements."

"Good."

"Bye."

"Bye."

I hang up my phone and stuff it in my pocket. "My parents are coming."

FORTY-SIX

Brooklyn

And here we go again.

Wyatt dropped Gizmo and me off after the call with his dad last night. Said he had to go to Glacier Point to finish up some paperwork and make sure there's a suite available. Neither one of us wanted to leave Gizmo alone since he just got here, so I stayed behind.

I swear every time something comes up with his dad, it puts Wyatt in a tailspin and he doesn't resemble the man I love to spend every minute of my free time with.

I'm not looking forward to going into work today and saying hello to his dad in my housekeeping uniform. I can already picture the look of disgust on Mr. Whitmore's face.

I round the revolving doors and enter through the lobby.

"Good morning, Brooklyn," Mac says, flagging me down. "Wyatt's dad is here."

"I know."

He face-palms. "Of course you do. Hey, congrats on the dog. Big step."

"Thanks." As I walk away, I glance back, wondering how he knows. Surely Wyatt's been too busy to say anything that doesn't revolve around his father coming.

"Buzz Wheel," Mac says. "Someone snapped a picture of you two on Main Street."

I nod. Of course. What used to be a nightly ritual has fallen off. I suppose being left at the altar might have that effect, but I need to get back to reading it if I want to know what they're saying about Wyatt and me.

"Brooklyn!" On the elaborate staircase that winds down into the center of the lobby is Eva Whitmore. She waves frantically and puts up her finger. "Stay right there."

"Whoa, the mother," Mac says.

Eva walks down the stairs, dressed in a lovely navy pantsuit with heels. Her hair is styled to perfection in a sleek bob that ends right at her shoulders. "How are you, sweetie?" She wraps her arms around my shoulders.

"I'm good." I look at Mac over her shoulder as he watches with wonderment. "Hi, Mrs. Whitmore."

She smiles. "Eva."

"Okay."

"Say it."

This can't be happening right now. "Eva."

Her smile widens. "Great." She claps once and leans in. "I told Wyatt I wanted you to have the day off so you could take me around this cute little town of yours. We drove down Main Street, and it's adorable. If it was snowing, it'd be like being inside a snow globe." Her excitement escalates as she talks. "But you know Wyatt, he said you'd never go for that."

"He's right. Everyone is relying on me, but I'm off tomorrow."

"Perfect." She smiles. "And I saw a little bottle of lavender oil next to my bed. That's yours?"

I shrug. "I'm sorry."

"Why? I'm going to use it when I take a nap later. I can't wait."

"I know, but Mr. Whitmore—"

"Stop with all the formalities. Abe won't even notice, believe me."

I smile politely and lean closer to her. "I work here. I can't call you both Eva and Abe while I'm under this roof."

Her hand runs down my arm and back up. "Understandably so." She looks around for the first time, seeing all the people pretending they're doing something else while watching our interaction. "How about we have lunch? Wyatt is with Abe the entire day. Feel free to bring another employee if you want."

"That's sweet but—"

"Please? We can have it at the restaurant in the hotel here. Our time was cut short at the wedding. I saw your brother is doing well."

"You did?"

"He was on the news, but when I searched for Lake Starlight, I found this sweet little blog. Um... I don't remember the name."

You've got to be kidding me. "*Lake Starlight Buzz Wheel*?"

"Yes." She points at me like "Bingo" and smiles.

I close my eyes and inhale to try to achieve a Zen state.

"It mentioned his rehab, and every time I check there, there's usually at least one mention about someone from your family. I saw your other brother is opening a restaurant. And I loved seeing Wyatt so happy last night when I checked."

My heart pounds. How on Earth did she find that blog? I step away, needing to get to work and not having the time to fight her any longer. "I better go clock in. But how about twelve thirty?"

"Of course, don't want to get you in trouble with the boss." She winks and waves as I beeline through the "Employees Only" door.

Once I'm secure in the locker room, I grab my uniform and head to a changing room, but I overhear heated conversation on the other side of the wall. I can't make out any actual words, but Wyatt's voice is the louder one. I grimace. I guess things aren't going well with his dad.

After changing, I head up to the housekeeping department, thinking of how uncomfortable it will be for Molly to serve me with Mrs. Whitmore at the table. And do I really want Mrs. Whitmore walking through downtown Lake Starlight, where people will tell her my entire life story? No, I do not.

Reagan's already pushing her cart out of the department area. "I heard the in-laws are in town."

I shake my head. "And guess what? We have a lunch date."

"I told you, I'm not into threesomes. Plus, Devon might have a problem if we don't invite him."

Thank you, Reagan.

I chuckle at her lame joke. "Mrs. Whitmore wants me to have lunch with her and you're coming along so people don't judge me and stare."

She shakes her head. "Don't you remember your oath?"

"Nope." I slide by her and fill my own cart. "Oh, don't

put any of my stuff in the rooms. I don't want Mr. Whitmore to be upset."

She rolls her eyes. "Sure thing."

I mentally note to double-check. Reagan probably doesn't give a shit what Mr. Whitmore thinks.

Twelve twenty-five comes as I finish my last room. I have to wait for the others with late check-outs to leave, so it will be an exhausting afternoon.

Reagan rolls her cart in and washes her hands. "I'm ready, sweetie. Do you think she'll like me?"

"What's not to like?"

We laugh and walk down the hallway. Right before we step into the elevator, our walkie-talkies go off.

"Housekeeping to Banquet Room B please," Neil says over the radio.

Reagan and I look at each other. We're not stupid. It's the same protocol that took place when we were told the hotel sold.

"Do you know anything?" she asks.

"No." I chew on my cheek.

The elevator stops on the main level. Other departments are filing into Banquet Room B, leaving what I'm guessing is a skeleton crew.

"I'll be right there," I say. "I just want to tell Mrs. Whitmore we can't make it."

"I'll save you a seat." Reagan gives my hand one big squeeze.

Dread weighs me down as I make my way to the restaurant. Mrs. Whitmore is chatting with Devon, a row of six wine glasses in front of her.

"That's the pinot." Devon points, smiling at me.

I weave through the tables. "Mrs. Whitmore, I have to be in a meeting that just got called so I'm sorry, but I won't be able to join you."

Her smile falters. "Oh, okay. No worries. I'm trying the wine selection." She giggles. "Dinner tonight though." She points at me.

"Definitely."

I hear Devon's phone go off. He scrambles to discreetly silence it.

"Don't worry about me. I won't tell the boss." Eva laughs.

"Okay, gotta go. See you tonight," I holler through the empty restaurant, waving.

I jog to the banquet room and slide through the door. Wyatt's up front and he eyes me coming in late. As quietly as I can, I find Reagan and slip past everyone until I'm seated beside her.

"Okay, let's get this started. We're going to talk to everyone in two rounds, so once you leave this room, you'll be heading back to work and those who are there will report here." Wyatt glances at his dad, who nods. "First, I'd like to introduce the owner of Whitmore Hotels, my father, Abe Whitmore."

His dad stands, but his eyes meet mine first, a smug look on his face.

Wyatt steps away from the microphone, leaving room for his dad. The few inches Wyatt has over his father is more obvious when they're close, and it's clear they share many of the same facial features.

"Hello, everyone. We'll make this fast since we have a hotel to manage. As you all are aware, I sent Wyatt here to get the full scope of how the hotel operates. We've dissected everything from numbers to employee attendance, to the systems in place and projected revenue. Unfortunately, it's not feasible to get this hotel back in the black without major renovations. I'm not confident even that will turn it around. Wyatt has convinced me that closing in a week would put many of you in a bad situation, so we've settled on closing in a month."

Grumbles and whispers spread like wildfire through the room.

"Did you know?" Reagan asks me.

I shake my head, my eyes on Wyatt—the man who has yet to look at me. He's not meeting anyone's gaze. Did he know this entire time that the plan was to close Glacier Point?

Abe holds up his hands. "There is some good news."

The room quiets down, waiting to hear the silver lining.

"Whitmore Hotels has purchased the resort in Sunrise Bay. It's currently undergoing its own renovations and will be reopening shortly under the name Koko Kayuh Resort and Spa. With the expansion, we'll need a bigger staff, so in two weeks, interviews will be held up there." He steps back from the podium.

No one asks questions or responds to the news. The resort in Sunrise Bay has always been our biggest competition, but Lake Starlight is a far better town.

"Wyatt, do you have anything to add?" his dad asks over his shoulder.

Wyatt stands, still not making eye contact with anyone. He approaches the microphone, and my heart aches for him if he really didn't have any idea. "That's it. We would appreciate it if you didn't tell anyone while changing shifts. We hope you all come out in two weeks for the interviews. Thank you."

He steps back, and his dad whispers in his ear.

"Did you know, Brooklyn?" Lyle from the kitchen staff asks.

I shake my head.

"Yeah, right. She's probably got the head housekeeping job at Koko Kayuh Resort and Spa," Alisha chimes in.

"Leave her alone. She's just as surprised as all of us," Reagan says.

"Let me know how it feels when you're broke and she's enjoying spa days at the new place," someone else says.

Alisha and Lyle sneer at me and walk out of the room.

I glance over my shoulder, finding Wyatt concentrating on whatever his dad is saying. Leaving quietly with Reagan, I wonder where this leaves us. Did I lose a job and a boyfriend all at once?

FORTY-SEVEN

Wyatt

After the second meeting, I'm thankful to leave my dad with my mom at the restaurant and seek out Brooklyn. She's on the sixth floor, in the penthouses, when I find her.

"Hey." I come up behind her and kiss her neck. The one thing about her working in housekeeping is that her hair is always up in a ponytail, her bare neck teasing me.

She pushes the cart and slides away from me.

"I checked. No one's around."

She stops the cart outside the next room and opens the door, ignoring me. I figured she wouldn't be happy, but she's yet to hear the good news. I can't wait to see how happy she'll be when I tell her.

I follow her in, and she heads to the bathroom.

"Did you know?" she asks, picking up the dirty towels.

"You mean before this morning?"

"Yeah."

"No. I knew my dad would think my suggestions to bring Glacier Point back weren't enough, but I thought he'd give it some more time."

She cocks her eyebrow at me. I've made a point not to talk to Brooklyn about the numbers and finances of Glacier Point. Mr. Clayton tried. He really did. But before Whitmore Hotels stepped in, the damage was done and we lost any chance of a quick return to profit.

"I swear." I put my hands up in a placating gesture.

She faces the sink. "There's really no other choice but to close the doors?"

"My dad doesn't think so."

"What about you?" She swivels back around, scooping up the washcloths. "Do you agree with him?"

I run a hand through my hair and sit on the edge of the luxury jacuzzi. "It's not my call."

"If it were?" She whips around again, training her vision on me as though she wishes she had the capacity to shoot lasers out of her eyes.

"I think it would take time. I'm not sure how long. But I have no say in this. My money isn't in the game."

She walks out of the room, discards the dirty towels on the cart, and piles shampoo, conditioner, and body wash into her arms. She positions the bottles precisely how she wants them on the counter. "You're being vague."

"It doesn't matter what I think." I stand and cage her in.

She stares at me through the mirror, her anger seeming to diminish a bit with my proximity. "You know how many people depend on their jobs here?"

I nod. "Since I signed their paychecks last week, I do. You have to understand it was a tough decision, but I have some good news."

"I'm not sure what good news you could possibly have."

I entwine our fingers and walk back over to sit on the tub with her next to me. I close my hands over hers. "My dad has agreed to give me a chain of hotels."

She smiles hesitantly. "Congratulations. I know you really wanted that."

"And guess what my first order of business will be?"

"What?"

"I want every room to be stocked with a sleep aid essential oil. In the suites, maybe a kit of four. I thought I'd talk to the owner of Earth's Potions and see what she thinks."

Her smile grows but doesn't last nearly as long as I thought it would. "And where do we do this from?"

This is the hard part. "I can't do my job here. I have to be in New York. I want you to move there with me."

Her hands slide from mine, and she walks out of the room.

This is not how I thought this would go.

I follow her, but she's already on her way in with fresh towels.

"Brooklyn, talk to me."

She folds them over the rack with the precision of someone who's done it a thousand times. "You want me to leave Lake Starlight and run off into the sunset while all my friends and coworkers are left to struggle?"

I come up behind her, stopping her from adjusting the towels. "Talk to me please."

She slowly turns. I'm not prepared for the tears. Strike that, tears of happiness I was all for, but these aren't those.

"I think the man standing in this room with me isn't the one I'd want to move to New York with."

I rear my head back. "What?"

"How could you be this selfish? You get your hotels, I

get my business, and we leave all these people to scramble and *maybe* get a job in the next town over? It's not lost on me that they have to interview for jobs they're already doing. I'm curious, why would you want me to move with you?"

"Because I think I'm fall—"

"Because surely you don't know me if you thought I'd be all for this plan. I told you I don't want to move away. It's the reason Jeff left me."

I swallow past the lump in my throat. "I thought maybe I'd be enough."

"Spoken like an egotistical jerk."

Her insult throws me off and I step back. "I have no idea why you're so mad."

"Wyatt! Do you not realize what you're asking?"

"Yes, I do, and I thought you felt the same way about me. I thought we wanted to see where this thing between us went. You knew my life was in New York."

She puts her hands on her hips. "And you knew mine was here."

"But I'm offering you a way to grow your business. A way to really make something huge out of Earth's Potions." I throw my hands in the air, not understanding why she's being so difficult when I'm handing her her dream on a silver fucking platter.

"I know that, and I love that you've thought of me, but you're asking me to abandon the Glacier Point family. If you knew me at all, you'd know I can't do that."

"For a family, they haven't been very supportive of your choice to date me."

She narrows her eyes. "Go back to work. I need to work this out in my head."

"So you'll think about it?"

She sprays the mirror and wipes it down, staring at me in the reflection. "I can't see my answer changing, but I need to work. We can discuss this tonight after I've thought about it."

"Okay." I step back. "I'll be in my office."

"Wyatt?" she calls, and I walk back into the bathroom. "It'll be longer than a few hours."

I inhale a deep breath and nod. Leaving her in the room, I'm certain Brooklyn and Wyatt are no longer going to be kissing in a tree, and I honestly have no fucking clue why not.

FORTY-EIGHT

Brooklyn

"So he wants to make all your dreams come true?" Reagan asks, raising her hand to Nate for another round.

"Pretty much," I mumble.

"And you told him no?" Savannah asks.

"I told him I had to think about it."

"I can't believe they're closing the hotel." Juno sips her beer. She's probably thrilled that Wyatt turned out to not be my prince.

"Tell me about it. The hotel in Sunrise Bay is going to be some posh hotel with a spa. How am I supposed to fit in there?" Reagan says.

I say, "You'd fit in great."

"Thanks. Guess we'll see. Back to you though... I think Wyatt just wants you to have everything. You two have definitely grown closer." Reagan slides shot glasses around.

"We've only been dating a hot minute."

Savannah raises her eyebrows then looks at Juno. "You've been dating for months."

"No, we haven't." I down my shot. "I was getting over Jeff for months."

"You were dating without the sex. You two acted like you were in a relationship—dinners, movie nights, him helping you with your business. I mean, not a lot of guys would go with you to your garden and help you pick and plant flowers," Juno says, surprising me. She's been the captain of team "I Hate Wyatt" recently.

"You're like a teeter-totter when it comes to your feelings about Wyatt and me."

She shrugs. "I knew this day was coming. He's being selfish, taking what he wants and bolting out of town without looking at the wake he's leaving in the rearview mirror, but he does want to make it right for you, so I can't hate him too much."

My head falls to the table. "What do I do?"

"Go," Reagan says, and I glance at her.

She's serious. Here is someone who will be directly affected by Wyatt's father's decision and she's telling me to go live my dream? I reach over and squeeze her hand. She's a great friend, and that's precisely why I won't just up and leave.

"Savannah, could Bailey Timber purchase...?"

She knows what I'm implying and her eyes flick to Reagan then back to me. "I don't know. I'd have to talk to Dori, but I don't think so."

I nod.

"Can I ask you a question?" Juno interrupts. "Do you love him?"

Do I? "Um..."

"She does," Reagan confirms. "More than Jeff."

I look at my good friend. I guess I'm that transparent, because I've felt something for Wyatt for a long time. We clicked. When I think about being happy, he's front and center in that picture.

Savannah and Juno look at me.

I nod and steal Savannah's shot, downing it. This time I'll be breaking my own heart.

Leaving Lucky's, I walk along the lake to head home, much to my sisters' chagrin. But I need to think this through, and if I know Wyatt, he's waiting for me to get back to the apartment.

Our time together runs through my mind. From hitting him in the head with the book to us sitting by the lake and talking about life, to his confession about what it was like to grow up in his family.

Is Wyatt enough for me to move to New York? Of course. When he asked, my heart swelled—but the thought of leaving my family dampens any excitement I may have momentarily felt. To not be here when Austin and Holly or any of my other siblings have kids? To be the aunt they see once in a while when she's in town, versus being able to be at their games and recitals, birthdays and holidays? My parents' death taught me that time is never guaranteed. You're not promised tomorrow, much less a year. No matter how intense my feelings for Wyatt are, it's not enough to leave my family. I'm not sure anyone could ever be enough for me to leave my family.

I sit at the lake's edge and pick up some pebbles, tossing them into the water. My head is a jumbled mess.

"Hey." Wyatt's voice from behind surprises me. "I didn't want to startle you, but Juno texted me and said you were walking home."

He sits next to me and puts Gizmo between his legs. Tears prick my eyes.

"I just wanted to think." I pet Gizmo's head.

"About my offer?"

I shake my head, sitting up straighter. "You make it sound like a business deal."

"Is that why you don't want to come to New York with me?"

I turn my head, resting my cheek on my forearm. "I think I want to talk to your dad about keeping the hotel open."

He chuckles until he realizes I'm serious. "Nothing will change his mind. I tried, believe me. I have a feeling his plan this entire time was to close Glacier Point so it wasn't in competition with his new baby up in Sunrise Bay. It sucks, but it's just business."

"I hate that you say that. It's not just business. It's people's lives. People I've known my whole life. People who have spent their whole careers at the hotel. What will Molly do? Or Reagan? Or Mac? How can you work alongside those people every day and not worry about them now?"

He stares out at the lake. "I'm going to try to get them all a spot at the new hotel, but there's nothing more I can do. Does it suck? Yes. But this is our chance, and I really want you to come with me."

"I don't think I can," I whisper.

"Can I ask you a question? Would you come if the hotel was staying open? Am I enough?"

A tear slips from my eye. "It's not about being enough. I do have feelings for you. Strong feelings. As shitty as it sounds, stronger than I ever had for Jeff, a man I was going to marry. My heart is already breaking from the idea of us not being together, but I'd be giving up my family if I go to New York."

"We could come back all the time. We'd make it work."

I smile at him. "But there would be no impromptu cookouts. Grandma Dori is getting older, and I'm not sure how many more years she'll have left. I'll miss the Sunday dinners."

"You'll gain Sunday mornings with me and late nights of filthy sex." He waggles his eyebrows.

I can't fight my smile.

"But it's not enough, right?"

I huff. "It's not about being enough. I don't want to choose between you and my family. It's been what? Five months? What if we get to New York and you decide you don't want me? What if the business grows too fast and I can't keep up? I appreciate you wanting to be some white knight who saves me, but I don't need saving. You've shared your knowledge and helped me gain footing. You gave me the best thing ever—you gave me my self-confidence back. I can never repay you for that."

"Is this your nice way of turning me down?"

I look at the lake before I place the spike in the beating heart that is the two of us. "I can't go to New York with you."

"I can't stay here," he says, sounding torn.

I want to ask why? Why do I have to leave everything I love? I could twist this around and say why am I not enough for him to stay? But I don't want him to feel like he settled by staying here. He has so many opportunities waiting for him in New York, even if he doesn't like his dad.

"I guess that means we're going our separate ways." My chin hits my chest and I fight back tears.

He stands, picking up Gizmo and tucking him under his arm. "Let me walk you home. Maybe something will change after a good night's sleep. An alternative we're not thinking of."

He wraps his arm around my shoulders, and we walk the path back to the apartment in silence. We both know nothing's going to change in the morning. If anything, daylight will only make it that much clearer that we can't stay together.

FORTY-NINE

Wyatt

We woke up the next morning and nothing had changed except the distance we'd put between us. Brooklyn made excuses that she was too busy to hang out because of all the orders she had to fulfill. I offered to help, but unlike before, she didn't take me up on it.

So here we are, three weeks later, and I'm packing my office with one week to go in Lake Starlight. A knock sounds on my office door.

"Come in," I say, stacking papers.

"Did you not see the light dusting of snow that fell this morning? You better have Mac throw some salt out there before some old lady like me falls and breaks her hip. She might sue this place." Grandma Dori walks in with Savannah in tow. She flings her hand in Savannah's direction. "You can wait outside."

"I think you should just call yourself Thelma,"

Savannah grumbles and grabs the knob. I don't understand the reference, but I don't have long to think about it before she says, "Hi, Wyatt."

She shuts the door before I can say my hello.

"Hi, Dori." I motion for her to take the seat across from me.

Her eyes fixate on my half-filled box. "Packing up, huh?" She sits down.

I eye the wrapped box in her lap. "I am. We're shutting down next week and I'm going back to New York the day after."

She nods. "It's a shame. I wish Bailey Timber could bail out the hotel, but we can't. All these people losing their jobs."

I lean back in my chair. "We were able to employ half of the current employees at the new place in Sunrise Bay."

"That's probably a good average for you guys, right? Fifty percent."

I clasp my fingers, smiling. "You're being very polite today. You can say what you really think."

She smiles. "That's why I've always liked you. You're a smart boy."

"Thanks?"

"From day one, you knew what you wanted."

"How so?" I tilt my head.

She leans forward. "Our Brookie. You liked her from the get-go, didn't you? When I first met Mr. Bailey, he told me when he saw me across the frozen pond, he got this feeling in the pit of his stomach. He thought he ate too many meatballs." She giggles. "He wasn't exactly a man who was smooth with words, but he loved me something fierce."

"You must miss him a great deal."

"That's why I wonder, for such a smart boy, why you're being so dumb."

Her insult catches me off guard, and I blink a few times.

"Don't act insulted. You love Brooklyn, but you're going back to New York."

I steeple my fingers. "I need to make a living."

The two of us have polite smiles, but it still feels like a showdown.

"Well yes, I understand that. My husband didn't want to take over the timber company from his dad. He wanted to build something for himself. Now, he eventually did take the reins, and I like to think he loved what he did with the company. Most of that joy came later in life, when he got to show the ropes to Tim, Brooklyn's dad. But in those early years, I'd find him watching the boats going out with longing in his eyes. He'd wanted to be a fisherman and captain his own boat. Back in that day, we would have struggled without a steady paycheck."

I nod. Her story is endearing, but I'm wondering when this stroll down memory lane will end.

"Life is about chances. Taking an opportunity and running with it. Now I don't know much about you and your father's relationship, and to be honest, right now your father is on my shit list. But I've witnessed what the pressures of a family business can do to the relationship between a son and a father. I wish things would've been different for Mr. Bailey and me. I wish I would've told him to live his dream of being a captain. Now, he was such a great man, he never resented me for working for his dad. We had a wonderful life together. But as a wife, I feel it was my job to push him. To tell him to take the risk, I wasn't going anywhere."

"I'm sure he was happy with what the two of you made together."

She looks me right in the eye. "As scary as it is, if you take a leap of faith, sometimes it pays off."

I nod, not really sure how that applies to me.

"Anyway, I suppose I should go. Savannah's probably out there tapping her toe to get back to the office. Hopefully she finds someone to drill the energy out of her one day."

I laugh.

"Oh." She places the box on the desk. "A goodbye gift for you."

"Thanks." My fingers move to unwrap it.

"Not yet. When I leave."

I stand. "Thanks for coming, Dori. Maybe our roads will cross again." I round my desk and put my hand out between us.

She leans in and pats my stomach. "Oh, they will. I guarantee it." She smiles and opens the door, then steps out of my office. "You look like a fine fellow. What's your name?"

"Neil," he answers.

"Does she scare you?"

"Seriously, Grandma? Let's go," Savannah says.

"I get it. She needs a man who can give her some tough love. I don't think you're him."

"Thanks?" Neil says, confusion in his tone.

Then I overhear Dori saying things to people about how if they don't have jobs, come apply at Bailey Timber after they burn this place to the ground.

I close my door and stare at the wrapped gift.

Curious, I unwrap the blue paper and find a set of mugs. I open the box and pull them out. One has an outline of the state of Alaska on it, and the other an outline of New

York. A dotted line with the words, *Never too far apart. Maybe in distance but never in heart* is printed on each. Inspecting them, I see Brooklyn inscribed in the New York outline and Wyatt in the Alaska one.

She really is a class-A meddler.

I stuff them back inside the box and place it on the shelf behind me.

As impossible as it feels, I need to put Lake Starlight in my rearview mirror.

FIFTY

Wyatt

S tepping off the elevator of my condo building in New York, I feel as though I can only remember my time with Brooklyn here. From the years I've spent riding that elevator, walking down this hall to my condo, all I can seem to recall are the few times Brooklyn was at my side. How there wasn't enough room for us to walk side by side, so I slid back for her to go first and admired her ass in the dress she wore to my sister's wedding rehearsal dinner. How excited I was to peel it off her before realizing she was nervous and I had to take my time.

How did everything unravel so quickly? My heart aches from missing her. For the first time in my entire life, I took the coward's route because I feared I'd make a fool of myself by begging her to get on the plane with me. What was I going to do? Try to convince her money and wealth trump family?

It took a ten-hour plane ride to be thankful I didn't try to convince her. Brooklyn isn't impressed with tickets to shows on opening night or reservations at the "it" restaurants. She prefers the boisterous parties with her family and walking downtown, catching up with people she hasn't seen in a while. It might take her a half hour to do one errand, but she doesn't care. She's never in a rush.

We're from different worlds.

I insert my key in the door and walk into my condo. I sigh, finding my lights on. My mom's curled up on the couch. *Fuck. What happened now?*

"Mom?" I ask, dropping my bags and shutting my door.

She peers up from the couch. "You're home," she says with a smile.

"Yeah. Why are you here?" I sit across from her.

She keeps the blanket over her lap and sits up. "I was waiting for you."

"Why? I was going to come by in the morning. Dad said the paperwork would be ready for me to sign then. Did he change his mind about giving me the chain? Is he not—"

She shakes her head. "No, but I wanted a little alone time with you beforehand. He's flying back from Texas tomorrow morning, and I figured you'd be too tired to come over tonight."

"Is something wrong? Haylee? Bradley?" I swallow. "You?"

She smiles. "We're all good. What I'm wondering is, are you?"

I huff, standing with the hopes I have some sort of alcohol here.

As if she read my mind, she say, "I brought you some beer."

I open the fridge, finding only that. "I need groceries."

"Do you?" she asks.

I tilt my head. "Let's cut the chitchat. What's up?" I pop off the top of the beer and head back to the couch.

"When I was sick, you were so young. Too much responsibility was placed on your shoulders. If I could take one thing back, it would be that. But you were my little boy, and I was so scared of losing you and Haylee forever, I didn't want to fight for you to live your life while I was fighting for mine."

"Mom, stop. You were sick. Don't feel guilty about that."

"Your dad should've been there to make sure you didn't feel responsible for making me happy. But you and Haylee... I'm not sure I would have continued fighting if not for you two." She looks out the window at the New York skyline sprinkled with lights.

"Why are we talking about this?"

"Because you're about to do something I think you feel like you *have* to do, but I'm not sure you really *want* to do. I need to make sure you understand exactly what you're getting yourself into before you sign those papers and take on that hotel chain."

I sip my beer, because I have no idea where the hell she's going with this.

"When your father and I married, we were so in love, but your father's first love is this company. I'm not blind to that. Never was. He's come a long way in the years since I was sick." She waves. "I know you and Haylee don't see it because he's not one for open displays of affection. But he has. We're working on it."

"But still work takes priority over you."

She nods.

"And you're okay with that?"

"I am. I signed up for it, and for a long time, you and Haylee were my priority. You probably still are."

"That's different."

She shrugs. "Maybe. But you're not your father. You're not a man who wants to work eighty-hour weeks and travel all the time for business. You don't get that same high your father gets when a deal is closed."

"I know I never took this seriously before, but the last few years—"

She shakes her head. "You're not irresponsible, that's not what I'm saying. I have a feeling you want this chain of hotels for a reason other than you've dreamed of it your entire life."

"What are you talking about?" I sip my beer, and she stares at me as though I should already be catching on. I stand and head to the window. "This isn't about Dad."

"Isn't it?"

"No. What else would I do? I was born into Whitmore Hotels. This is what I always knew I'd do."

"But you fought it for most of your life. I remember when you were growing up and you wanted to be a fireman."

"I was six."

She laughs. "Well. You never dressed up in a suit and said, 'Take me to work with you, Daddy.'"

"Like he would have anyway." I down the rest of my beer. Man, that went fast.

"That's not the point. Wyatt, I don't want to pressure you, but is leaving Lake Starlight something you want to do? You had no feelings for Brooklyn at all?"

If I tell my mom the truth, I'll disappoint her.

"I know I meddle. I know I pushed you to bring a date, and if you felt forced to and that's why you brought Brooklyn, okay. But that night after the announcement about Glacier Point, when she didn't join us for dinner, I saw it on your face. You're always in a bad mood around your father, but it was something more than that."

"Did I ever tell you that you nitpick and make assumptions about everything I do?"

She laughs. "Tell me my mother's intuition is wrong."

I turn away from the city and meet her gaze. "I can't."

"That's what I thought. Then why are you back here fighting for something you don't want? To throw it in your dad's face? To prove to him that you're just as good as or better than him? That you somehow deserve to spend your life running a business that wasn't your dream in the first place? Come on, Wyatt."

"I never said I didn't want it." I toss the empty into the recycling bin and grab another beer. The memory of my dad's hands on that woman eats at me. Does she know what a complete scumbag he is? I can't keep it in any longer. She deserves to know. "Mom, there's something you should know."

She holds up a hand. "If you're about to say what I think you are, you should know I know your father is no saint. But I've put the past behind me, as has he. We've been to counselors and done the work, and yes, your father is still a workaholic and hard to please, but he's not the same man he was so many years ago."

My head hangs down. She knew all along and she chose to forgive him?

That makes one of us, I suppose.

She rises off the couch and comes over to the breakfast bar. "You're a better man than your father. You have nothing to prove. Don't let the resentment of who he is—or was, in some respects—deter you from going after the life you want."

I close my eyes and bite my lip staring anywhere but at her. "That would mean leaving you too."

She lays her hand on mine. "I'm a big girl. According to my driver's license, I'm old enough to take care of myself and not too old to need long-term care."

"But—"

"Nope. We're not going to live worrying about the future."

"Mom—"

"Do you love her?"

I look her in the eyes and take a deep breath. I've never been in love, so I have no idea, but the fact is I almost didn't get on the plane. The minute I landed, I wanted back on one that would take me to her. "I do."

She walks away from me. "Then you're going to fly back to her right now."

I contemplate doing what she says, but I still have business to work out with my dad. "I have something I have to take care of first."

My mom tears up. "Did I ever tell you how much time you used to spend playing with Lego? You always loved building things from the ground up."

I nod. "Yeah, and it's about time I did that again."

FIFTY-ONE

Brooklyn

G lacier Point is officially closed. Wyatt's car is no longer in the parking lot at my apartment building.

I climb the stairs, and when I reach the third floor, I pause before opening my door. It's going to feel different in my apartment now that Wyatt is gone. He didn't live with me, but he was always here, and the fact that he's returned to New York feels like a gaping hole in my chest.

I thought he'd at least say goodbye.

I open my door and stop, finding a gift bag on my kitchen table, Wyatt's key to my door next to it. Dropping my bags, I sit at the table and take out the tissue paper. I inhale a deep breath, trying to keep it together.

I pull out a mug with a letter stuffed inside. I smile at the outline of the state of New York. The heart. My name on the inside.

When I open the letter, my heart leaps when I find Wyatt's handwriting.

Brooklyn,

I didn't want to be a coward, but I couldn't stand to say the word goodbye to you. These past four weeks of being close to you, yet not nearly as close as we've become is what I imagine prison feels like. So many times, I wanted to knock on your door and beg you to come walk around the lake with me. At work, I wanted to tuck that loose strand of hair behind your ear, corner you in a room, and tell you you were being stupid. But I didn't. Because I could never live with myself if you came with me now and hated me later. I wish things were different. Your grandma gave me this set of mugs, and I have one with Alaska and my name in it. Although we can't be together, I'll smile every morning knowing you're having coffee and you might be thinking of me, because I'll definitely be thinking of you. I did leave my heart in Alaska with you, after all.

Love,
   Wyatt

I fold the piece of paper back up, though I want to read it over and over again. I can hear his voice reading it to me in my head.

A knock sounds on the door. Without me answering it, Savannah, Juno, and Holly walk in. Holly's in her overalls and carrying gallons of paint and a bucket holding brushes. Savannah's in yoga pants and a sweatshirt, and Juno's wearing sweats and a U of Anchorage sweatshirt.

"What's going on?" I ask.

"We're here to redo your coffee table," Holly says. "Fresh start."

"And drink." Juno holds up two bottles of wine.

"And eat." Savannah lifts two bags of junk food.

"Thanks, guys." I put the mug and letter into the bag and escape to the kitchen to hide it. Some things are meant for just me.

Besides, coffee mugs and Savannah don't mix.

"You okay?" Juno asks, meeting me in the kitchen to open the wine.

"I'm good."

Five minutes later, Holly's getting started on the table when my door opens again. In comes all my brothers, including Kingston, who just got home from a long summer and early fall of putting out fires.

"I heard there's a party," Austin says.

"A pity party," I say.

"Nah, just a 'Wyatt's an asshat' party." Kingston winks.

"Denver will be up shortly. Liam's helping him up the stairs."

Rome can't even finish his sentence before Liam walks in with Denver in his arms, his crutches hanging from his hands. "Put me down. No need to show off how strong you are."

"Is that any way to treat your new husband?" Liam asks and deposits Denver slowly so he can put his crutches on the floor. "I'll be right back. I forgot the beer."

The door shuts with Liam's departure, and I sit on the couch. They start the same party they had for me when I got stood up at the altar, and I can't help feeling sick of being the Bailey project. It's time for it to be someone else's turn.

"I gotta ask. You knew the score, right?"

I scrunch my eyebrows at Kingston.

"Like, you knew his life was in New York, so why get involved?" he clarifies.

I eye Rome. "Someone told me he'd make a great rebound."

Everyone's eyes shoot to Rome.

Savannah hits him on the back of the head. "You're such an idiot."

Rome holds his head. "What? It's what any guy would say."

"Not to Brooklyn. Maybe Savannah with her cold heart, but Brooklyn?" Juno hits him.

"I'm fairly sure you just insulted me," Savannah says, pouring a glass of wine.

"Take it as you're tough." Juno pretends to flex like a bodybuilder. "But in your mind."

"In that case, I'm sorry." Kingston pats my knee. "That you went to the dumbass brother for advice."

"Whoa, whoa, whoa..." Rome holds his hands in the air. "Brooklyn, are you over Jeff?"

I nod. "Yes."

"Mission complete." Rome wipes his hands clean and heads into the kitchen.

The door opens and closes, and Liam enters holding

two cases of beer. I kind of want to bury myself in a hole right now, but whatever.

"You've got a hot new neighbor." Liam nods toward the hall.

"Joel said he was putting the place up on Airbnb," I say.

"What's she look like?" Rome asks as he and Kingston run to the door.

"She's gone, guys," Liam says.

"Not to mention if she wants any Bailey, it's going to be the famous one." Denver puffs out his chest a little, using another chair to rest his leg on.

"How about the one who owns his own restaurant?" Rome adds.

"The guy who risks his life every day to fight wildfires?" Kingston points at himself.

"Or the stunning tattoo artist with the heart of gold?" Liam says, and Denver throws his beer cap at him.

"That's about as truthful as saying you're a virgin," Savannah snipes.

"Maybe I am." Liam laughs. "What do you think, Savannah, wanna take my virginity?"

She rolls her eyes. "I'd be more worried I'd take something else from you. Like an STD."

Quietly, Holly works on the coffee table with Austin by her side. Gizmo cuddles in my lap until Juno picks him up and dances with him. As they talk, laugh, and razz each other, I can't stop thinking about Wyatt and where he is right now. What's he doing. Most of all, how much I wish he was here.

FIFTY-TWO

Brooklyn

L ovely of my family to leave me with a mess to clean up. I wipe my hands and open the apartment door, holding it open with my hip to take out the case of empty beer bottles.

"You had a party to celebrate my leaving?"

I look up and my heart leaps. Am I still half-drunk from last night?

"Wyatt?" I gasp.

He eyes the beer bottles again, wanting an answer.

"Maybe."

"That's upsetting. Maybe I should head back to New York then?" He stuffs his hands into his pockets and heads toward the stairs.

I drop the box and the bottles clank. "Why are you here?"

"Because I love you."

I suck in a breath and my eyes close. A tear trickles down my cheek before I even realize my eyes have welled up. "What?"

He breaks the distance, cupping my cheeks, his thumbs brushing away the tears. "I'm scared to death to find out whether these are happy tears or not."

I stare into his blue eyes. Did I know the first time I saw him that he was supposed to be mine?

"It's crazy, and if you need more time, done. I realize you ended things with Jeff not that long ago, but I've never felt anything with anyone remotely like what I feel when I'm with you. I love you. So much."

Those are the words I'd hoped for so long to hear from him, but I'm afraid to hope again. "New York?"

"I'm moving to Lake Starlight for good. In fact..." He holds up a set of keys. "I just opened a business here."

"You did?"

"A hotel. The old owner sold it to me, so it's mine now to rebuild and make something special. But I have to be honest. I had to clean out most of my trust fund to make it happen, plus take a loan from my father—courtesy of my mom making it happen. So if it doesn't work out and turn a profit, we're going to be pretty much destitute."

I chuckle. "If anyone can make it work, you can."

"Your confidence is inspiring." He places a chaste kiss on my lips. It doesn't last long enough. "Now, weren't you in housekeeping? Would you like a job?"

I shrug. "I think I'm retiring from that. Plus, we shouldn't work together."

"Why not?" His forehead wrinkles.

"Because I shouldn't sleep with the boss." I smile, and he wraps his arms around my waist.

"Which means?"

I grab his shirt and pull him closer. "Which means, I love you too. I'm like the Welcome Wagon. Want to come inside and I'll officially welcome you to Lake Starlight?"

"As long as I'm the only new resident you welcome."

I laugh against his lips. "Definitely."

I step back, and his lips don't leave mine as we secure ourselves behind apartment door three twenty-two. Maybe it was fate all along.

EPILOGUE

SIX MONTH LATER...

Brooklyn

All of our faces are glued to the window of the restaurant. Wyatt's hand is on my hip, his face right above mine.

"I'm not sure we should be watching," I say.

"Then he should've done it in his Jeep behind Lucky's," Savannah says.

"I'm with Savannah. You don't want witnesses, don't do it in public," Rome chimes in.

Austin has Holly in the gazebo in the middle of the square where Rome's new restaurant is located. It's late winter and it's still cold out, though not as frigid as the past few months. Snow falls around them and they're all bundled up. He goes down on one knee and Holly's hands fly to her face.

"It's so romantic. Who was in charge of photos?" Juno asks.

We all scramble, looking around.

"Austin is going to kill us," Sedona says, jogging out the door with her cell phone.

"Glad I still have an excuse." Denver is sitting in his chair, not as enamored with Austin's proposal as the girls in the family are.

"I need to head back to the kitchen if you guys want to eat," Rome says.

Grandma Dori smiles out the window with a satisfied grin.

"They better give me some promo work. They might be my very first marriage." Juno rests her chin in her palm.

Phoenix shakes her head.

"For the millionth time, you didn't get them together," Kingston says.

"I did. And these two." Juno thumbs toward Wyatt and me.

We look at one another.

"I guess she did dodge out of the way of the book that hit me." Wyatt shrugs before going to sit next to Denver. They clink beer bottles.

"I got them together," Grandma Dori says from the window. "I'm the one who told him to look out for her *and* I gave you those coffee mugs."

"You gave Wyatt coffee mugs?" Phoenix asks.

"Uh-huh. He was supposed to go back to his lonely New York apartment and put that pretty mug with Alaska on it next to what I assumed would be a purchased set of new coffee mugs and remember he was missing out on being where people love him. Lake Starlight."

I glance at Wyatt, who raises his shoulders in a shrug of agreement.

"Do any of you listen to me?" Grandma asks. "A man with matching coffee mugs is a man no one loves."

We all nod.

"Got it, G'ma." Juno pats Grandma's shoulder. "Just keep those keepsakes away from Savannah."

Savannah flips her off. "Oh, he's sliding the ring on her finger!"

Juno, Savannah, and I all sigh.

Holly wipes tears from her face and jumps into his arms. He picks her up and backs her into one of the pillars while they kiss frantically.

"Do you think they realize what they're doing? I mean, they're going to be in the Buzz Wheel tonight for sure and it won't be the announcement of their engagement. It'll be a picture of them half naked with their tongues down each other's throats." Savannah shakes her head.

We move back to the table Rome arranged so we could have dinner together before his opening next week. We all sit down, talking over one another, asking for this or that to drink.

Holly and Austin come in a while later, Uncle Brian and Karen following. Sedona trails behind, looking like a wet dog from the snowfall and having no coat or hat.

"Good thing I had backup on the picture thing. You'd think after raising all of you, one of you could take some pictures."

We ignore Austin, but all the girls jump up and hug Holly, then our brother. The guys fist-bump Austin and lightly hug Holly, welcoming her to the family.

"We all know who's next," Austin says, sitting down with Holly on his lap.

"Do you plan on eating your entire dinner with her on your lap?" I ask, ignoring his comment.

I'd love to be married to Wyatt, but I'm not rushing into anything this time around. When we do decide that it's time, I hope that Wyatt's in agreement that we should either have a small wedding or sneak away, just the two of us. Right now he's still working hard to make the resort what he envisions, and I'm still getting my own business off the ground.

"Since I really want to lay her out on the table and feast on my soon-to-be wife, you should be happy she's just sitting on my lap."

Holly shoves his chest but then kisses him, the two going way overboard in the PDA department as always.

"You guys ready?" Rome calls from the kitchen.

"I'm hungry, and I have to get back to the center before the roads turn icy," Grandma Dori says.

"It's okay, Wyatt's driving you in his brand-new truck," I announce.

Wyatt's cheeks flush.

Kingston laughs. "Now you're a true Alaskan."

"Aw, trust fund boy had a little extra in the bank to pay for a new vehicle?" Denver says with a grin.

"Piss off," Wyatt says and tosses a napkin in Denver's direction.

"I hope it's not too high because—" Austin stops when a rush of cold air hits the table.

The door of the restaurant opens, and in walks an attractive blonde with a baby on her hip. She catches my eye. I smile and stand to see if I can help her with directions or something, but her eyes fixate on Denver.

"I'm sorry, this is a private party. Family only," Savannah says, sliding out of her chair.

"Well, then I guess we're in the right place," the woman says.

We all exchange looks, but everyone is confused.

Rome walks out of the kitchen with a plate of beef and places it on the table. "Why is everyone so quiet?" He looks over at the woman and child.

The woman's face falls, her mouth hanging open, and she has to prop her daughter higher up on her hip. "There's two of you?"

Denver tilts his head, and Rome rounds the end of the table to get closer.

"I'm sorry, how can I help you?" Rome asks.

The woman's eyes narrow. "You can tell me which one of you is the father of my little girl."

For the first time in Bailey family dinner history, the entire table is dead silent.

One of the twins is a dad?

Buzz Wheel is going to have a field day with this.

THE END

COCKAMAMIE UNICORN RAMBLINGS

Wow... This book was the one that wouldn't end. In a good way, the characters just would not stop talking to us. Every time Rayne thought she could wrap up their happily ever after, something else arose. She went way past the set deadline, but we try to always keep true to the characters and their story—whether that's a 70K story, or in this case, a 90K story.

Even though Rayne would groan each time she had to go to Piper and say it still wasn't done, Piper and Rayne agreed to see it through and Piper would make the adjustments as needed on her end.

As our faithful readers know, we like to see the couple in steamy situations and by the time we said The End, Brooklyn and Wyatt only had one detailed sex scene. We found ourselves once again biting our lip, contemplating if we were disappointing our readers.

We even included four betas this round to make sure we were delivering a good story. In the end, we decided to stand by our couple and their unique strangers-to-friends-to-lovers (Piper's coined phrase) trope. Brooklyn's character is not one who would rush into another relationship or into bed with a guy after being left at the altar. And in order for Wyatt to truly change he needed to show the slow growth he did after falling for her.

A few behind the scene tidbits about plotting to paper with this story...

1. Wyatt's identity was going to stay hidden from readers for the first 50% until Rayne found herself writing his POV the first time and thought how are we going to accomplish this? *Cue emergency call with Piper*

2. Gizmo and Brooklyn's dog socks were added only because while searching for reader box items, Piper found some specific socks we wanted to include.

3. Rome's role of "The Bailey Vault" just came out during writing. It wasn't planned ahead of time in either Lessons or Advice.

4. After writing a nighttime scene with great lines about moonlight between Brooklyn and Wyatt, we realized this is Alaska and during the summer there's 18 hours of daylight.

Many thanks to everyone below. Without them we'd be lost!

Danielle Sanchez and the entire InkSlinger family!
Ellie from My Brother's Editor for line edits.
Shawna from Behind the Writer for proofreading.
Sarah from Okay Creations for the cover and branding for the entire series.

Sara from Sara Eirew Photography for the loving picture of Brooklyn and Wyatt.

To our four betas: Dani, Lourdes, Ceej and Gabri. Thank you for taking the time with notes and thoughts about our story.

Bloggers who consistently carve out time to read, review and/or promote us.

Piper Rayne Unicorns who shout from the rooftops about our new releases and love our characters like we do.

Readers who took a chance on our book with so many choices out there.

Hugs to everyone!

I think we've teased you enough about Birth of a Baby Daddy, so we'll leave it with this...

Who's the Daddy? Find out 5.2.19! Don't forget to head over to lakestarlightbuzzwheel.com for the latest gossip in Lake Starlight!

Xo
    Piper & Rayne

ABOUT PIPER & RAYNE

Piper Rayne is a USA Today Bestselling Author duo who write "heartwarming humor with a side of sizzle" about families, whether that be blood or found. They both have e-readers full of one-clickable books, they're married to husbands who drive them to drink, and they're both chauffeurs to their kids. Most of all, they love hot heroes and quirky heroines who make them laugh, and they hope you do, too!

ALSO BY PIPER RAYNE

The Baileys

Lessons from a One-Night Stand

Advice from a Jilted Bride

Birth of a Baby Daddy

Operation Bailey Wedding (Novella)

Falling for My Brother's Best Friend

Demise of a Self-Centered Playboy

Confessions of a Naughty Nanny

Operation Bailey Babies (Novella)

Secrets of the World's Worst Matchmaker

Winning My Best Friend's Girl

Rules for Dating your Ex

Operation Bailey Birthday (Novella)

The Greenes

My Twist of Fortune (FREE)

My Beautiful Neighbor

My Almost Ex

My Vegas Groom

The Greene Family Summer Bash

My Sister's Flirty Friend

My Unexpected Surprise

My Famous Frenemy

The Greene Family Vacation

My Scorned Best Friend

My Fake Fiancé

My Brother's Forbidden Friend

The Modern Love World

Charmed by the Bartender

Hooked by the Boxer

Mad about the Banker

Complete Set (all 3 books)

The Single Dad's Club

Real Deal

Dirty Talker

Sexy Beast

Complete Set (all 3 books)

Hollywood Hearts

Mister Mom

Animal Attraction

Domestic Bliss

Bedroom Games

Cold as Ice

On Thin Ice

Break the Ice

Complete Set (all 3 books +)

Charity Case

Manic Monday

Afternoon Delight

Happy Hour

Complete Set (all 3 books)

Blue Collar Brothers

Flirting with Fire

Crushing on the Cop

Engaged to the EMT

Complete Set (All 3 books)

White Collar Brothers

Sexy Filthy Boss

Dirty Flirty Enemy

Wild Steamy Hook-up

The Rooftop Crew

My Bestie's Ex

A Royal Mistake

The Rival Roomies

Our Star-Crossed Kiss

The Do-Over

A Co-Workers Crush

Hockey Hotties